the rojocci papers

The
Kingdom Within You
by
R. J. Graves, Jr.

Cover design by: BETIBUP33 Designs

the rojocci papers
THE KINGDOM WITHIN YOU
Copyright © 2017 by R. J. Graves, Jr.
Published by R. J. Graves, Jr.
Pensacola, Florida 32503

Visit us at www.facebook.com/rojocci
www.therojoccipapers.com
ISBN-10: 0-9984073-3-3
ISBN-13: 978-0-9984073-3-3
Christian Fiction
$13.95 USD

Printed in the United States of America.

Titles in The rojocci Papers series:

Hidden Within You

Freedom Within You

The Kingdom Within You

This book is dedicated to my parents,

Bob and Betty Graves,

who endured many youthful shenanigans from

my three brothers, my sister, and myself,

yet raised us with the education, discipline,

and respect of loving parents.

Thank you both for all you've done for all of us.

I love you from the depths my of heart!

Acknowledgments

Several people have helped me with many aspects of this book, none more than my precious wife and editor, Susan C. Graves, whose tireless efforts and extreme attention to detail have been a wonder to behold. She is truly the most remarkable person I know and the love of my life. Heartfelt thanks also to Betty Graves, Mike Parker, Kathy Coker, Sarah Whipps, along with Frank and Bernice Osborne, for their most helpful input and encouragement during the many revisions.

Although I will no doubt, inadvertently leave many others out of these acknowledgements, I do want to thank my friend, Doug Gehman, who first suggested and encouraged me to consider writing.

"The kingdom of God cometh not with observation:

Neither shall they say, Lo here! or, Lo there! for, behold,

the kingdom of God is within you."

Luke 17:20-21 KJV

-prologue-

During the second week of July 2017, the weather
was as expected for the Gulf Coast, hot and
humid. I had scheduled a meeting with the
older gentleman whom I had given the nickname "The Man-
With-The-Kind-Eyes" for Thursday of that week. Having
telephoned me early on Wednesday, he confirmed that he
and his wife, Annalisa, would be arriving around ten o'clock
the following morning. I was excited about their visit.
Having released their second book a month before, we were
about to begin working on the next one.

Hearing their knock on our door, my wife, Susie, and I
invited them from the steamy climate outside into the
coolness of our air-conditioned home. I am fully convinced
that over three-quarters of the population of the South
would live elsewhere in the summer if it weren't for the
invention of chilled air. We settled in our family room and
enjoyed a lively conversation until lunch. Immediately
following our chicken salad sandwiches, chips, and iced tea,
I invited Alan into my office. It is the tiniest room in our
modest home and the one I have nicknamed—The Fruitful
Vineyard. The moniker is much more a confession of faith,
than an actual garden replete with grapes hanging from

bountiful, woody vines. Although to be honest, it has, to my own consternation at times, produced various and sundry fruits of an internal sort. I am well acquainted with frustration, irritation, and annoyance, as well as patience, endurance, and determination. The latter I have found to result in much more pleasant relations than the former. In short, the work I do in The Fruitful Vineyard has been stretching.

It is a brief commute to this study, no more than a few steps down the hallway with a left turn into the room. Alan chuckled as he entered into the ten foot by ten foot, sparsely decorated room. His eyes darted around from wall to wall as he caught a glimpse of what is my purposefully paltry existence for five, sometimes six days a week. I am a visual person who finds some decorations to be distracting. For instance, there is a large, framed photograph upon the wall in our family room of a man standing directly outside the door of a lighthouse. Looming immediately behind is an enormous wave poised to come crashing down upon him. I find it mesmerizing and have gazed at it for more than an hour at a time. This is the type of distraction I do not need in The Fruitful Vineyard.

My desk is a foldable, steel table I found at a garage sale, centered upon its plastic surface, rests my laptop, ever beckoning me to tickle its impatient keys. On one side, amid several reference books, including a concordance, a dictionary, and a thesaurus, stands the ever ominous *Chicago Manual of Style*. This lone volume supremely reigns as a judge in his courtroom. At the other end, a stack of manuscripts in various states of revision lie haphazardly, along with a few proofs of Alan's books. On the wall above, an assortment of post-it notes remind me of important thoughts to include in Alan's current book as well as other manuscripts I am working on.

Stationed in several locations around the room are two inch tall signs with the following typed upon them: $2.12. Alan looked at these curiously and asked, "What do these mean?"

I explained briefly that a number of years ago I had been an entrepreneur. Toward the end of my first year in business, I found myself with a checkbook balance of only $2.12 and was fully convinced I would be out of business by the end of the week. To my mixed surprise, I wasn't. The following week I continued to be amazed as, somehow by God's great mercy, the doors were still open. The process was repeated over and over for the next few weeks and months. To my amazement, the business eventually prospered, and I sold it a dozen years later.

"And?" asked Alan leaning forward.

"The little sign is a constant reminder to persevere, never give up hope, and never quit, because I just don't know what God may have in store around the very next corner."

"Good for you," he affirmed. "You're definitely a **rojoccian**."

"Thanks, Alan. I take that as a compliment."

He nodded, and then asked, "Why do you call this stark room The Fruitful Vineyard? It seems to me to be a contradiction in terms."

"Because it is producing fruit, even though most of the yield can't be seen. But believe me, it's there and I know it's growing."

"How can you be so confident?" he probed with a smile, giving indication he already knew the answer.

"The pruning," I confidently replied, raising my eyebrows. "You know, Gospel of John, fifteenth chapter, where Jesus tells His disciples that if they bear fruit, His Father will prune them so they can bear more fruit. It's like if I have a little patience, He directs or allows situations to come my way to help me grow and develop even more— that's my Fruitful Vineyard."

"I understand," he concurred with a wink and a grin.

I acknowledged with a chuckle.

"Oh, before I forget, here's a copy of the paper from P. D. in Bend, Oregon." Alan handed me a large envelope containing a single sheet of what appeared to be parchment-like paper. I pulled it part way out, viewing the upper half only.

"You mean?"

"Yes, but let me tell you the whole story first, okay?" he bartered.

"Absolutely," I agreed.

His eyes returned to roaming around The Fruitful Vineyard. They located something in the midst of the menagerie of notes posted prominently above my laptop and directly in my line of sight when I'm working. It is a section of Scripture I entitled "The Writer's Creed". He got up and stepped over to my desk. Leaning forward to better view the document, Alan steadied himself with one hand atop the desk. He then softly read the verses out loud.

"The words of wise men are like goads, and masters of these collections are like well-driven nails; they are given by one Shepherd. But beyond this, my son, be warned: the writing of many books is endless, and excessive devotion to books is wearying to the body. The Book of Ecclesiastes 12: 11, 12."

Alan smiled, nodding his head as he eased back down into the only seat in the room other than my desk chair. "There's wisdom in those words. Perhaps this should be our final book. What do you think?"

"I concur with one caveat; if the Lord were to do anything significant in the future, we should leave the door open to record it."

He considered my suggestion as he turned to gaze out the only window in my office, which looks out onto the front porch, the lawn, and to the street beyond. After nearly a minute, his concentration was broken by a passing minivan.

"Yes, I think that's a good idea," he agreed. "Let's bring our story up to date, to 2017. Then, if our Lord indicates He has something else He can use, we can always cross that bridge when we come to it."

"Perfect," I nodded with a smile.

"Now, with that settled, where were we?" Alan questioned with a look of curiosity on his weathered face.

"We had just finished up the summer of 2003 with your daughter Julie and her boyfriend, Roger, graduating high school. They had stepped into your living room and had made, what appeared to be, a very disturbing announcement," I replied gently, not yet aware of the magnitude of Julie's news.

"Yes, I remember now. I had just committed myself to seeking the Lord and His Kingdom with all of my heart.[1] At the time that was no easy matter. I had so much to ferret through. That summer proved to be incredibly difficult. In fact, so was the following year."

Knowing how much he loved his children, I glanced down at the floor in deference to him. Alan again gazed out the window from the rocking chair. Then, turning to me with those kind eyes and soft wry grin, he quietly asked, "Are you ready for this?"

-one-

Both the best and worst in a person are glaringly on display in the midst of difficulties. The greater the suffering, the greater the manifestation of what's hidden within. This revelation sometimes surprises, yet at other times is completely expected. Character is made to be exposed, and it doesn't have a choice when the time for its unveiling arrives. Old and new qualities alike will come to light, often without warning.

Similar to the wildfires of the American West, the hurricanes of the Deep South thin out the old growth to accommodate the new. This, to be sure, is an unpleasant experience. But those who have been through many of these tumultuous events seem to handle the stress, inconvenience, and discomfort better than the neophyte. For to one who is inexperienced, it looks and feels like random devastation. To the discerning eye, however, this pruning is precise and the intent is clear. Granted, while in the midst, storms can be quite intimidating and alarming, nevertheless, the lasting effects bring change and renewal. In a very real way, Alan Browne was finding this to be all too true and entirely too personal.

September 2004 began like any other September in Pensacola, Florida—sunny, hot, and humid. But within two weeks, an entirely different forecast was predicted; a Category 5 hurricane called Ivan dominated the headlines and was taking aim at Pensacola. Whoever decided to name a hurricane Ivan, must not have been a student of history. Have historians ever recorded anything referencing Ivan the Friendly, or perhaps Ivan the Benign? No, the name Ivan and the word Terrible have been linked together for centuries. Therefore, when a hurricane is dubbed the title Ivan, its legacy surely has been predestined. In this regard, the storm of the same name was determined not to disappoint. And it didn't. Hurricane Ivan was terrible!

Two days after the storm had ravaged the area, Alan walked their property in Myrtle Grove, a mostly residential district within the city, surveying the damage. There were numerous branches of varying sizes strewn throughout the yard. A corner of the standing seam metal roofing on his home had been pulled up and curled back, as if a large hand of enormous strength had peeled back the lid to a tin can. Behind the house, a neighbor's pine tree had snapped off like a toothpick twenty feet above ground and had fallen across their wooden privacy fence, smashing many of the boards like popsicle sticks. Their two car, detached garage, which he used as a woodworking shop, had a broken window as well as a couple of missing planks of lap siding. Surprisingly, other than those issues, he and his family had come through Hurricane Ivan with very little loss. Although it was difficult to be happy about damaged property, when considering what could have happened, he was truly grateful.

Removing the last of the plywood covering the windows, Alan stacked each piece neatly in the rack he had made years ago. They were once again prepared for the next storm. With the help of his dear wife, Annalisa, and their children, Richard and Emily, it took Alan most of the day to carry all of the fallen branches to the street to await removal by the City of Pensacola's debris pick up crews. At one point, as he passed his wife while hauling branches, he asked if she had heard from their other daughter Julie.

"No," she replied. "But I'm not concerned, Alan. She and Roger were at the hospital with his mother. I'm sure she's fine."

"Then why hasn't she contacted us?" he asked with a tone that expressed more worry than annoyance.

"Alan, the phones still don't work. She's okay and will call when she can."

"Yeah, well, why don't they drive over here then?"

"Honey, you know the roads are probably blocked in many areas. Maybe they tried and had to turn around."

"I think they may be doing this on purpose," Alan protested with a scowl. His insecure thoughts were finding an exit through his words.

"Alan, that was over a year ago. They're not vindictive people. I think our Lord is just prolonging this test to get the most He can out of it. It's for your benefit, you know." She was smiling as she kissed him on the cheek. The softness of her lips were in sharp contrast to the stinging effect of her words upon his heart.

Watching her walk away, his mind began to drift back to that awful day. It had started out nice enough. He was feeling light, free, and in a pleasant mood. He and Annalisa were sitting on the sofa in their living room enjoying one another's company when Julie and her boyfriend Roger strolled in. After exchanging pleasantries, she had announced some rather devastating news.

"It's true," he whispered to himself as he scooped up the last batch of branches in his arms. "It took me quite a long time to recognize Roger and Julie's situation was a test God was using in my life too."

Interrupting his thoughts, Annalisa called from the porch of their turn-of-the-century farm house that she was going in to prepare lunch. He acknowledged and told her he would be in the garage trying to fix the broken window. Moving the big, plastic, trash barrel over to the window, he began carefully removing the shards of glass from the eight by twelve inch pane within the wooden window. While cleaning out the old window putty, his mind once again wandered back to that terrible day last year. His daughter Julie had been the spokesperson for Roger and herself. It had angered Alan that her boyfriend would take advantage of her in that way. Alan had accused. Julie had defended. Roger stood silent. He had his arm around Julie's waist and was staring at the floor. Annalisa had taken up the role of peacemaker. The entire encounter hadn't lasted ten minutes, but the rift between them had lasted more than a year. Alan didn't realize it yet, but these are the dynamics that our nefarious enemy loves to exploit and to continue capitalizing on through much watering, cultivating, and fertilizing. He is a master gardener of all things divisive and evil, nurturing where we feel hurt, offended, and justified. Later, we are surprised at our harvest full of prickly weeds.

Noticing a splotch of bright red on the white wood window, Alan was somewhat awakened from his reflective daydream. Carelessly, he had ripped open the end of a finger on a shard of glass. He casually walked to the first aid kit hanging on the wall across the garage. While cleaning the wound to the tip of his left ring finger, he gazed at his wedding ring. Although a tiny circle of metal, it symbolized so much more to him—his relationship with the love of his life, Annalisa. He stopped cleaning the cut and compressed it tightly between two fingers as he pondered why this particular finger had sustained the injury. A quiet thought breeched his mind like a whale breaks through the surface of the sea.

"The detailed care with which you are attending the minor cut on your finger should be used for a much more serious wound."

The thought landed with a massive splash upon his mind, disseminating waves even as far away as his heart. It was so precise in its intent that it shook Alan, sending him shuffling across the sawdust covered floor to his desk chair. Once seated, he quieted his heart and asked the Lord for clarification to this latest revelation. However, his mind kept drifting back to that awful day more than a year ago. Eyes closed, he sat stone still while he replayed the conversation several times. He remembered the words that were announced, in the calmest of tones, by his daughter. Grimacing, he also recalled his own harsh words and attitude. It hurt to watch this scene unfold in his mind yet again.

"You declared you wanted to seek first My kingdom," whispered the nearly silent thought.

"Yes, Lord, You know I want to walk with You all the days of my life."

"This is what it means to walk with Me and seek My kingdom."

"But, dear Lord, they're doing the wrong thing. They're going the wrong way. If I don't tell them, who will?"

Glancing around his shop, Alan sensed he had overstepped and decided to apologize quickly. "I'm sorry, Father. That was completely inappropriate for me to act as if I'm the only one through which they could hear from You. I'm sorry, that was wrong of me. Please forgive me . . . Thank you for your forgiveness."

"Judge not lest you be judged[1]," responded the soft voice of love in his thoughts.

For Alan, this hit right at the heart of the matter. He had judged his daughter and her boyfriend. Actually, he hadn't even let them finish explaining their situation. He had interrupted and brashly declared his opinion, which he had, of course, considered to be the only correct and valid one. Before he had had a chance to finish his comments to them, Julie had wagged her head in exasperation. She and Roger had turned and angrily stormed out. That was the last real conversation he had shared with his daughter. Since then, he had received only short answers to his questions with "fine" being the favored response.

Leaning forward, while still holding his throbbing finger, Alan shuddered. His mind rehearsed the moments immediately after Julie had slammed the front door, when

Annalisa had pointedly expressed a couple of observations trying to enlighten him to a different perspective. A heated argument had ensued between them resulting in her stomping up the stairs and slamming their bedroom door. Fuming and standing alone in the living room, he felt completely justified. Julie and Roger were the ones in the wrong. He most assuredly was faultless in the matter. After all, he was the one seeking God, right?

Within minutes, however, as he was walking out to his shop, a Scripture had popped into his mind, like high beam lights on a lonely, dark road.

> "But the goal of our instruction is *love* from a pure heart and a good conscience and a sincere faith."[2]

This thought had nagged at him all that afternoon and well into the evening. Somehow, he hadn't previously connected this Scripture with his particular situation. The Lord had indeed given the remedy, yet he hadn't applied it. So it festered, like any unattended wound would. Had he, at the expense of his relationship with his daughter, valued being right, being justified as more important? Based on the Scriptures, could one's pride ever be elevated above one's love? An ever so subtle breeze began to breathe across his slowly increasing awareness. In God's economy, relationships are infinitely more important than the insignificant matter of who may be right or wrong. "I mean, in the light of God's majesty . . ." Stopping himself mid-sentence, he began to comprehend that he had been completely duped by the wretchedly deceitful enemy.

He leaned back in his chair and looked down at his injured finger. Removing the bloodied gauze, he discovered the cut had stopped bleeding. He dabbed it with some antibiotic ointment and gently wrapped it with a band aid, carefully assuring the non-sticky surface was directly covering the wound. Then closing his eyes, he began to pray. But just before he formed the words, a quiet thought came to his mind.

"If you had only taken the same care with your daughter that you did with your finger, the wound would have healed quickly."

"I need to fix this," Alan declared out loud as he stood up with his eyes wide open. "This has gone on way too long. It shouldn't matter what their issue is . . . that's between them and God. My attitude, my response, and my words are what I'm responsible for, both to them and to my Lord."

Grabbing the pad of drafting paper and a pencil, he began jotting down some notes. Certainly, cleaning this situation up was what God wanted him to do, and he wanted to assure he didn't miss a single detail. First, he needed to make things right with Annalisa. Once that was settled, then he would work through the mess with Julie and Roger. This was definitely going to be a challenge, but that's what faith is for . . . the tough times. And it is because of love that faith is exercised.[3] If he didn't love God and others, he wouldn't be using his faith to work through these issues. He would just keep convincing himself that he had been wronged and that he was justified in holding to his position, thereby letting the injuries continue to fester and allowing the relationships to drift further apart.

"Love is the ultimate goal of everything He is trying to teach me,"[4] he stated aloud. "It is the pinnacle of any relationship with Him. God is love.[5] It is His essence. It is who He is. And along with faith and hope it is considered one of the three most important elements in the universe.[6] It is declared as the two most important of all the commandments.[7] Love is everything. And everything should be used to develop and enlarge it in my life. Love is the central point of His kingdom, the kingdom within me."[8]

Once he had determined what God wanted him to do, Alan took action immediately. He marched across the driveway and into the kitchen where Annalisa had just finished preparing their lunch. He gently took her hand and led her into the living room where they sat down on the sofa. He tenderly explained to her what had just happened in the garage, holding up his bandaged finger as evidence. Further, he expressed how the Lord had convicted him regarding his insensitivity, pride, anger, and selfishness. Humbly apologizing, he confessed that he was wrong and was sincerely sorry. Finally, he asked for her forgiveness, which she gladly gave with tear filled eyes. She then slid her arms around his shoulders.

"Thank you, Alan. I can't tell you how much this means to me."

"Why, honey?" he asked softly. "And why are you crying?"

"Because I was offended and felt like you had wronged me. It was driving a wedge between us. And not only us . . ."

23

"I know, honey. As soon as I see them, I'm going to apologize to Julie and Roger too."

"That's a good start, Alan. But it's more than that. I think the enemy has really had a field day with this situation.[9] Think of the wonderful relationship we used to have with our daughter and her boyfriend before this all started. They were over here all the time eating dinner, playing games, and talking. You even said he was like a son to you. Now what? We hardly ever see them, and when we do the conversation is short and to the point. There's no longer the exchange of ideas, hopes, and dreams. They don't talk to us. You don't talk to them. And truthfully . . . I didn't feel much like talking to you either."

"Oh, honey, I'm so very sorry. I never meant for anything like this to happen," he lamented.

"I know, my dear husband, but it has, and now you need to fix it. Strange, I think it may have started when you declared you were committed to seeking first the Lord and His kingdom. Shortly after that, I began to notice an attitude in you. It was very subtle, but it was there. I sensed it in what you said and how you said it. You know, like you thought you were better than everyone else because you were seeking the Lord."

"Oh no, really?" he asked, his eyes brimming with unshed tears.

"I wasn't sure, honey," she whispered. "Until that day, when it came out in living color. After that, there was an invisible wall between us, so I never really felt I could tell you. Meanwhile, our daughter has been walking around deeply wounded."

At this point, both Alan and Annalisa broke down and allowed the tears to flow freely as they sobbed upon one another's necks. God was healing their hearts, their relationship, and the spirit of their marriage. They acknowledged that Alan had indeed committed himself to pursuing the kingdom of God, but what they hadn't realized was how His kingdom actually grows—through brokenness. This, coupled with the fact that the Lord had used a very natural circumstance with his daughter to help Alan see his faults, came as a revelation to them both. He quickly determined, as he and Annalisa prayed together, that he would strive to never again be prideful regarding seeking the Lord and His kingdom. Nor would he ever impose upon others his opinion about what they should do with their lives.

"God knows what's right for each individual, not me," he confessed. Then while still holding her close he prayed, "If they should ask me, Lord, I'll look to You for an answer before responding. But I will not blurt something out that has not been sought by another."

"Me, too, Lord," agreed Annalisa quietly.

Then the two of them in unison said, "Amen."

No sooner had they walked back in the kitchen and sat down at the table for their lunch than Annalisa spoke up. "I feel like a huge burden has been lifted off my heart, Alan. I'm really proud of you for humbling yourself. To me, this is what seeking first His kingdom in our lives is all about."

Nodding his head, Alan swallowed a bite of his turkey and cheese sandwich. "Yes, my love, I think our gracious Lord has set up His kingdom, so it can only expand and grow in a life through practical experience. No matter how much you study, that which you have discovered isn't a reality in your life until you have actually lived it."

"How true," she confirmed. "Otherwise, it would belong to the smartest or most learned among us."

"Hmmm . . ." he acknowledged with a full mouth.

"It kind of levels the playing field," she continued. "No one is above another if these Christ-like characteristics are developed by experience because what one suffers in one event may be entirely different for another in a similar situation. If one is willing, however, God can enlarge him as quickly as the person is able to let Him do so."

"I agree, honey," smiled Alan. "It's ingenious really. It doesn't matter how much time you study, if your intent is other than implementing what you've learned. It's sort of like someone who has been learning to swim, but once they jump into the water, they resort to flailing around instead of using what they've been taught. They may have put forth a lot of effort in their searching, but if they don't put into practice the knowledge that they have gained, it doesn't produce the desired effect and they end up on the bottom."

"Alan, that's awful," she chided, throwing a dish towel, which landed squarely on his face.

"Sorry, honey. But, it's true," he quipped stuffing the last bite of sandwich in his mouth.

"Well, I don't like your metaphor. However, I do think what you're saying has some truth to it."

"Yeah, and it's precisely where God has me right now. I need to find Julie and Roger, so I can make this right. That wicked enemy has had way too much sway. His insidious fun, you know, his plans, are about to come to an abrupt end."

The route Alan drove to the hospital was every bit as serpentine as it was arduous. What normally took fifteen to twenty minutes to drive, was now bordering on an hour. Evidently, Hurricane Ivan had had its way with more of Pensacola than he had realized. There was devastation everywhere. He spotted downed trees, roofs blown off, damaged traffic signals not working properly, and power lines lying across the roads as well as many housetops. The military, donned with M-16s, had taken up positions at major intersections. At one such crossroad, a station wagon full of children and their frantic mother had stopped in the middle of the intersection. Alan wondered why the vehicle had come to a halt until he observed her rolling down her window. What he saw next made a lasting impression on him. In the midst of the chaos that was her world, the harried mother reached out and handed the weary soldier directing traffic a bottle of water. The kind and generous act was so convicting it brought tears to Alan's eyes.

"I need to be helping too," he challenged himself out loud as he turned into the hospital driveway.

Finding one of the few available parking spots, Alan pulled in and hopped out. Then he headed to the oncology floor. The elevator doors opened revealing a different world. One of life and death, pain and relief, hope and despair. Medical staff were rushing about, purposeful in their every move. Alan asked a young nurse if she knew which room Mrs. Ballinger was in. She advised him of the room number and pointed down the hall. Praying before he stepped inside, he found the room empty except for Roger's mother and all of the equipment attached to her through the various cords, tubes, and wires. Not seeing any sign of Julie and Roger, Alan greeted Mrs. Ballinger with a smile. After the usual pleasantries, he apologized for any hurt he had caused during a time in her life already wrought with pain and uncertainty. He confessed his self-absorbed attitude and his failure to be a strength to her and her son. At that point, he humbly asked for her forgiveness. She was quite surprised but very appreciative as she had heard of the entire unfortunate debacle through Roger many times. Alan sat down in the chair next to her bed and listened.

She spoke candidly of her youth and her early years of marriage before Roger's father had left her and their only child to live in Costa Rica with his old college girlfriend. It had been devastating, but with the passage of time she had found it within herself to forgive him. However, she was sure Roger never had. She thanked Alan profusely for leading her son to Christ. Although she had attended a church in downtown Pensacola for more than thirty years, she never felt quite confident enough to open up and share her faith with her son. She reached across to hold Alan's hand as she told him she would be forever grateful to him for sharing the words of eternal life and the gift of salvation with her son.

"You know," she panted as her breathing became quite labored. "Roger will be all alone when I die. He will inherit my house, car, and a life insurance policy, so he'll be well taken care of financially. But he won't have anyone, except your precious daughter Julie. They love each other so much, you know."

"Yes, I know they do. And I'm glad they have one another during these days."

"Roger wants to marry your daughter," she submitted frankly. "I've told him he needs to wait until he has a place to live and a stable income. The day I die he'll have all that and more."

"Really?"

"Yes. And he used to admire you. He really looked up to you as a father figure, the father he never had. You need to make it right with him, Mr. Browne. That boy of mine needs you. Believe me, soon, and very soon, he's going to need you even more."

The sharp twinge of her words sunk deep into his grief-stricken heart. When a heart has been softened due to sorrows, words have the power to cut more deeply than when it is joyful. He determined immediately that he would not rest until he made things right with both Julie and Roger.

For nearly an hour more, Alan continued to visit with Roger's mother. Then, noticing she was getting extremely tired, he asked if he could pray with her. After praying together, Alan gave her a hug and said goodbye. Once in the hallway, he headed for the elevator. As he passed the oncology floor waiting room, someone familiar caught his attention

P eering through the glass that enclosed the waiting room, Alan could discern that the young couple in one another's arms was distraught. Both appeared to be weeping uncontrollably. Watching this pitiful sight made him feel absolutely ashamed of himself. The severity of the situation came crashing down on him like a tsunami of regret. His eyes welled up with tears as the full realization of the chasm between them overwhelmed him. He should have made this right between the three of them long ago. He doggedly determined he was not going to wait any longer. It had taken months, but today was the day. It was time to take back the ground he had so readily given to the enemy. And further, he would tear down the stronghold that wretched one had built between his beloved daughter, Roger, and himself. Alan was learning how to fight the good fight of faith.[1]

Praying as he opened the waiting room door, he proceeded inside. The room was empty with the exception of the three of them. He walked across the dingy, carpeted floor unnoticed by the two on the little sofa in the corner opposite the door. He picked up a chair on his way toward the couple and set it down quietly in front of them.

"Dad, what on earth?!" yipped Julie, trying to wipe the tears from her eyes.

"Hi, honey," he empathetically responded with tears in his eyes. "Hi, Roger," he gave a single nod in acknowledgment toward the young man.

"Hi, Coach Browne. What are you doing here, sir?"

"I came to apologize and make things right. I cannot express to you how ashamed I have felt since the Lord recently convicted me about the way I handled things between us over a year ago. I thought I knew what was best for everyone involved, but I was dead wrong. I treated you two harshly, and I was so self-centered I couldn't see any other opinion but my own. So if you can find it within your hearts, will you two please forgive me?" Alan pleaded with all the sincerity in his heart. "I know I have hurt you both deeply, and I feel terrible about it. And I promise, I will never do that again."

"Oh, Dad," cried Julie as she leapt across the gap between them and into her father's arms.

Alan waved Roger over to join in the hug. He complied immediately. Afterward, the three talked through all that had caused the awful misunderstanding. Alan thought it imperative to clear this up completely, thereby no longer giving the enemy room to inflict any further damage. After nearly an hour of discussing the situation and its many peripheral issues, smiles were once again seen on the tear stained faces. Realizing they too had played a part in the rift, Julie and Roger confessed their faults, asking for her father's forgiveness as well. It was a wonderfully precious time of healing for all.

As Julie left to freshen up in the restroom, Roger confided in Alan.

"I am so glad we got this straightened out, Coach. I wasn't sure what to do. I have all these terrible decisions I will be forced to make shortly . . . you know, when Mom dies. I think it will only be a day or two. I'll be lost without her."

"Don't worry, son. I'm right here with you, and Jesus is even closer. We've got you."

"Thanks, Coach. I can't tell you how much that means to me. I'm really scared, you know? I don't know what to do with the house, the bills, and all of the money from the insurance. What do I do with all of that?"

"We'll work through it one day at a time, Roger. Just take it slow, okay?"

"Okay, Coach, I'll try. There are so many things I need to talk with you about. Uh . . . especially Julie."

"What about her?"

"Well, I'm sure it's no secret . . . I mean, you must know that I love her, right?"

"I kind of figured you had some strong feelings for her."

"Yes, I do, and I would like to marry her someday, uh . . . with your permission, of course."

"Let's take one thing at a time, Roger. You have enough on your plate for the foreseeable future. Besides, I would want us to work through a couple of projects together first."

Roger's head dropped as he stared at the floor silently. Alan realized he had deflated the young man. He knew this could be quite detrimental especially following such an important time of healing and renewal among them.

"I will say this to you, Roger. If you ever marry my daughter Julie, I think you would be the finest addition our family could ever have."

Roger's countenance lit up. "Really, Coach? The finest? Really?"

"Yes, I do, so let's just be patient, okay. God will bring about the perfect timing. And when He does, I'll be the least of your worries," smiled Alan as he patted Roger on the back.

The two walked into the hall just as Julie rounded the corner. After they exchanged hugs, the younger two headed for Roger's mother's room and Alan for home. Driving past one of the many emergency relief distribution stations, Alan felt a check in his heart. As a result of what he was sensing, he quickly decided to drop by the ice and water supply trailer.

After receiving his allotment of one bag of ice and one case of bottled water, he asked if they needed any volunteers to help. The middle-aged woman wearing a Red Cross hat and vest laughed, stating they were in desperate straits with very little help. In the same breath, she asked when he could start.

"If it wasn't for this ice, which will melt in my car, I could begin immediately."

"Put it back in the trailer," she replied. "We'll save it for you. By the way, I'm Wanda. Please follow me."

She sized him up for a hat and vest and introduced him to the others. Alan enthusiastically dove right in. From the second he started helping others, he felt a tremendous sense of blessing. He worked hard, jumping in wherever help was needed. Before he knew it, the trailer was empty, and it was well past seven p.m. Wanda asked if he could come back in the morning, explaining they had another trailer scheduled to arrive at five o'clock. Alan quickly agreed.

Hopping into his car, without his bag of ice, he smiled with satisfaction knowing he had helped his neighbors. His smile slowly faded into a worried expression when he remembered Annalisa always had their dinner ready at six. Pulling into their driveway shortly before eight p.m., Alan noticed Roger's car parked over by the garage.

"Uh, oh, now I'm really in trouble," he chided himself.

No sooner had he opened the side door than Annalisa threw her arms around him and planted a long, deep kiss upon his lips. "I love you with all my heart, you wonderful husband and father you. I am so very proud of you, honey."

"Thanks. I love you too, uh . . . with all my heart, too."

"Julie and Roger are in the living room, and they can't stop talking about you. It's Dad said this or Dad did that. It's amazing. It's like they aren't even the same people or something. You're really special, Alan Michael Browne. And may I remind you again? I love you with all of my heart," she smiled and then gave him another long kiss.

"Uh . . . sure, keep reminding me for as long as you like," he laughed just before she kissed him again.

"I love you with . . . uh, wait a second. Where have you been anyway? You're quite late."

"Well . . . I was helping folks with the ice and water at the emergency distribution trailers."

"Good for you, honey. Wow, you're really trying to implement what you've been reading. Aren't you?"

"Trying," he replied with a tone of uncertainty, wondering if he could continue to change.

The rest of the evening was especially enjoyable with the four of them talking by candlelight until almost midnight. It was so congenial that Alan even invited Roger to spend the night, on the sofa downstairs. Without hesitation, Roger accepted. Once upstairs and in bed, Alan and Annalisa continued to talk until the wee hours of the morning. What a difference forgiveness makes in the lives it touches. It's no wonder our enemy hates it.

Having been married for nearly twenty-five years now and quickly approaching their fifties, Alan and Annalisa both had a vast array of life's experiences to draw upon. They had spent almost half of their lives loving one another. She was still petite and a very pretty woman. She wore her auburn hair, which had just a sprinkling of grey, in a much shorter style now. To him, her expressive, deep brown eyes were one of her greatest assets along with her smile that could still light up a small city. Enjoying running since her youth, she continued with daily forays of about two to three miles. Alan too had been a very competitive miler who continued to delight in a jog alongside his wife a few times each week. Almost a foot taller, he still had a wiry physique although he wasn't nearly as fit as he wanted to be. His sandy brown hair and slate blue eyes, coupled with his ruddy complexion, made him quite the handsome specimen, even as he approached the half-century mark.

Moving to Pensacola, Florida, from the San Ramon Valley area of Northern California ten years ago, had taken some adjustment. The weather, for example, not to mention the occasional and unwelcome visit of a hurricane, was mild throughout the very short winters, but hot and humid during the long summers. Spring and fall were very pleasant, but relatively short. This was a huge contrast to that of San Ramon. However, whatever Pensacola lacked in climate, it more than made up for in its people. Never had Alan and Annalisa found friendlier folks than along the Gulf Coast. Generally, they were sincere, kind, and willing to lend a hand whenever needed. Alan decided the phrase "Southern Hospitality" must have been invented to describe the folks who live in Pensacola.

Before leaving California, Alan had sold his three bicycle shops. Upon arriving in Florida, he began working at a cabinet and furniture shop owned by his good friend Joey Hinote. A few years later, Alan had opened his own woodworker's business and had taken on a part time job coaching Track and Cross Country at the local high school. Shortly thereafter, his dear friend Betsy Taft had passed away, leaving her house in Arlington, Virginia, to Alan and Annalisa. Living nearly a thousand miles away, the offer by Betsy's attorney to purchase their newly acquired asset had come at just the right time. Once this sale closed, Alan had found himself, for the first time in his life, with a very large sum of money. Now came decisions he never thought he would have to make. After much prayer and discussion with Annalisa, he decided to close his woodworking business. Since then, he had made it his focus to seek the Lord and His kingdom. He did this by studying as much as eight, nine, even ten hours a day. He sometimes sequestered himself for days in his shop, hunched over his desk, digging in the

Scriptures and taking copious notes. At times, he memorized whole Psalms as well as chapters of some of the New Testament books. He tried to absorb himself wholeheartedly in the Scriptures, even to the detriment of other issues, including his family.

One day Annalisa had chastised him for his lack of attention to her and the children stating, "Our Lord told us there are two commandments more important than all the others.[2] The first is to 'Love God with all your heart, soul, mind, and strength.' And the second is, 'Love your neighbor as yourself.' If you declare you're seeking the Lord, then why aren't these teachings important to you?"

The sting of her words had rung in his ears for months. Try as he might, it was difficult for him to think of others before himself. He would have some moderate success for a week or two. Then sadly, he'd fall right back into his own insecurities, which revealed themselves as displays of self-centeredness. This waffling had continued for so many months that it was becoming more of a chronic problem than an acute flare-up. That was up until the day after Hurricane Ivan blew ashore when he had cut his finger. God had used the event as a wondrous living illustration which opened a flood gate of personal revelations and the grace to help him do what needed to be done.

Now his months of studying and memorizing the Scriptures suddenly presented their worth, as one by one, like a ticker tape at the stock market, they scrolled through his mind. First, the verse in Proverbs stating, "Reproofs for discipline are the way of life."[3] Closely followed by the Scripture that explains how God created mankind with a "spirit, a soul, and a body."[4] No sooner had those passed through his mind than, "God is spirit and those who worship Him, must do so in spirit and in truth,"[5] caught his attention.

"Because He is Spirit, it appears that God prefers to speak to me on the spiritual level, Spirit to spirit. If, for whatever reason, I can't hear His Spirit speaking to my spirit, then because He loves me He will choose to speak to me on the level of my soul. Hmmm . . ." He rubbed his unshaven chin as he pondered those thoughts.

"My soul," he continued out loud, "is the way I express myself to others and they to me, as it is the faculty that houses my personality. Yes, my mind and my emotions as well as my will. But suppose I don't hear what God is trying to say to me through other people or through emotionally stressful situations, then what?"

Sitting in his chair as quietly as he possibly could, Alan was trying to sense any thought that resembled the Holy Spirit speaking. His eyes were closed to hinder any visual distractions.

"Lord?" he whispered.

Just then a softly quiet thought crossed his mind, "You cut your finger."

Opening his eyes, Alan glanced down at his bandaged finger. His mouth dropped wide open while one of God's many mysteries slowly dawned upon him, like the pleasant fragrance wafting from a rose garden in spring. It was new and fresh, lifting his awareness and awakening his spiritual senses.

"First, my spirit."

"Next, my soul."

"Lastly, my body. That's how He disciplines in a progressively firmer fashion."

Leaning back in his chair, he slapped himself on the forehead. He slowly shook his head in disbelief as a broad smile spread across his face revealing the thoughts swirling in his mind.

"Wow, how could I have missed this? It is so simple, so practical. Whoa, there's my answer . . . He always keeps it plain enough that even a child can understand. It's we adults who seem to complicate it," he chided himself.

"Now let's see, my Father in Heaven is a Spirit and therefore prefers to speak to my spirit, my conscience first and foremost. How come I've never seen this before?" he asked in disbelief. "So if, after several attempts, I don't hear or perceive what He is wafting across my spirit, He will speak to my soul often using other people or even circumstances as His mouthpiece. From my experience, Lord, this usually isn't a pleasant encounter." Alan had slipped into his half-talking-half-praying thing, as he had a habit of doing.

"Finally," he continued with a smile and a shake of his head. "If I don't hear You by these avenues, You can resort to something physical, even bodily discomfort. Wow, 'discipline is the way of life', and I think I'm just beginning to scratch that surface. But thankfully, You are helping me to see what I have not seen."

Glancing around his shop, his eyes came full circle to once again rest upon his damaged finger. "Such a minor thing as a cut on my finger. What else have I missed when

God has been speaking through circumstances? If only I had the spirit to perceive. What might I have discovered of the magnificent mysteries of God and His majestic kingdom? Think of it, the possibilities are absolutely endless."

This revelation coupled with the knowledge that everything God was trying to teach him, all of it, served the same purpose—to bring him to the goal of love.[6] Love for God and love for others.[7] There is no higher calling he decided. In fact, love is the calling. That very day, Alan had marched across their driveway and into the kitchen determined to make things right with his family, starting first with his precious wife Annalisa. That was the first day he could recall that all of the discipline made sense. Now he comprehended a bit more why Christ's disciples are call 'disciplined ones.'

As the weeks flew by after Ivan, everything was continuing to heal in their family as well as throughout Pensacola. Little by little, the city was being restored and renewed to that which they had grown to love and enjoy. The same was true in Alan's life. It did appear to him that many times it took a storm to make things right. In the aftermath he was glad, even thankful, but during the tempest the winds were full of misunderstandings, hurt, and pain.

Remembering back, he once again recalled how the conversation had started calmly enough that day over a year ago. His daughter had declared that she and her boyfriend, Roger, would not be accepting their full scholarships to a university education. Without thinking, Alan had abruptly jumped up from their living room sofa and bellowed forth his decree, proclaiming in no uncertain terms that they were making a colossal mistake. He had already conclusively determined that they should accept the free rides to a four year education and had judged any other idea as ludicrous. Julie had tried to explain her situation, but her father had turned a deaf ear and would hear none of it, even though she had pleaded with him. Without having had the opportunity to fully explain herself, she and Roger had left feeling frustrated, discouraged, and angry.

Immediately following their departure, Alan had quickly justified his position to Annalisa declaring that Julie was probably pregnant. In fact, he had concluded, with as much time as the two lovers were spending alone, he was absolutely positive that was the situation. Annalisa had been thoroughly disgusted with his attitude. She let him know, in her unmistakable way, what she thought of his theory. When they were pretty much through with their shouting match, she had stormed up the stairs and slammed their bedroom door shut. Alan had retired to his solitude, the shop in his garage.

Days later, Alan had discovered the terrible truth behind Julie's announcement. Roger's mother had been diagnosed with pancreatic cancer the previous day. Her chances for survival were minimal. To his credit, Roger had decided to forego his scholarship to stay home and take care of his ailing mother. Julie had committed to do the same thing. Although this new piece of information changed things, Alan still thought he knew best. He wouldn't give up his staunch position in favor of humbling himself and accepting that only God knew what was best for others, even his daughter.

For the past thirteen months, this wound had festered, affecting everyone in their family, until Alan cut his finger. The revelation he had from this minor event caused him to humble himself, apologize, and ask for their forgiveness. From that moment forward, the atmosphere had changed. The sky was clear of storm clouds, and the harsh winds had calmed to a delightful breeze. Thankfully, the enemy, who had wreaked such havoc, was defeated. The entire family enjoyed one another again. However, those who are knowledgeable with regard to hurricanes, recognize there's always the threat of the huge storm spawning a tornado or two.

Less than a month later, Roger's mother passed away.

The ripple effect brought many issues to light for all, especially Roger. He confided in Alan about most every matter from the funeral, to the transfer of property titles, to the surging emotions of one who has lost someone whom he held most dear. These were incredibly difficult days for the young man and, therefore, for his girlfriend Julie. As Alan and Annalisa had counseled them often, God would comfort and heal them, but sometimes it just took time. No sooner had the situation with Roger begun to settle down, than a second whirlwind launched into Alan's fragile camp.

Sitting on his front porch the first week of December 2004, Alan was reading a book and enjoying the warm Florida sunshine when his phone rang.

"Hello?"

"Hey, Alan, how are you doing today, my brother?" It was the unmistakable voice of his best friend Joey Hinote.

"Loving this weather. You?"

"Yes, it's awesome. Pam wants to have a picnic in the backyard, so we're going to grill up some hamburgers later for dinner. How about you guys?"

"We're having a chicken pasta dish. It's one of my favorites."

"Nice," Joey concurred. "Hey, something has come up. You got a minute to talk?"

"Yeah, man. What's going on?"

"Well . . ." hesitated Joey, "I've got some good news, and I've got some bad news. Which do you want to hear first?"

-three-

The phone was silent while Alan tried to determine if this was a serious matter Joey was presenting or just another one of his riddles. Not being fond of negative news, especially right on the heels of all he'd been working through with Roger, Alan laughed and teasingly told Joey he had mistakenly called "The Good News Only Hotline." Therefore, he was only able to listen to good news on this phone call.

"Okay," replied Joey. "I've taken . . ."

"Wait!" interrupted Alan. "Although I can't really handle any bad news right now, I would rather hear it first, so I can chase it down with some good news. What's the bad news Joey?"

"The bad news is that Pam and I are moving."

"What?! When, where, why?"

"Well, that's the good news. Remember all the furniture refinishing projects I did for those hotels?"

"Yeah."

"They want me to run their refurbishing jobs for all of their hotels. They're headquartered in Birmingham, Alabama, so it's a requirement that I live there. It's a great opportunity. They have just under a hundred properties throughout the Southeast and are committed to remodeling each one every twelve years or so, on a rotating basis, of course."

"Man, that is awesome, Joey! How on earth did you get that job?" Alan asked enthusiastically, trying to hide his utter disappointment that his best friend would be moving away.

"I was finishing up my last project in Destin when their V.P. of Operations, Ms. Bowes, showed up. We got to talking, had lunch, and on the way back to the hotel I shared some ideas with her as to how they could make these projects run more smoothly and save quite a bit of money in the process. She called me two weeks later and asked if I would come to Birmingham for an interview. It was pretty intimidating. I mean, several board members and the President of the company were in the meeting. They had a slide show, you know, one of those fancy Power Point deals, indicating the locations, types of hotels, and a schedule for remodeling each and every one of those properties. When it was finished, the lights went back on, and they started firing questions at me."

"Why? What were they asking you?" inquired Alan in a somewhat serious tone.

"They wanted to know how I would schedule the projects, and if I had any ideas to save them time and money. I mean, everything from the big picture of a multi-year timeline to what kind of varnish endures the longest. They even asked about my knowledge of Microsoft Excel. I felt like I was being grilled. It wasn't until later that evening at dinner with two of them that Ms. Bowes slid a folded sheet of paper across the table in my direction. When I inquired as to what it was, she replied that it was an Offer Letter. It was incredibly difficult to contain myself when I unfolded it. Alan, it was for more money in a year than I would normally make in three years."

"No way. Are you serious?"

"Yes, I'm as serious as a heart attack. My title is Director of Revitalization."

"Wow, Joey, congratulations! That is absolutely amazing," Alan cheered, trying hard not to reveal his disappointment. It was a very difficult pill to swallow.

The two talked the better part of an hour before hanging up. Alan then sat quietly on his front porch, discouraged. Even though they regarded one another as equals, Alan relied on Joey, who was about ten years older, for encouragement. Now, his friend would be nearly five hours away in another state. After a morning of exercising and reading, Annalisa sat down on the porch next to Alan. He shared Joey's situation and his own feelings with her.

"Don't be downcast, honey," she coaxed. "It seems God has people moving here and there on a regular basis. They'll probably be back in a few years. Who knows, we may be moving."

"What's that supposed to mean?" he chided.

"It means, you just never know. That's all. Besides . . . oh, I almost forgot. You have a message on the answering machine. Sounds like that guy you met at the church in Thomasville, Georgia, last month when you were speaking there. He mentioned something about P. D. in Bend, Oregon, and a particular **rojocci** paper. He wants you to call him back."

"Thanks, my love. I'll call him after dinner. I'm kind of glad those speaking engagements have slowed down a bit. All that traveling was starting to wear me out."

"Me too, Alan," she smiled, reaching to hold his hand. "I like you being home. It's been what, a year and a half now since you started receiving requests to come share about The **rojocci** Fellowship?"

"It was shortly after we sent out The **rojocci** Manifesto mailer. I hope we get more invitations to speak, just not so many at a time. Forty-three in eighteen months is a bit hectic."

"Well, make sure you call that guy back, okay?" she reminded.

"I will. What's his name again?"

"Uh . . . I think it's Leonard Smitley."

After dinner, Alan moped around the house, finally coming in for a landing on the living room sofa next to Annalisa. He wasn't depressed, but he wasn't chipper either. After being asked for the third time if he had called Leonard Smitley, Alan decided to move into the kitchen to make the phone call. It was a cordial conversation and seemed to be winding down when Alan asked what kind of **rojocci** paper Leonard had discovered. From that point forward, the conversation was a monologue with Alan emitting an occasional grunt of acknowledgement in response to Leonard's latest statement.

"Well, how'd that go?" questioned Annalisa as he plopped down on the sofa nearly ninety-five minutes later.

"That fella sure can talk," he sighed. "Nice enough guy, but he sure is a talker."

"Why didn't you tell him you had to go?"

"I was going to, except I couldn't get a word in edge-wise. I'm not kidding you. When he gets on a rail and runs, that thing is to the west coast and back before I get a chance to ask him the first question."

"Honey . . ." she started to say when Alan interrupted.

"He did have one very curious tidbit though," he confessed, glancing at her as a way of apology for cutting her off.

"What's that?" she smiled accepting his contrite gesture.

"He mentioned that someone in Bend, Oregon, had some kind of historical document. P. D. are the initials this individual goes by. He encouraged me to travel to Oregon and look this person up to see what the artifact is all about."

"Why doesn't he go?" she jabbed with a chuckle.

"He doesn't have the money or the time. I think Leonard is probably in his latter years. Kind of sounds like it on the phone anyway."

"Oh, I'm sorry." Annalisa was much more sincere in her response this time feeling she had misjudged Leonard.

"Yeah, sad. I would like to go at some point, if we can find some more evidence that something **rojocci** actually exists in Bend, Oregon. Although, we have heard about this before, I just can't remember when."

"We could fly to San Francisco and visit my Mom and my sister, Alan. Then we could drive to Bend. It can't be that far, can it? What do you say to that? We haven't been back since Dad died."

"Yeah, maybe. But before we go off on some chase down a rabbit hole, I would want to know we at least had a chance of discovering what we went there to find."

"I agree. But tell me we'll at least go see my Mom and sister sometime soon, okay?"

"We will," he smiled. "At least, I think we will."

"Alan?"

"We will, honey. I promise."

With the end of the high school Cross Country season, Alan found he had more time on his hands, so he sequestered himself in his shop either studying the Scriptures or creating something out of wood. His latest creation was a rocking chair for Annalisa he hoped to finish by their anniversary in May.

The first few months of 2005 were fairly uneventful with the exception of Joey and Pam moving to Birmingham. Unfortunately, Alan's high school Track team wasn't doing very well. They had only won four of their ten meets so far and hardly any of his athletes qualified for the Florida State Championships, a far cry from when Roger and Julie were on his teams. Hoping to endure until his younger children, Richard and Emily, were old enough, Alan had pushed aside the thought of quitting. However, with Richard only a sophomore and Emily a freshman, he wasn't sure he could hang on. Besides, Richard preferred soccer and Emily wasn't really interested in running. Therefore, as the losing season grinded to a close, he tendered his resignation.

That summer Hurricane Dennis charged ashore with the eye moving directly north over the Pensacola Bay and quickly into Alabama. Though the Category three storm had the same rating as Ivan had registered the previous September, it was not nearly as destructive. This made sense to those who experienced both storms, for who ever heard of Dennis the Terrible?

Shortly after completing the clean up around his own property, Alan hustled down to the emergency distribution area to see how he could help. To his surprise and delight, the city appeared to be in much better shape overall this time around. In fact, the folks lining up at the ice and water trailers were a much smaller crowd. After a few days of handing out bags of ice and cases of bottled water, he walked around to the side of the trailer to eat his lunch. Catching a glimpse of someone moving toward him, Alan turned and recognized a man he had helped after Hurricane Ivan had left its mark on the city.

"Well, hi, R. J., how are you?" resounded Alan as he thrust out his hand in my direction.

"I'm doing fine, Alan," I responded. "Make it through the storm okay?"

"Yes, we had very minor damage compared with last time. You?"

"Lost six shingles off the roof. No leaks though. Thank the Lord for that."

"I hear you, brother," acknowledged Alan with a grin.

"Listen, Alan, I was hoping I would run into you. Would you be open to grabbing a coffee sometime?"

"Sure. Name the time and place."

"Okay. How about next Wednesday, nine a.m. at the Starbucks on Bayou Boulevard?"

"Which one?"

"Uh . . . oh yeah. The one by the theater. The one by Chic-fil-A has a really bad parking problem."

The following Wednesday Alan and I sat down over a hot latte and a black coffee. I'd guess I'm close to ten years younger than Alan, so I'll let you guess who ordered which beverage. After a few sips, I asked Alan a question. Over the next hour, I began to unravel his most unique saga. While finishing my now lukewarm latte, I asked if he would be available next week for another visit. This pattern continued for several weeks. Each meeting we followed a similar format. I asked questions. He opened up and poured out of his well everything from The **rojocci** Fellowship to his latest discoveries in the Scriptures. It was fascinating, and a time I looked forward to every week.

On one such visit, a lunch at The Cactus Flower Mexican restaurant, I revealed to Alan that I was a part-time author. I then asked for his permission to write his and Annalisa's story. At first, Alan was very much opposed to the idea. However, two weeks later, after much prayer and many discussions with Annalisa, he consented.

"But only as a fictional work. That's a condition I'm not willing to budge on."

Upon agreeing to this, I set about getting the story down on paper. Strangely, soon afterward, I got extremely busy with my daytime job, which lasted for several years. You see, I worked in management for a large homebuilder and we were in the midst of a housing boom. And as they say in our business, "You have to make hay while the sun shines." I did, however, telephone Alan about twice a year, explaining I had made very little progress on his manuscript.

Eventually, we lost touch with one another. Unfortunately, his story lay dormant within my laptop for ten years, although Alan and Annalisa's story continued to develop.

With the passage of time, their son, Richard, graduated from high school and was accepted to a small Christian college outside of Jackson, Mississippi. A year later saw their youngest child, Emily, off to a school in Birmingham, Alabama. That same year Julie and Roger both graduated with honors from the University of West Florida in north Pensacola. A day later, the whole family had a wonderful celebration at the Browne's home including delicious, slow-roasted pork tenderloin, corn-on-the-cob, potato salad, sliced tomatoes, and some tasty Key Lime pie for dessert. Shortly after the cleanup was complete, Roger sat down next to Alan on the front porch.

"Uh, Coach?"

"It's okay to call me Mr. Browne, Roger. I haven't been a coach for three years now."

"Well, I kind of like calling you coach, Coach."

"Fine," agreed Alan ,who actually kind of liked it too.

"Anyway, Coach, I've been thinking. I've finished my degree and all. Uh, although I don't have a job yet, I have some money and a house, you know, a place to live. I have a pretty good car too."

"What's your point, Roger?" asked Alan acting as if he didn't know where this was heading.

"My point, Coach? Well, uh . . . I would like your permission to marry your daughter?"

"Which one?" teased Alan.

"Which one? Now Coach . . ."

"I was just kidding, Roger. I know you're talking about Julie." Alan paused and then teased Roger again. "Right?"

"Of course, Coach!"

"So you want my permission to marry Julie? Well, she does seem to care for you and you for her. Correct?" Alan glanced at Roger to let him know the conversation was now officially more serious.

"Oh, yes, sir. Absolutely."

"Her mother and I have both noticed how well you appear to get along with each other. Although, you are an only child, and she is a first born. You could have some head butting days ahead. But if you love each other?"

"So I have your permission then, Coach?"

"Well, hold on just a second. Remember what I told you at the hospital that day?"

"No, sir."

"Hmmm . . . that's not encouraging."

"Sorry, Coach. Wait. Was it something about working through a project together?"

"Yes. So let's talk about that. I want you to do some research. Find out what Julie's name means, her middle name too. You know, the definitions. Write them down on a sheet of paper along with why their meanings are special to you. Once you have that completed, I want you to articulate in writing twelve characteristics you love about her. Now, I don't mean the color of her eyes or the way she wears her hair. I'm talking about meaningful qualities, lasting virtues, like patience, boldness, determination, or even joyfulness. Then, explain how you lack those particular qualites. Finally, explain how being married to her would create a strong and stable union, you know, how you would round each other out. You got that, Roger?"

"Yes, sir."

"When you have those items complete, set up a time with me, and we'll look it over together."

"And then?" Roger's voice had an expectant tone of hopeful anticipation.

"And then, we'll work through it together. By the way, this remains between you and me, understand? If I hear Julie learned of this, I won't be happy."

"Sure, Coach. Absolutely."

"Roger, be thorough. But remember, the sooner you get this done, the sooner you may obtain permission," encouraged Alan as he smiled at the young man he already considered a son. In his mind, Alan had already given his hearty approval to Roger. However, he was sure this would be an exercise that Roger and Julie would benefit from and would take with them throughout their entire married life.

Later that evening, as they prepared for bed, Alan whispered all that he and Roger had discussed. Annalisa was extremely excited for their daughter, stating several times, as they lay in bed, "Oh, I love a fall wedding."

Three days later, Roger pulled into their driveway. Hopping out of his 2003 Ford Taurus, he spied Alan working in his shop. Sitting down in the chair by Alan's desk, Roger handed three typewritten papers to Alan. He took his time to read through each one carefully. Then, Alan nodded his head as he was finishing up. "Now," he requested, "present it to me."

It took Roger between fifteen and twenty minutes to complete his detailed presentation.

"Very nice, Roger. Only one more thing."

"What's that, Coach?" Roger asked with a tone signifying he was ready for anything.

"Before you ask Julie to marry you, share this with her just like you presented it to me. That's very important, more than you could ever know now."

"Okay, I will," complied Roger.

"Roger, listen to me carefully. That presentation is my engagement gift to my daughter. Do you understand? I cherish that precious girl. I know you can't possibly comprehend this right now. But someday, if you have a daughter and are in my position of giving her away, the very one you have poured so much of your life into, you will find out how hard it is. You may have loved her for three to four years, but I have loved her for more than twenty-two years."

"I don't know what to say, Coach."

"Don't say anything," Alan smiled with tears flowing down his cheeks. "Just assure me you will, with great care, communicate with your whole heart what you have shared with me today."

"I will, Coach. I will."

"Thanks, son. I can't express how much I appreciate you."

"Really, Coach? I mean, I have your permission, your blessing?"

"With that one condition we agreed upon. I can't stress enough how important this will be to the two of you. You may not think so today but two, five, ten, twenty, or even fifty years from now you'll be very grateful you did. Trust me; you'll be very glad."

"I do, Coach. So I have your blessing then, right?"

"Yes. And Mrs. Browne's blessing too. Now, I think Julie is in the house. You want to go get her?"

"Yes, sir. I'm taking her out to a spot on Perdido Key beach. It will be perfect."

"I'm sure it will, son."

-four-

Other than planning for their daughter's wedding, life had quieted down for Alan and Annalisa. When their youngest, Emily, headed off to college, just the two of them were left to ramble about the house. They were, what many folks call, "empty nesters." Their daily routine consisted of rising early, studying the Scriptures, and praying until breakfast. Then they usually exercised and did the household chores until lunch. Afternoons often found them running errands or returning phone calls, letters, and emails. Once or twice a month, Alan continued to receive invitations to speak at a church or Christian retreat. Sharing the Scriptures and using The **rojocci** Papers as an allegory to his message evidently was a unique and refreshing change for some of his listeners. A few churches had asked Alan back to speak several times, especially the one in Wiggins, Mississippi, where Teddy Wilbeam was pastor. So it came as no surprise to him when he answered the phone Saturday morning and Teddy was on the other end.

The consummate Southern gentleman, Teddy was tall and rangy with flowing silvery-white hair and a neatly trimmed beard to match. He had a booming voice without even a hint of harshness anywhere in his speech. A conservative dresser, more as a result of his lifestyle of faith than his tastes, Teddy was always neat and clean. Some might even say polished. In his late twenties, he had begun his ministry as a traveling evangelist. Years later, with his health suffering from too many years on the road, he decided to accept a position for a small congregation in the Southern Mississippi town of Wiggins. The same day he was ordained as pastor, he celebrated his fifty-third birthday. Now, more than twenty-five years later, he was calling his longtime friend Alan Browne to see if he was available to speak in two weeks.

The two had first met many years ago when Alan and Annalisa's pastor had invited Teddy to speak at their church in California. Afterward, they welcomed him into their home for lunch and had an enjoyable time of fellowship. He and Alan had become fast friends; for years they kept in touch off and on. Eventually, the phone calls and letters became less frequent. That is until the day Alan mailed Teddy details of The **rojocci** Manifesto. Upon receiving the document and Alan's newsy letter, Teddy immediately picked up the phone and invited Alan to come and speak to his congregation. Apparently, Teddy and the church had appreciated what they had heard because every two to three months Alan had received another invitation, just like the one today. After the usual pleasantries, Teddy asked a curious question.

"Alan, can you bring Annalisa for this visit?" he inquired.

"Sure, I think so. Why?"

"Well, there's some folks here I would like the two of you to meet. I think you would really enjoy them. Can you arrive Saturday by lunch?" urged Teddy.

"I don't see why not. We'll meet you at your house at noon two weeks from today," assured Alan.

"Oh, just meet us at the church. See you then. Lord bless y'all."

Slowly hanging up the phone, Alan turned toward Annalisa, who had just entered the kitchen. "Well, that was a little bit strange, even for Teddy," chuckled Alan.

"What's that, honey?" she asked as she sat down at the table.

"Teddy wants me to bring you when I go up there to speak in two weeks."

"What's strange about that? I've been there several times, just not the last two," she remarked with a shrug.

"He said he had some folks he wanted us to meet. And when I told him we'd arrive at his house by noon on Saturday, he told me to go straight to the church instead. Doesn't that seem a bit odd to you?"

"Not at all. Maybe they're having a church work day, or perhaps he needed to tidy up some things in his office. I wouldn't worry about it, honey," she assured. "Are you ready to take me out to lunch for some barbeque?"

The next couple of weeks dragged by slowly as Alan was overly concerned about the visit to Teddy's church. It wasn't the speaking in front of the congregation that had him worried; it was the elusive way Teddy had asked if he could be there by noon on Saturday and to be sure to bring Annalisa along. He was sure something was up. But what could it be?

Two weeks later, as he and Annalisa made the turn into the church parking lot, his interest was more than piqued. It was on high alert. "I told you something was up, honey," he declared with a sense of satisfaction that his hunch had been proven to be correct.

"Oh, it's nothing, Alan. Let's just go on inside and see what's going on, okay?"

"Are you in on this?" he barked accusingly.

"What? Yeah, sure, honey. I tricked you into coming up here, so all these folks inside, whose cars are completely visible in the parking lot, could ambush you at the door. Come on, Alan, really?"

Walking through the unlocked front doors and across the sanctuary to a smaller meeting room, which the church had labeled Fellowship Hall, Alan and Annalisa were greeted by about a dozen people, including Teddy and Margaret Wilbeam.

Rising from his seat at the head of the table, Teddy proclaimed in a loud voice, "Okay, folks, we can have lunch now that our keynote speaker is here!"

Alan, with a surprised look on his face replied, "What keynote speaker?"

Teddy laughed, slapped Alan on the back, and commented that he was just kidding. Although they soon discovered that Alan would be addressing the group later that evening. Teddy quickly pulled Alan and Annalisa aside, waving Margaret over as the others began lining up for the pot luck lunch.

"Did y'all have a nice trip?" inquired Teddy with his wide, toothy grin.

"Yes. It was uneventful. That's always a good thing when driving," Alan replied frankly.

"Good. Okay, listen, you two, this is our annual Elder Board Retreat. We don't like to spend the money traveling someplace when many of our folks can't even afford a meal out. So we just hunker down here for the day. After lunch, I'll introduce you to each one. Then we'll continue our Board meeting. Just listen. You don't have to say anything, well . . . unless someone asks you a question," he chuckled. "Just enjoy. They're really wonderful, down-to-earth people."

"Okay. What about this speaking thing?"

"Oh, yeah. We'd like you to give a thirty minute message to wrap up our meeting this evening after dinner."

"What do you want me to say? I mean, what's the topic?"

"Oh, just do what you had prepared for the service tomorrow morning, but cut it in half," he smiled as he slapped Alan on the back leading him and Annalisa toward their seats at the table.

Alan glanced over at Annalisa giving her hand a squeeze. Her eyes widened and she shrugged her shoulders to indicate she didn't know what was going on either. The conversation around the table during lunch and all that afternoon was quite pleasing to Alan as he sensed the church was right on the fringes of some exciting discoveries and implementations. After Alan finished his mini-message later that evening, the group stood in a circle and prayed for nearly thirty minutes. With that, the Elder Retreat was adjourned.

Teddy handed Alan a key to his home, asking if he minded heading on over because he still had a few details to wrap up. Ten minutes later, Alan and Annalisa were sitting at the Wilbeam's dining room table with glasses of iced tea, waiting for their hosts to arrive. Before long, lights flashed across the front windows indicating a car had pulled into the driveway, and within a few seconds the front door swung open.

"Hey, you two, find everything you need?" asked Teddy cheerfully.

"Yes, sir. Hope you don't mind. We helped ourselves to some iced tea," confessed Alan.

"Oh, no, I'm so glad y'all felt at home," Margaret piped in. "Care for some peach cobbler with that?"

Alan and Annalisa glanced at each other then in unison exclaimed, "Sounds wonderful." Annalisa continued, "If it's not too much trouble, Margaret."

"Oh, no trouble at all, my dearies. Just be a minute. Any for you, sweetkins?"

"Sounds good, dear. Just a little though," requested Teddy with a sheepish grin.

Alan glanced at Teddy. "Sweetkins?"

"Yeah, she's called me that since elementary school back in Okemah, Oklahoma."

"Oklahoma? I thought you were born and raised in Mississippi?" Alan asked in a slightly higher octave.

"Well, yes, might as well have been. My father accepted a position at Southern Miss when I was twelve. When we moved, I never thought I would see Maggie again. At age eighteen, I walked into my first class at Southern Miss. It was an English composition course. Just after I found my seat, I heard this sweet voice a couple of rows back, 'Hey there, sweetkins.' I immediately knew it was her. We've been together ever since. That's going on fifty years now."

"Married forty-nine," confided Margaret as she placed the desserts on the table.

They enjoyed one another's company until sometime shortly after ten o'clock. Thinking they were getting ready to retire, Alan got up from the table.

"Do you two have just a few more minutes, Alan?" asked Teddy.

"Sure, I thought you folks were getting tired. We're okay, right, honey?" he glanced at Annalisa to assure it was fine with her. She nodded her agreement.

Teddy, with Margaret by his side, asked a number of questions regarding Alan and Annalisa's perception of the Elder's Retreat and some of the individuals in particular. Although it seemed friendly enough, Alan sensed there was more to this little question-and-answer session than met the eye. Finally, after several minutes, out came the question.

"So, you two, do you feel that God could call you here to help with this little work?"

The room fell silent for more than a few seconds as both Alan and Annalisa were processing the somewhat startling question. Annalisa, with a smile on her face, gazed across at Alan, looking for him to respond. Alan stared at Teddy, not at all sure he had heard him correctly. After several more silent seconds, Alan finally broke the tension in the air.

"Uh, would you mind repeating that please, Teddy? I'm not sure I heard you right."

"Sure. I realize this must come as somewhat of a shock. But I think there's something way down in your heart that confirms it. Look, I'll be seventy-nine in January. I have come to recognize that I can't continue doing this forever. So I've been praying, and your names kept coming to my mind. After discussing it with Maggie, I bounced it off the Board members. One of them suggested we have y'all up for our Elder's Retreat to see how we all get along."

"And?" asked Alan hesitatingly.

"They all love you. And the ladies love Annalisa even more than the gents love you, Alan," he laughed.

"We'll have to pray this thing through, Teddy. This is huge. I've never, uh . . . I mean, I wasn't expecting. I don't know what to say. I don't know how we . . . uh, could you give us some details please? When would we need to be here to start?"

"Well, that's open. But the sooner the better. There's no salary or anything. It's a faith position. Meaning, you live by faith. Do y'all understand this?"

Alan and Annalisa both nodded their acknowledgement in response to Teddy's question, although, if they were to be honest, neither was quite sure they fully understood.

"Simply stated," continued Teddy. "It means you look to the Lord for all your needs. Some of the folks here participate in a food co-op. Also, many of our families are enrolled in a share-the-expenses medical program. You're welcome to join those if you like. There's no salary, no housing allowance, no vehicle allowance, no retirement, or anything else. It's living by faith. And frankly, it's trusting our Lord."

"Well, like I mentioned, we'd really need to pray about this. But I do want you to know something that I feel is very important."

"What's that, Alan?"

"The church where we've been attending, since moving to Pensacola over ten years ago, decided to try something we thought was Biblical but completely outside the box of what most church going folks would call normal," stated Alan with a hint of timidity.

"What's that?"

"Well, several months ago our pastor left to take another position in a distant city."

"It's been a year, honey," Annalisa corrected gently.

"Okay, a year. We had been studying the Book of First Corinthians and were about at chapter twelve when he departed."

"The spiritual gifts chapter," smiled Teddy nodding his head.

"Yes, and so without a pastor for a time, we decided to rotate the sermons among a few of the men. After a few months, something started to become evident to us."

"What was it?" asked an increasingly curious Teddy.

"I'll get to that in just a minute," affirmed Alan holding up one finger.

Teddy nodded.

"Well, as you know," continued Alan, "there are two lists of spiritual gifts in the twelfth chapter. One list appears to be fill-the-need-of-the-moment kind of gifts, and the other list seems to be more of positional types. We do not see either of these as permanent roles within the Body of

Christ. The need may be just for a second or two, or for many years, but not something of an unending nature. I mean, you mentioned it a few minutes ago."

"What?" questioned Teddy.

"That you couldn't continue to do this work much longer."

"Yes, that's correct."

"You see, the first list indicates gifts like, the word of wisdom, the word of knowledge, healings, effecting of miracles, discerning of spirits and the like. The second group lists positions like apostles, prophets, healers, administrators, teachers, and others. It makes sense to us that these are all to meet the need at the time. There's another partial list in the Book of Ephesians[1] to back this up. It also includes pastors and teachers."

"I'm not sure what you're getting at, Alan," posed Teddy with a perplexed look on his face.

"Let's see here. May I use you as an example, my brother?"

"Sure," smiled Teddy as he glanced at Maggie then across to Annalisa.

"You were once an evangelist, correct?"

"Yes," replied Maggie. "And before that, he taught Sunday school for many years."

"Good," acknowledged Alan. "Later you became an evangelist and after that a pastor. Your positions have changed over the years, but something in you has never changed."

"What?" Teddy was leaning forward now.

"Why did you want to teach? To share the Gospel? To pastor a church?"

"Well, let me think. Hmmm . . . I would have to say, and you chime in here, honey, if you think of something, it had to be because I wanted to encourage others and give them hope."

"That's what I would have said as well, Teddy," Maggie confirmed.

"There you go," asserted Alan. "That's your spiritual gift."

"What is?" chuckled Teddy.

"You won't always be a Sunday school teacher, an evangelist, or even a pastor. But you will always be an encourager and an exhorter."

"That's an interesting proposition, Alan. How did you come up with that?" asked Teddy frankly.

"We had this huge vacancy in our church when the pastor left. We didn't know what to do, so we cried out to the Lord for direction. He showed us how vulnerable we were depending on only one person, especially when the Lord had provided so many gifts to strengthen the church. With all due respect, Teddy, the church was never meant to be directed by any one person other than the Lord Jesus Christ Himself."

"No disrespect taken," nodded Teddy. "In fact, I wholeheartedly agree with you. But how do you get the individual members of the body to take up the responsibility? Therein lies the difficulty, the rub."

"By showing them their worth; their great value in the kingdom of God. When they comprehend this, they take up their charge and put their shoulder to the wheel. Additionally, they do it voluntarily and with joy."

"I couldn't agree more. But how would you start? Where would you begin?" questioned Teddy with a wry grin as though he had found the death blow to Alan's side of the discussion.

"There's another list,"[2] asserted Alan.

"What are you talking about?" inquired Margaret.

"Romans, chapter twelve," stated Teddy.

"Yes, in this chapter God shows us another prominent list of gifts. He even calls them gifts in the sixth verse of that chapter. Listen to this grouping and tell me what's different from the other two lists, okay?"

Both Teddy and Margaret nodded their heads, remaining silent yet showing much interest.

Alan continued, pausing between the titles of each gift to allow the Holy Spirit to quietly speak to their hearts:

"Prophesying"

"Serving"

"Teaching"

"Exhorting"

"Giving"

"Leading"

"Showing Mercy"

Following the final one, Alan sat silently. He glanced from face to face. After more than a few seconds, Margaret spoke up. "They're verbs, not nouns. I mean, they're action words not a person, place, or thing."

"Yes," added Teddy, "They are actions not positions. They are gifts of action the Holy Spirit gives to individual members of the Body of Christ for the building up of itself in love. This is absolutely brilliant, Alan. I can see this is invaluable to the church today. But let me see if I understand you correctly. What you're saying is that someone who has the gift of Teaching could be in the position of pastor. We could call him a teaching pastor. And the one with the gift of Exhortation could be the pastor encourager. Another one may be the one with the gift of Service, showing everyone how to help others."

"That's the serving pastor," chirped Maggie.

"Yeah, and the one with the gift of Leading can organize folks," announced Annalisa. "In fact, in our church in Pensacola, we called the ones with this gift our Organization folks. And those with the Giving gift are great at helping to meet pressing needs."

"Well, I can see how the one with the Serving gift would assure that everyone had their needs met and was taken care of," stated Margaret shyly, adding, "I think I have that gift in living color."

"You sure do," agreed her husband.

"And the Prophecy gifted guy started the whole thing in the first place with declaring the truth. It works, Teddy. We've been doing it now at our church for several months, and I can assure you, it works," attested Alan with a nod of his head. "But to be honest, we don't call them pastors or anything else. They're simply members of the Body, who have a particular gift in serving the whole church. Every saved believer has at least one of these."

"To be candid," offered Annalisa, "it was a bit rough at first. It wasn't something any of the congregation had ever experienced before. However, after searching the Scriptures, they determined for themselves that it may very well be Biblical and God's intent for his church. It's not that the church doesn't need a pastor. It does. At least I think it does. But this way enhances and strengthens the Body because there are at least seven of what could be called lay pastors, all discerning an issue from seven different perspectives. And, just as important, you have the individual members really interested in participating."

"True," agreed Alan. "It rubbed some folks the wrong way. In fact, there are still some on the fence. But for the most part, we have seen harmony in the body of believers as well as the evidence of a few minor miracles in our midst."

"Alan, Annalisa," inquired Teddy. What are your gifts?"

"Annalisa is a great example of one who has the gift of Mercy with an additional bit of influence from some of the other gifts," stated Alan while looking fondly at his wife.

"And you, Alan, you have the gift of Prophecy, don't you?" Teddy stated confidently.

"Yes, sir, I have the Prophecy gift with a minor in exhortation," he chuckled almost apologetically.

"Are you embarrassed by that?" asked Margaret quietly.

"Well," Alan replied somewhat sheepishly. "It's not like someone who has the Teaching gift or likes to give. They have no problem expressing to others what they believe to be their gifts because those gifts are more clearly understood. However, when you tell someone you have the gift of Prophecy, the general response is that you're some kind of religious fortuneteller waiting around for something bad to happen so you can say, I told you so. Granted sometimes I sense the Lord warning me about something on the horizon, but for the most part I just have a desire to proclaim what the Scriptures declare and how it applies to real-life situations."

"Teddy," Margaret urged. "I absolutely love this."

"Look, you two," pronounced Teddy with some passion in his voice. "This is precisely why you have to come and be a part of the work here. These folks need this kind of message, this kind of teaching. They need your gifts, your examples, and your convictions to grow this church. So, what do you say? Are you up for another adventure with God?"

-five-

Arriving home from Wiggins late Sunday evening, Alan and Annalisa were exhausted. They had discussed the possibilities of Teddy's proposition from so many different angles that they had returned to the original starting point more confused than when they had begun. As they finished unpacking their suitcase, Alan suggested they place the matter in God's hands and try to get some rest. It was wise advice and would have allowed Alan to sleep through the night if he had heeded it. Rather, he tossed and turned until sometime after two a.m. when he decided to go downstairs for a glass of milk. Sitting at the kitchen table, he quietly asked his Father in Heaven what they should do. He waited silently for an answer.

Soon, a soft thought drifted across his mind. "No matter what happens, I have always taken care of you, and I will never leave you or forsake you."

"Yes, Lord, I know you have, but . . ."

"Read about my friend, Abraham."

Alan immediately found his Bible and opened it to the Book of Genesis. After reading the inspiring story, he turned to the eleventh chapter of the Book of Hebrews and read a very stirring phrase,

> "By faith Abraham, when he was called, obeyed
> and he went out,
> not knowing where he was going."[1]

Sitting ever so still, Alan meditated on these words for what seemed like more than an hour. He began to whisper a few certain words. "By faith . . . obeyed . . . not knowing." He emphasized these several times a bit louder. Just then, he sensed a prompting in his heart to read chapter four in the Book of Romans. Flipping the pages in that direction, his eyes caught a couple of lines as he passed through the Book of Second Corinthians,

> ". . . we are taking every thought captive
> to the obedience of Christ."[2]
> "You are looking at things as they are outwardly."[3]

Alan pondered these words as well for a few minutes before continuing on to Romans. Upon finishing the first five verses of the fourth chapter, Alan knew what he must do.

"I have my two or three witnesses, so I am confident of what the Lord wants me to do. The peace in my spirit certainly is a witness as well. However, I wonder what Annalisa will think. She most assuredly is the crucial piece to this decision. Well, tomorrow's a new day, so I'm going up to bed."

Catching a glimpse out the back kitchen window as he rose from the table, he noticed the sun's first rays were beginning to light up the sky. Glancing at the stove's clock, his mind confirmed what his eyes couldn't believe. "Oh no, I've been up all night."

Resigned to his fate for the day, he reached over and turned the coffee maker on. "She should be down in twenty minutes or so. Then we can work through this together," he thought aloud.

Two cups of coffee and forty-five minutes later he heard her prancing down the stairs. Swinging the door wide open, she made her usual cheery entrance into the kitchen.

"Good morning, honey, get up early?" she inquired in her singsong voice.

"Mmmm . . ." mumbled Alan, head in both hands.

"I was thinking of making us some granola and yogurt with some of those fresh peaches. Sound good?"

"Mmmm . . ." came an unenthusiastic reply.

"Or maybe an omelet? How's that sound, dear?"

"Mmmm . . ."

"Okay, if you don't really care, I'll make the yogurt, okay?"

"Mmmm . . ." This time Alan slowly nodded his head.

"Oh, thanks for fixing the coffee, Alan."

"Sure. Listen, I want us to work through this thing Teddy proposed to us."

"Oh, yes, Alan, me too. In fact, I had the most incredible dream last night, and I really think we should accept the invitation to help pastor their church."

"What? Are you serious? We haven't even talked about it yet."

"Yes, I am, uh . . . I mean, I know we hadn't come to a conclusion yet. But you see, in this dream I was like a farmer's wife living in the country on a farm somewhere. Although I knew I was married, I never saw my husband in the dream. But somehow I knew he was struggling to make ends meet. The harvest was approaching, and it was looking bleak. We didn't have anything left to eat except one last apple. Once we finished the apple, all that was left on the stark white plate was a stem and one seed. I took both, walked out into the front yard, cleared a small area about six inches in diameter, and planted the seed. Then, after covering it up, I stuck the stem in the ground right above it."

"Honey?"

"Wait a minute, Alan. Let me finish, okay?"

"Sure, dear."

"Next, in my dream, I prayed over it, asking our Lord to bless it," smiled Annalisa. "At this very moment, the neighbor lady, standing on her side of the fence, began mocking me by shouting out discouraging comments, 'It will never work! Nobody does it like that! It won't grow but will just wither away, and then you'll look like the fool you really are.' I mean, she was really nasty. Finally, after a few more of her remarks, I shouted back at her, 'Go away you foul and discouraging woman. Leave me alone.' She shut up immediately and went in her house."

"Wow, that's some dream, sweetheart," muttered Alan as he took another sip of coffee.

"Let me tell you the rest, Alan. The next morning, in my dream, I woke up and noticed the sun didn't seem as harsh. Instead, its light was somewhat filtered. I opened the front door and there, where I had planted that tiny seed and its stem, was a huge apple tree with hundreds of brilliant red apples hanging from the heavily laden branches. I couldn't believe what I was seeing. It was a miracle, an absolute miracle!"

"I'd say so. That's amazing, honey."

"Yeah, I know, right?! Then, I noticed something even more amazing. Everywhere an apple fell from this tree, shortly after it hit the ground, another tree sprung up bearing more fruit. At first, this happened maybe once every minute. But soon it began occurring several times each minute. After a while, the new trees began dropping some apples too, and when these hit the ground they became new trees as well. It was so incredibly amazing, Alan. So I think we need to move to Wiggins to help Teddy and Margaret with their church."

"What?" responded an astonished Alan. "How did you come to that conclusion?"

"Because God made it clear in my dream."

"Uh . . . I think I'm following you here, but my mind is a bit foggy because I've been up all night," confessed Alan softly.

"That's funny," she grinned, tilting her head to one side. "I slept like a log."

"Wonderful and I think I'm following your train of thought, but just to be sure let me hear your interpretation of this dream."

"Well, remember it's a dream, okay?"

"Of course," he nodded.

"I think the tree is the church in Wiggins. You are the seed. No, I think you are the stem. The seed is the message God has given you. Yeah, that may be more accurate. You and the seed are planted to help grow the church. Or something like that, I think. The fruit are the people of the tree; uh . . . I mean the apples are like the people of the church. As they grow and become ripe, they leave and others spring up and on and on," she explained while shrugging her shoulders indicating she wasn't positive about the interpretation.

"Okay, and who are you in this dream?"

"I'm me. You know, the person in the dream, that me is me."

"No, honey, I mean, what is your part in the dream. What do you do?"

"I planted the seed . . . and the stem. Why?"

"So you planted me and the message God gave me?" he smirked with the tiniest hint of sarcasm in his tone.

"Yes."

"Honey, what on earth are . . ."

"Alan," she interrupted. "Would you move to Mississippi and take up the work at the Wilbeam's church, if I thought we shouldn't go?"

"No, of course not. God would want us to be unified for a big decision like that."

"Exactly. So by me being the one in the dream who is actually doing the planting, I think it indicates that I am in full agreement, and that I have a very important part to fulfill in this ministry too."

"Yes, you do, my precious love. Without the two of us working side by side in the vineyard, the fruit of our labors would surely rot on the vine. We are a team that God had planned before the beginning of time. It is so evident to me that we were made for one another. If we were to take on something like this without each other's full agreement, it would be destined for failure. But what could the results be if we are agreed?"

"A huge tree with branches laden with fruit so ripe that the fruit falls from the tree and grows new trees wherever it lands," proclaimed Annalisa as she sat down on his lap, sliding her arms around his shoulders.

"I believe it too, honey. I think God is indicating that we should go. I'll call Teddy later today and let him know what we've decided. That is, after I take a nap."

"Didn't sleep well, Alan?" a giggling Annalisa teased.

Throughout the day and the rest of the week as well, Alan and Annalisa had some huge decisions to make, such as, what they should do with their Pensacola home. Should they try to sell it or rent it? Would they need both of their cars? How about their furniture? Surely they would be living in a much smaller home in Wiggins. How much should they keep? Should they give it away? Sell it? Put it in storage? And what about all of Alan's woodworking tools?

Some choices came easy to them while others seemed to fester for days. This move, they realized, signaled a major life change. It was even more pivotal than their move to Florida from California some twelve years ago. And the move from Virginia to California many years previous, paled in the light of that move. No, they decided, this wasn't just a change in location; this was a turning point in their life together.

Working through the many decisions one by one, they eventually came to the day of no return. They signed a lease agreement allowing a young couple to rent their home for

one year. The next day they traveled to Wiggins and signed
a similar agreement to rent a single story, two bedroom
house about a mile from the church and two miles from
Teddy and Margaret's home. They decided to stop by the
Wilbeam's on their way out of town. As they were about to
leave for Pensacola, Teddy asked Alan if it was okay if he
took a peek at their new home. Alan agreed, handing him
one of their two keys.

The next three days were an absolute blur to Alan and
Annalisa. They rented a truck to move their belongings.
Then, with the help of Roger, Julie, and several folks from
their church, they loaded it up. Alan tidied up of all the
utility bills, dropping by each office to finalize their
accounts. Several people also helped with the cleaning of
the house from top to bottom. Finally, they handed the keys
to the young couple and said some emotional and tearful
good byes to their close friends and family.

Arriving in Wiggins sometime after ten o'clock that
evening, they backed the truck into the driveway. Alan
pulled their mattress out of the truck and laid it on the shiny
hardwood floor in the room they had selected to be their
bedroom. After putting on the sheets, they fell into bed, fully
clothed, and were fast asleep within minutes. Upon waking
the next morning, Annalisa decided to make a quick trip to
the grocery store for some basics. Imagine her surprise,
when she opened the refrigerator door and found it fully
stocked with milk, meats, salad fixings, eggs, cheeses, and
even a homemade berry pie. Her eyes welled up with tears as
she praised their Father in Heaven for the gracious

generosity He had shown them through the kind folks in Wiggins.

Just then, her eye caught sight of something on the counter top across from the refrigerator. As she moved toward the counter, she counted no less than eight envelopes. Some had Alan and Annalisa's names written across the front. Others had a verse of Scripture. She opened the first one and discovered five twenty dollar bills inside. Another contained fifty dollars, and in another, two hundred. She knelt down on the kitchen floor and wept tears of joy. Her weeping continued as she praised and thanked the Lord for His unbelievable goodness to them. Deciding to leave the rest for them to open together, she headed into the living room. There on the fireplace mantel, she spied six more envelopes. She laughed and cried simultaneously.

"What's the matter, my love?"

She turned to see her half asleep husband moving slowly across the hardwood floor. "Envelopes!" she cried. "They're everywhere."

"What?"

"Yes, and each one has money in it. I can't believe how good our God is to us, Alan. It's absolutely unbelievable."

He held her tight, kissing her on the forehead several times. Then reaching across, he pulled an envelope off the mantel. "Wow, this one has five hundred dollars in it. But there's no indication as to who gave it. How will we thank them?"

"All of the envelopes are the same, honey," she sniffled. "Every single one has been given anonymously. I think they wanted God to get the glory, not themselves."

"Wow that's amazing. If we had any doubts as to whether this was the right decision, this sure helps alleviate them," he whispered with a smile.

"I just can't believe it."

"Well, let's gather these up, so we can look through them later. For now, we better get down to the grocery store to get a little food for breakfast."

"We don't need to," she cried aloud.

"What? Why not, sweetheart?"

Annalisa pointed toward the kitchen as she stood in the living room, shoulders shaking. Alan walked around the corner and into the kitchen.

"What on earth?! Did you see this?" he called from the kitchen.

Poking her head in the archway from the living room, Annalisa's tears began flowing again as she noticed Alan had all the cabinet doors open revealing canned goods, flour, spices, oils, paper towels, plates, and napkins. Her face, soaked with tears of joy, now radiated a cheerful smile as she pointed toward the refrigerator. Alan turned and swinging the door open, laughed out loud.

"God is so good to us!"

Annalisa nodded unable to speak.

"Look at this, honey. There are even a couple of meals in here. Looks like some kind of casserole with chicken and broccoli and another one that's definitely lasagna. Man, oh, man, I could eat a plate of that right now."

They held one another close as Alan lifted up a prayer of praise and thanksgiving for all that God had done. He slipped all of the envelopes in the back pockets of his jeans while they swayed back and forth in one another's arms. Before long, there was a knock at the front door.

"Oh, Alan, I'm not even dressed yet. Look at my hair." She quickly ran down the hall and shut the bedroom door behind her.

Looking out the window, Alan could see that it was Teddy and Margaret at the front door. He let them in and greeted them both with hugs.

"Uh, Alan, I thought I'd give you a heads up. Several of the folks will be here in along about fifteen minutes. They insisted on helping y'all get unloaded and set up. Now, you can do as you like, but if I were you, I would station Annalisa by the front door, so she can direct each one to the appropriate room based on the load they're carrying. Then, let the men put together the beds, tables, chairs, and the like while the women unload and set up your kitchen. I'm telling you, if you'll take my advice, before you know it, you'll be set up and ready to go."

"Okay, that sounds good to me," agreed Alan with a smile.

"Where's Annalisa?" asked Margaret quietly.

"Oh, she's probably in the bathroom. She'll be out in a minute."

"Now, Alan, I want you to know I've got this Sunday's sermon and the following Sunday as well. After that, we'll leapfrog. So you'll be speaking in both services two weeks from this Sunday, okay?"

"Yes, sir. I'll take care of it."

"Also, once you're settled in, let's sit down and work through how we should implement this spiritual gift approach to ministry. I think most folks will be open to it. I'm excited to see what the Lord will do. Aren't you?"

"Yes, sir."

"Well, good morning, Annalisa, how are you, darling?" asked Margaret as she noticed a more presentable version of Alan's better half emerging from the hallway.

"Oh, long day yesterday," she confessed giving them both a hug. "However, I'm afraid we're only half done. But what a blessing to find the cupboards full, and the refrigerator stocked with more than we need! Please convey our heartfelt thanks to everyone."

"I thought you folks might want to do that yourself this Sunday," proffered Teddy. "We have a time during each service where folks can share testimonies. I think it would be real encouraging for the folks to hear how the Lord has blessed y'all. What do you think?"

"That sounds perfect," acknowledged Annalisa as Alan nodded his agreement.

"Good, looking forward to it," replied Teddy. "Well, dear, we better get going before these folks put us to work," he chuckled.

"Oh, you'd just get in the way," teased Margaret. "Besides, I don't think they'll need any help."

Annalisa smiled and glanced at Alan as the older couple turned to leave. "What did she mean by that?" she whispered.

"I'll tell you in a minute," he mouthed silently.

A moment later, several cars and pickup trucks pulled up. Some of the people headed for the moving van while others started for the front door. Alan smiled at Annalisa, who had a near panicked look on her face. Taking her gently by the shoulders and maneuvering her to a spot just inside the front door, he quickly explained her new role as traffic controller.

"Please, honey, just stay right here and tell each one where to place their load, okay?"

"Uh, I guess so," she answered meekly.

Placing a kiss on her forehead, Alan beamed, "Trust me, honey. You're going to love this."

-six-

With more than a dozen helpers, the house had become a home in a matter of two and a half hours. With a sense of relief and gratefulness, Alan and Annalisa flopped down on their sofa together and rested their weary feet upon the coffee table, which stood between the sofa and the fireplace. They had done it. They had moved to Wiggins and started their new life, helping in ministry. Sipping on their iced teas, neither said a word because both knew what the other was thinking. After another swallow, she broke the silence.

"Okay, honey, now what?"

"Uh . . . how about a nap later this afternoon once we've finished hanging the pictures?"

"No, Alan, I mean, what do we do next, you know, in this new life?"

Glancing at her with a smile, Alan shrugged. "I'm not sure. Although I've always felt somewhat of a calling, I've never been a pastor before. I mean, not that I'm a pastor, but I am, kind of, right?"

"I think so," she replied.

"Well, I guess we'll lay low today and tomorrow. Perhaps on Sunday Teddy will give us an idea of what I need to be doing,"

"That sounds good to me, honey. I could use a day or two to recover."

Sunday came and went with no guidance from Teddy whatsoever. In fact, the entire week passed without so much as a word from the senior pastor. This was a bit confusing and disconcerting for Alan because Teddy had mentioned they would get together to start planning how to present the new approach to ministry. On Tuesday, Alan dropped by the church and left a note on Teddy's office door. After not hearing anything for a couple of days, Alan drove to their house. Teddy wasn't there. He spoke with Margaret for nearly twenty minutes trying to relay his concerns. However, he still heard no reply from Teddy.

Sunday morning dawned bright and sunny, but Alan sensed a dark cloud over his relationship with his mentor, Teddy. After the morning service, while Alan and Annalisa were talking with another couple, he noticed Teddy and Margaret driving away. That evening, as the service was wrapping up, Teddy approached Alan.

"You got it next Sunday, right?"

Alan acknowledged with a nod and a, "Yes, sir."

"Good, let me know if you need anything." With that, he slapped Alan on the back and quickly headed out the front doors of the sanctuary.

Alan stood there completely astonished as he watched Teddy, Margaret, and another couple on the front steps of the church laughing and talking.

"You okay, honey?" asked Annalisa in a whisper.

"I'm not sure what to think," he confided quietly. "Let's talk about it later."

This same scenario of little to no communication between Alan and Teddy continued for the next couple of months. Alan presented messages every other Sunday, and Teddy did the same on the alternate weeks. He mentioned to Alan about getting together to begin working on a few things, but he never actually set a time to meet with Alan. Having tried more than a dozen times to connect with their pastor, Alan finally gave up, determining it was better to coast from Sunday to Sunday, than to live a life of frustration and discouragement.

Meanwhile, Annalisa traveled to and from Pensacola several times. She absolutely loved these days she spent with Julie planning her upcoming wedding. The time seemed to fly by as they scheduled everything from the church to the wedding cake and everything in between. The date finally arrived, Saturday, November fifth. The weather started out overcast but by the time the two o'clock ceremony came around, it was a gloriously sunny day. The small chapel was decorated with purple and lavender carnations interspersed with white roses. Each pew displayed a beautiful bouquet with bows to match.

Stunningly beautiful in a simple yet elegant, white satin gown trimmed with delicate lace, Julie was a beaming picture of loveliness. Her three bridesmaids wore soft lavender gowns with deep purple highlights. Dressed in a white tuxedo, Roger looked handsome as he stood at the altar of the little Beulah church, anxious to catch a glimpse of his bride-to-be. His three groomsmen stood by his side, donned in their charcoal grey and black formal attire. When the time arrived, Alan proudly walked their precious daughter down the aisle before taking his place next to the officiating minister.

Both Julie and Roger had written their own vows and articulated them to one another with love and heartfelt sincerity. It was a precious time and very meaningful to all who attended. Afterward, there was a catered reception in the church fellowship hall. The selection of several of the local favorites, including Southern seafood and Cajun dishes, delighted everyone. The celebration lasted well into the evening hours. Alan and Annalisa didn't arrive back home in Wiggins until the wee hours of Sunday morning.

Exhausted, but joyous, they arose three hours later to attend the service. Although tired, somehow they made it through and then quickly left, so they could take a much needed nap. After waking from his afternoon rest, Alan reflected on the earlier church service and realized Teddy hadn't asked how their trip went nor had he even waved in their direction.

Already in their fifth month of living in Wiggins, Alan felt nearly convinced they had made a wrong decision in moving there. While eating lunch one Saturday, he broached the subject of moving back to Pensacola with Annalisa. Thinking he almost had her convinced, he was surprised when she presented a very reasonable assertion.

"Look, honey, we can't move back there for another seven months. Remember, we leased our house to that young couple for one year. So let's try to stick it out for another few months, okay?"

"Oh, I don't know. I feel like I have absolutely nothing in common with these folks. It's not because I haven't tried either. They just don't seem interested in getting to know us. I think we're like an add-on to their congregation or something. You know, like when the Kensington's did that addition to their forty-eight hundred square foot house. They really didn't need it. That's us, honey; we're really not needed here."

"You don't know that, Alan. Something could happen tomorrow, next week, or next year that would change everything. Be patient. God is at work. None of this is a surprise to Him. Now, how's your foot? Can you run in the morning?"

"No, I better not. This plantar fasciitis is really flaring up."

"Hey, maybe that's part of the problem. You haven't been able to get out and run. Perhaps you should go for a walk?"

"No, I'm not walking. I'm a runner, not a walker."

"Suit yourself. I'll be hitting the road about seven-thirty," she grinned, knowing full well her goading would spur him to action.

Sure enough, the next morning Alan was out walking before Annalisa left for her morning jog. He was delighted to discover he didn't have any pain in his foot. Walking to the end of their block, he turned the corner and headed for the downtown area. He crossed over the railroad tracks and continued further into an unfamiliar area. Deciding he had ventured far enough into this unknown zone, he made another turn and within a few blocks came to Magnolia Drive and the little business district. Striding along Magnolia, he passed by a coffee shop. A dozen steps later he turned around, having decided a mocha latte sounded perfect.

Latte in hand, Alan found a seat at the table by the front window and soon became lost in his thoughts. So much so, he hadn't really noticed the noisy table at the back of the little shop where four men were seated having a rather candid discussion about politics. But when the good natured clamor at their table penetrated Alan's reverie, he found he quite enjoyed the lively, somewhat animated comments made with a most pleasing Southern accent. The whole theater of it all caused him to smile and completely forget what had overwhelmed his mind just minutes ago. Finishing his latte, he continued to eavesdrop on the group's spirited chitchat. He could hear the conversation morph from politics to family matters and then on to religion. All of it was intermingled with laughter and friendly teasing. Obviously, thought Alan, these men had known one another for many years. They had been pontificating when he had arrived, and they were still jawing when he left to head home. Thoughts of the four men reminded him of something Norman Rockwell would have desired to paint. The picture brought a smile to Alan's face on and off throughout the day.

Having mentioned the scene to Annalisa several times, it wasn't a shock to her that he was up and out the door early the next morning. Under the guise of a walk, he made his way straight toward the coffee shop with more than a hint of intent. Opening the shop door, he was not at all surprised to see the same four men, at the same table, in the exact same seats as yesterday. In fact, Alan was certain before he arrived that this would be the case. This time he ordered a white chocolate mocha and took a seat at a table closer to the talkative quartette. The ubiquitous conversation seemed to be along the lines of current events but quickly moved to politics. At times, the decibels of the harmless banter got so high that the coffee shop owner, an older, grey haired woman barked, "Y'all hush! Getting too loud over there!" Each time she turned to Alan with an apologetic smile. Alan thought she had to be related to one of the men because of the familiar way she spoke to them. When the men heard her, they blamed each other with a good-natured slap on the shoulder and an accusatory snicker, "It was, Willy!" or, "I told you to quiet down, Jimmy!"

It was always quickly responded to by the shop owner, "I don't care who it was. It's getting too loud, so y'all hush up."

The whole atmosphere absolutely delighted Alan to the core of his being and was so pleasing that he kept coming back each day for more than a week. To him this was real life at its most genuine level without the many layers of façade most folks have accumulated. During the second week, he began choosing a seat a bit closer to the group every couple of days. Finally, one Tuesday morning, nearly three weeks after discovering the entertaining foursome, he had a front row seat. Trying to be inconspicuous, he sat with his back to their table initially. However, the very next day he took a seat facing them, and it was as good as if he was part of their dramatics. At one point in their animated discussion, the oldest among the group, a man Alan had determined was named Willy, nodded in his direction. When Alan nodded back, Willy stopped the other three with a proposition.

"Come on, y'all, let's ask this man." Then turning back toward Alan, Willy inquired, "So what do you think? Is President Bush listening in on our phone calls?"

"I don't know," replied Alan. "What do you guys think?"

"Well," chuckled Willy, "Beldon and Jimmy say he does. But John over there," pointing toward the youngest at the table, "he say he don't know nothing about it."

"What do you think?" Alan asked Willy directly.

"I think there ain't no way that man could listen in on all them phone calls. He's just checking on folks that may be bad apples."

"Does it bother you guys that our President may be listening to your calls?" inquired Alan.

"Yeah, it do," exclaimed Beldon and Jimmy together.

"Why?" asked Alan curiously.

"Because he ain't got no business knowing what I'm talking about to my old lady or anybody else," replied Jimmy with a frown.

"Y'all hush up over there," admonished the shop owner.

"We just talking, Bertha," defended Willy. "We ain't hurting nobody by talking."

"Maybe not, but keep it down or take it outside."

"Look, man," chimed Beldon, "I agree with Jimmy. I don't care who he is. He ain't got no right to listen in on my phone calls."

"Do you think he wants to hear what you be saying?" laughed Willy. With this rhetorical question the whole table broke into a holler, which included some high fives and slaps on the table.

"I'm not going to tell y'all again," threatened Bertha from behind the counter.

"Y'all be cool," admonished Willy.

"Or maybe the more important question," posed Alan. "Are you saying something you know he wouldn't want to hear?"

"Nah, man, he ain't listening," replied Beldon.

"That may be true, but someone is," proclaimed Alan with a grin.

"What you mean by that?" questioned Willy.

"I mean the President may not be listening, but *He* always is." Alan glanced upward when he said, "He always is."

"Yeah, you got that right," agreed Willy with a nod and several shakes of his head. Then turning to Alan, he asked his name.

"Alan Browne, and yours, sir?"

"I'm Willy Jarvis. That there is my brother, Jimmy. Beldon is our cousin and John Abercrombie is my momma's neighbor. Well, before she pass on. That was about a year ago."

"Nice meeting y'all. My condolences regarding your mother, Willy."

"Oh, she in a better place. She with Jesus."

"Yes, she is. You guys come here often?" inquired Alan. This brought more than a few snickers from the four men.

"Yeah, since we all lost our jobs over the last couple years," volunteered Willy, "We've been coming here each morning when Bertha and I open the shop. We sit and talk. Misery loves company. You know what I mean?"

"Yeah, I do. Well, kind of anyway. I just moved here a few months ago."

"What brought you here, Alan?" asked Willy.

"Oh, I help out at a church," shrugged Alan.

"Which one?" probed Jimmy.

"The one out close to Highway 49."

"You mean old Teddy Wilbeam's church?" corrected Willy.

"Yes, sir. You know Teddy?" queried Alan curiously.

"Sure enough do. When he first moved to town, oh, I suspect it be more than twenty-five years now, he used to hold a once a year revival meeting out at a farm in the country. I used to go to them meetings with my momma. I got saved there," volunteered Willy. "How old Teddy getting along?"

"He's almost eighty, so I'm sure he's a bit slower than twenty-five years ago. But he seems to be doing alright," assured Alan.

"So, what you do at that church, Alan?" questioned Beldon, leaning forward.

"Oh, I just help out as I'm needed."

"You get paid for that?" asked Jimmy.

"Jimmy, you shut your mouth. That ain't none of y'all business," snapped Willy at his brother.

"It's alright, Willy. No, it's not a paid position," confessed Alan.

"So you in the same boat with us then," teased Beldon with a smirk on his face.

"Hmmm . . ." mumbled Alan. "Yeah, I guess you could say that."

"Are you a preacher?" quizzed John Abercrombie. These were the first words the youngest in the group had spoken since Alan had entered the conversation some thirty minutes ago. Alan was hesitant to reveal he was a pastor for fear the men would hold back from including him or would put on airs trying to impress him. He soon found his fears were completely unfounded.

"Uh, yes, I guess you could call me that."

"Come on, Alan, you a sure enough preacher man?" laughed Willy with the others following suit. "You ain't look nothing like no preacher I ever known."

"Oh, I guess I'm kind of new at it," ventured Alan sheepishly.

"You got that right," nodded Willy. "Man, look at you, old nasty sweatpants and sneakers. Where you get that shirt, my brother?" he teased.

"I'm just out for a walk. I don't dress in my Sunday best for some exercise. Do you?" demanded Alan with a wry grin. His sharp reply bordered on sarcasm.

Willy immediately turned serious. "I'm wearing my Sunday best. In fact, it's my everyday best."

"I'm sorry, Willy. I didn't mean anything by it. Seriously man, my sincere apologies, okay?"

"Yeah, it's okay. Don't worry about it. It's just, we been without a job so long I got little hope that anything ever going to be different," confessed Willy.

At this point, the other three men got up, shook hands, and said their good byes. Willy moved across to Alan's table and waved Bertha over to freshen up their coffees. After she left, Willy turned to Alan.

"Look, Alan, life's been hard these last couple years. I lost my job, lost my momma, lost my car. If Bertha hadn't started this shop five years ago, we'd have nothing. As it is, we ain't got much."

"How'd you lose your job?" Alan asked gently.

"Oh, I don't even know no more. My boss and me had this argument on Friday because he told me I would get a raise, but I didn't see it in my pay. That weekend I was playing softball on my church team. When I slid into second base I broke my ankle. It was bad, bone sticking all out. Well, I was on them pain pills and come Monday forgot to call in. On Tuesday morning, which I actually thought was Monday, I called to tell my boss I broke my ankle and would have to be off a few days. He would hear none of it and said he done fired me on Monday when I didn't show up for work."

"I'm real sorry, Willy."

"Yeah, when Bertha got home that day she drove me down there, but he wouldn't even see me. I can't ever find no job since. Then, couldn't make no payments on my car neither, so they towed that away. Without no car it's hard to get a job. Me and Bertha walk here every morning."

"Do you have a place to live?"

"Yeah, me and Bertha live at my momma's house with our four kids. My brother and his wife Ella live there too with they kids."

"How many children do they have?"

"Two. They have two kids. I didn't buy that house, so it ain't mine. We share it with my brother and them. We all fall on tough times, and we left they church too."

"What do you mean you left the church?" inquired Alan quietly.

"Well, after we had lost so much, I couldn't pay them tithes, and I felt like they didn't want us there no more."

"What? Did someone say something to you?"

"Oh no, nobody say nothing. But you know what they be thinking."

"Willy, listen, you don't know what they were thinking."

"I sure enough do," declared Willy with more confidence than Alan had noticed previously.

"How? How could you possibly know what they were thinking?"

"Because nobody helped us."

Alan slumped back in his seat when the sound waves from this last comment hit his ears and registered in his brain. His thoughts immediately started running at a thousand miles per hour. First, one zipped by creating a guilty sensation. It was followed quickly by another one causing him to defend himself. Then another, leading him to excuse his position of guilt because, he reasoned, he wasn't at fault for any of this. Therefore, he didn't have any responsibility to do anything. This all happened at light speed, or more accurately, thought speed. Regardless, here was a person in need and Alan believed he should do something, but what? Within seconds, Alan spoke up.

"Do you have any idea, Willy, why all of this happened?"

"No, not really. But I haven't been back to church since."

"Okay, but how is your relationship with the Lord?"

"What relationship? He turned His back on me, so I turned my back on Him."

"Why do you think He turned His back on you?"

"Look at all what happen to me, man. He sure enough turn His back on me. I was going to church, reading my Bible, paying them tithes. I never beat my wife or slap my kids, didn't cuss or get drunk neither. I mean, I was a hardworking man. I never go out carousing or nothing. Why the Lord do me like that? Huh, Alan, can you tell me? Why He want to do me like that?"

"You ever read the Book of Job, Willy?" inquired Alan gently.

"Oh, years ago. Why?"

"Job was a good guy too. He went to church, so to speak, paid his tithes, prayed, and was good to other people. He had some pretty bad things happen to him too. Don't you think?"

"So?" replied Willy indicating he thought Job had nothing to do with him and his situation.

"Look, Willy, my wife, Annalisa, and I went through some really terrible times many years ago. We thought we weren't going to make it. In fact, at one point it was so bad I didn't want to live. I won't bore you with the details, but trust me, it was awful."

"You lose your job too, Alan?"

"No, much, much worse," whispered Alan with a pained expression. "We lost a child."

"Aww man, Alan, I'm sorry. I ain't never had that. I think I die if I lost one of my babies."

"Yeah, it's incredibly tough, Willy. But listen, my wife discovered something in the Book of Job as we were wrestling through our sorrow. We had come to a place where we could have easily fallen into that black hole of bitterness and despondency. You know what I mean? But just then, she found a precious secret in the Book of Job that set her free. I don't mean free in terms of physical bonds or shackles, but free on the inside, in her heart."

"What she find?" asked Willy leaning forward.

"Well, instead of me telling you, why don't you go home tonight, pull out your Bible, and read the Book of Job. Ask the Holy Spirit to show you, to reveal to you, if you are bitter or angry at God or anything like that. He loves you, Willy, and He'll show you."

"Alright," nodded Willy slowly. "I guess I can do that. I guess I could give Him one last chance."

"Now, I won't be dropping by the coffee shop over the next couple of days. I have a quick trip to take. Then I'm speaking this Sunday at church. But I'll be back here on Monday. We can talk again then, okay?"

"I think I'd like that, man."

"Me too, Willy. Seriously, I have enjoyed this more than I could ever express to you. Thanks so much for the conversation . . . and the coffee," he smiled, waving at Bertha as he got up from the table.

"Alright then, Alan," expressed Willy stretching out his hand in Alan's direction. "Looking forward to Monday then."

"Me too," agreed Alan as he shook Willy's hand. "Oh, and one last thing, Willy," Alan called across the vacant room.

"Yeah, what's that?"

"When you sit down to read, anytime it refers to Job, go ahead and take his name out and replace it with another name."

"What name?" called Bertha as she gazed at her husband with a knowing grin.

Alan shouted back as the door was closing behind him, "Willy!"

seven

Early the next morning, Alan and Annalisa were on the road. Stopping first at a restaurant in Jackson, Mississippi, they had a delightful brunch with Richard. After spending most of the day with him, they were back on the road for the three and a half hour trip to Birmingham, Alabama, where they enjoyed dinner with their sweet Emily. Shortly after ten o'clock that night, they pulled into Joey and Pam Hinote's driveway. The two couples were so happy to have someone familiar to converse with that they stayed up until the wee hours of the morning doing nothing but talking. After sharing their own story for more than an hour, Joey turned to Alan and with a smile asked,

"What alchemy have you worked to transform yourself from a humble carpenter to a shepherd of God's people?"

"Oh," shrugged Alan, glancing at Annalisa, "It was no magic; it was just a little ole giant leap of faith."

"Well, I think it's absolutely wonderful," cheered Pam. "And I want to hear all about it."

From that point, until nearly three in the morning, Alan and Annalisa shared their adventure while Joey and Pam peppered them with questions. With a four and a half hour drive ahead of them, they had originally planned to leave for

Pensacola sometime around eleven the next morning, but with sleeping in until ten-forty-five they decided maybe noon would be a more attainable departure. The good byes were bitter sweet, with all four of them recognizing how difficult it is to find those of kindred spirit. Even so, they were determined to depart no later than twelve-thirty.

The atmosphere in the car was quiet, even somber with neither Alan nor Annalisa saying a word for the first two hours. Both were exhausted, but were also lost in their private thoughts. Finally, Annalisa spoke up revealing fully what had been occupying her mind.

"Are you happy, Alan?"

"Whoa, my love, that's a huge question? Could you narrow it down a bit?"

"What do you mean narrow it down?

"I mean," he reiterated, "am I happy about what? Am I happy with this trip? Our marriage, our kids, this car? So could you narrow it down for me instead of just asking if I'm happy."

"Are you happy with our decision to move to Wiggins and help out at the church?" she replied frankly, revealing the intent of her original question.

"Well, that's a loaded question. Generally, I'd have to say I'm not happy with the overall situation with church and, more specifically, my relationship with Teddy. I guess I thought he would be more of a mentor. I hardly see the man, much less have a conversation with him. I really need his guidance, I mean, having never been a pastor before; I don't know what to do."

"What did you expect from him?"

"You know, a once a week meeting. A time where we could compare notes, so to speak, and more importantly, I could ask him some questions. "

"Well, he must think you're doing a good job, or he would say something to you."

"It's not just that, honey. It's the people. I mean, for the most part they're very friendly and generous, but I sense they're lacking any real depth. Now, I don't mean all of them, but generally speaking, they don't seem to have any spiritual interest more than just being saved. I'm not judging here, okay? I'm concerned. And as the Lord's under shepherd assigned to this flock of believers, I think I have that responsibility."

"What do you mean, that they're shallow or something?"

"No, uh . . . I'm not sure. It's like . . . they have little to no interest in maturing spiritually. There's more of a sense that they want the church to have a sort of social club feel. I think maybe it's because Teddy was an evangelist for so long and feels comfortable giving those types of messages each week."

"What kind of sermons?" she questioned with a curious expression.

"The evangelistic themed addresses where folks get saved. Don't get me wrong, that preaching is absolutely needed in our society. However, what I sense is needed in the church is more meat and potatoes and less milk and creamed corn."

"Alan, honestly."

"I know you don't like my metaphor, but I think there's at least a little truth behind it," he smiled as he patted her hand.

"Well . . ."

Alan interrupted, "You know what I just realized as we were talking? I haven't had any true fellowship, like we just had with Joey and Pam, since we moved to Wiggins. In fact, I'll go one step further than that, I enjoyed my couple of hours the other day with Willy, Beldon, Jimmy, and John more than I have enjoyed our six or so months at this church."

"Really? Are you serious, Alan?"

"Absolutely. I felt more life, more like the Holy Spirit was leading the conversation with those guys, than I have with most folks at the church."

"Wow, honey. Why do you think that is?"

"I don't know. It's probably me. It's been very frustrating though. I'm not kidding you, sweetheart. I feel totally useless at this church. Granted, I stand up and give two sermons every other week, but besides that, what do I really do? Nothing."

"Alan, I think maybe it's because Teddy is perceived as a father figure. I mean, he and Margaret not only look the part but have that kind of demeanor too. I don't know, but I'd guess they're really nice grandparents."

"Yeah, but remember, he asked us to come here to grow this church. I don't think he meant more people either. He sensed they needed something more substantial than what's-her-name's apple pie."

"Mrs. Utterback," asserted Annalisa.

"Yeah, her. Uh . . . although I must confess, Mrs. Utterback's pie at the pot luck picnic was really good. Don't you think?"

"It sure was. I need to get her recipe. That was a fun day, except for that softball game," grimaced Annalisa.

"Yeah, that got kind of ugly. But that's what I mean. If they had eyes to see and hearts to perceive, that scene at the ballgame would have spoken volumes to them of their need to grow spiritually. But there seems to be more interest in showing up for some food and play time, than for sitting down and working through some issues in a Bible study. Don't get me wrong, honey. I love to play too. More than most I'd dare say. But frankly, I thought we came here to do something more than that. So no, to answer your original question, I'm not happy at this church and therefore with our move to Wiggins."

"Are you thinking of quitting, Alan?"

"No, I've never really seen much good come out of quitting. Besides, we still have a few months left on our one year lease. When that comes up for renewal, I think we should ask ourselves some hard questions."

Their discussion was put on hold as they pulled into the driveway at Julie and Roger's home. The young couple was sitting on the front stoop anxious to welcome their parents into their cozy home. After hugs and smiles, everyone settled down on the back porch with iced tea while Roger grilled up some juicy hamburgers. The conversation was so lively and light that it actually added fuel to Alan's position of being dissatisfied with their move. The next morning was every bit as pleasant as Julie and her mother were in the kitchen preparing a sumptuous breakfast of blueberry pancakes and sausage patties. Alan and Roger sat in the living room talking about life.

From what Alan could gather, Roger was considering attending a seminary with hopes of going into the ministry. When asked regarding what he was sensing from the Lord, Roger replied that they would be missionaries somewhere in Africa or perhaps South America. He wasn't asking for Alan's advice, so Alan withheld counseling his son-in-law in one direction or another. However, later over lunch the topic came up again, and Annalisa had plenty to say. She didn't try to dissuade them but gave the young couple more than enough to consider for many weeks to come.

After such a lovely visit with their daughter and her husband, Alan and Annalisa were sad to leave. However, the two and a half hour drive would put their arrival in Wiggins just before four o'clock that Saturday afternoon. Alan didn't have the sermon responsibility the following day, but he was scheduled to lead the worship. The maestro of apple pie and church pianist, Mrs. Utterback, had arranged for a worship rehearsal at four o'clock. She was every bit as fastidious regarding rehearsals as she was about her famous pies. Alan didn't dare arrive late.

Walking out the front door Monday morning, twenty minutes earlier than normal, Alan arrived at the coffee shop about quarter to eight. He nodded toward the table in the back. As expected, Willy, Beldon, Jimmy, and John were seated, sipping their hot coffee and already jabbering away. Alan noticed an extra chair at their table.

"How are you this morning, Mr. Alan?"

"Oh, I'm just fine, Miss Bertha. How was your weekend?"

"We doing good. We doing real good," she remarked as she handed across a tall cup of white chocolate mocha.

Alan reached into his pocket and pulled out three dollars. Stretching out his hand toward Bertha, he looked at the amount indicated on the cash register.

"Oh, no, Mr. Alan, this one on the house."

"What?"

"Yes, sir. And thank you so much, Mr. Alan."

"For what?"

"Oh, I'm sure you're going to hear right about the time you sit down with them at that table. They been waiting for you," she smiled with tears in her eyes.

As Alan turned toward the men seated at the table, he heard Bertha call over to her husband and his friends, "Y'all be as loud as you want today. Oh, yeah, this here a good day, an amazing day." Then she broke into her own rendition of the old hymn "Amazing Grace." The other gal behind the counter, who was Jimmy's wife, joined in the singing too, followed by Willy, then Jimmy, and the others. Finally, Alan lifted his voice as well. When they completed three stanzas, the men quieted down as Bertha and her sister-in-law continued to hum the melody. Willy turned to Alan.

"Will you pray for us, my brother?"

"Sure."

Not knowing quite what had happened to his new found friends over the last few days, Alan prayed a rather long prayer trying to cover all of the bases. When he finished, all at the table and behind the counter exclaimed a hearty "Amen." Immediately, Willy started right in.

"God did a miracle in my heart. I've been born again, again."

"Wow, praise the Lord. Tell me what happened," urged Alan.

"Well, I was backslid real bad. Jimmy too, huh, Jimmy? Bertha tried to get us back to church, but I didn't want nothing to do with it. I told the fellas too. We all agreed we ain't never going back. But when you told me to read that Book of Job . . . well, I couldn't believe it. God healed that nasty bitterness and showed me how that old enemy done got ahold of me. I told Bertha what I was fixing to do, and she knelt down there too."

"What were you going to do?"

"Pray, repent, and get right with the Lord. So we be there on the floor in the living room when Jimmy and Ella walked in. That's his wife, there she is behind the counter there. The Holy Ghost got ahold of them too. They both start crying too, so we invite them down on the floor to pray with us. Man, we was praying and crying and crying and praying for what, pert near an hour wasn't it, Jimmy?"

"I don't know. It was awhile though."

From behind the counter Bertha shouted, "Oh, Lord have mercy. Thank you, Jesus!"

"Yeah," continued Willy, "and the Holy Ghost told me I had to tell Beldon what had had happened. So I got up off that floor and walked over to Beldon's and laid it all out to him and Linda, his girl he been living with. They both set out to crying too, so I grabbed they hands and pulled them down to the floor and we all prayed right there. Man, we all was crying, wasn't we Beldon?"

"We sure was."

"We no sooner get up off that floor, than Beldon say he got to make it right. So he took Linda by the hand, and they marched all the way down to the courthouse and got themselves married."

"Thank you, Jesus!" shouted Bertha again, this time with her head in the refrigerator.

"What? Really?" laughed Alan with more than a hint of delight. His delight was in what Willy was communicating. His laughter was due to Bertha's enthusiasm.

"While they be down at the courthouse," resumed Willy, "I walked back home praising the Lord for all He had done. But what you think I found when I got home?"

"I don't know."

"Jimmy had sure enough gone next door to fetch John, and they were on that living room floor in my house praying up a storm. I'm meaning, a Holy Ghost storm! Bertha and them were down there too, so I jumped right on in. It was a miracle, brother Alan. Oh, yeah, it was a sure enough miracle."

"Somebody say, 'Jesus!'" praised Bertha as she and Ella stepped out from behind the counter headed toward where the men were seated.

The others were nodding their heads and praising God for what He had done in their lives and the lives of their families. Willy went on to testify that each one of all of their children had been saved as well. It had all started with Willy humbling himself. Who would have ever thought? One fifty-five year old, unemployed man, angry and bitter, resenting all he thought God had done to him had, with the most simple of acts, opened the door for so many others to receive salvation and eternal life. Now this once hardened and opinionated character, turned to Alan and in a meek tone asked a question that Alan had longed to hear ever since moving to Wiggins.

"What we do next, brother Alan? I gots to go deeper, you understand? I can't stay here lest I fall again. I'm not sure I could be born again the third time."

"Would you gents be up for a Bible study?"

"Sure enough," responded Willy and Jimmy together.

"Me too. I'm all over that," nodded Beldon.

"I would like that too," replied John quietly.

"Okay," consented Alan. "How about we meet here tomorrow morning at seven o'clock? Everyone bring your Bible."

"Man, I ain't got no Bible, Mr. Alan," confessed Beldon.

"Okay, number one, no more calling me mister anything. We are all brothers and sisters in the Lord, equal in His sight. So either call me Alan or brother . . . or brother Alan," he smiled. "Got it?"

They all laughed and nodded their agreement. Just then, Bertha leaned over and asked, "Can we sisters get in on this too?"

"Absolutely," cheered Alan.

All the men were thrilled to have them join in. However, upon further thought, Bertha asked if the study could be started at eight o'clock as her shop's busiest time was between the hours of six and eight each morning. All were in favor of the later start time. Then Alan asked an important question,

"Who needs me to bring them a Bible tomorrow?"

That afternoon Alan and Annalisa drove to Hattiesburg to purchase several Bibles and a dozen little notebooks. On the way there, Alan told Annalisa the whole tale of how Willy and his friends had come to Christ. She laughed and rejoiced right along with Alan. During the drive home, she decided she wanted to be a part of the Bible study too. Alan wholeheartedly agreed. The next morning the two of them walked through the coffee shop door at ten minutes to eight. Willy had pulled four tables together and arranged eighteen chairs around them.

"Expecting company?" teased Alan with a smile.

"You never know," asserted Willy. "I figure it better to be safe than sorry. Besides, it look more inviting this way if they already an open seat there."

"Good thinking," encouraged Alan.

The meeting opened with prayer. Alan led a very interactive study of the Bible. Since it was their first time together, he went over many of the basics of the faith with them. Touching here and there on the major themes in the Scriptures, he wound it to a close by asking if there were any questions regarding what they had discussed. Several raised questions about particular issues but none too personal until John spoke up.

"I can't tell you, Mr. Alan, how much I need this. I mean, I don't know nothing about nothing. Can we do this again tomorrow?"

"If you stop calling me mister, I don't see why not. But that's up to you guys, not me."

They talked it over together for a few seconds. Then all agreed to meet again the next morning, same time, same place. They gathered the following day too and every morning that week. The depth and sincerity of their questions many times brought tears to Alan and Annalisa's eyes. They adored these folks. They were so real, so hungry, and so very sincere about putting into practice whatever was discussed in the study. There was an amazing sense of awe in the little coffee shop. More than once, a customer, upon being invited over, sat down and listened until they closed the meeting with prayer. Two of Willy and Bertha's children along with Jimmy's oldest daughter showed up and joined the group. The following week John's son joined in the study too. They had given away all of the Bibles previously purchased, so Alan and Annalisa drove back to Hattiesburg and bought more.

After dinner Friday evening, Alan and Annalisa sat down in the living room across from the fireplace where a crackling fire glowed. Holding hands, they scooched close together on the sofa and decided to spend some time praying for the little coffee shop group. They went around the table in their minds, lifting each one and their needs before the Throne of Grace and asking their Father in Heaven to continue to fan the tiny flame that burned within the group. When they finished, Alan confessed to Annalisa what was on his mind.

"Honey, I sense the Holy Spirit impressing upon my heart that we are responsible for these folks. By that I mean, more specifically, we need to find them a church. They need a place where they can be fed more than what I can offer and not only that, but somewhere they can begin to use their gifts to build up the Body of Christ."

"I was sensing that too, Alan. Why don't we invite them to come to our church next Sunday? You're speaking that week. I think it would be a very natural transition for them."

"Uh . . . I don't think that's a good idea."

"What? Why not?"

"Because I think they may feel uncomfortable there. And just as important, I think several, who are already in the church, would feel uncomfortable. Look, honey, our friends in this little group are so real, so genuine. What I'm trying to say is, they're so transparent that some folks might be critical of their sincerity. I would never want Willy and them to go through something like that."

"I know, Alan, but their transparency and sincerity are so beautiful."

"You and I think it's beautiful, but I think some of the folks at church, at least the ones with a few thick façades of their own, may find it . . . uh, may find them, somewhat offensive."

"Well, that's their problem then," chided Annalisa. "It's not ours and it's certainly not Willy's."

"Yes and no. I agree that our Lord would desire to stir up the church to love and good works. However, I also believe the unity of that same church is of paramount importance to God. We really need to be prayerful and careful about doing something that could shake things up. We don't want to end up on the wrong end of this with the Lord."

"Of course not."

"So let's keep praying and asking Him to show us what we need to do. I sense He knows what's best for them. Don't get me wrong. I would love to have every one of them at our church. I think it would bring so much life. Not that it's dead or anything. Perhaps it just needs to be stirred up a little. You know, to wake it up or something. But I think it's best to leave how to accomplish that in God's hands. I hope I've learned my lesson about trying to tell people what I think they should do. It does make me smile, thinking of old Willy and sweet Bertha up there singing their hearts out and praising the Lord at the top of their lungs. Can't you just see the look on Mrs. Utterback's face?"

Annalisa slapped Alan on the arm as he snickered. "Stop it, Alan. You're awful," she reproved with a hint of a chuckle. "Although to be truthful, I would love to see that scene too."

The following Bible study hosted fourteen people and more participation than they had experienced to date. Just after finishing up, Willy and Bertha, along with Beldon, Jimmy, John, and a couple of others approached Alan and Annalisa.

"Hey, y'all, before y'all go, you got time for one last question," posed Willy with a serious look on his face.

"Sure," agreed Alan with Annalisa by his side.

"Well, we were talking last night over at John's house. He had us by for some biscuits and gravy. Anyway, we was all talking, and we decided since we had read that verse in Hebrews 'Not forsaking the assembling of yourselves together'[1] that we should probably be getting to church on Sundays. What y'all think about that, Alan?"

"I think it's very important to be a part of a body of believers. It's an essential part of growing up, of maturing in the Lord, and a place where you can be helping others."

"Yeah, you right. That's what Beldon was saying last night too. It would be good for us . . . for all of us. But we kind of scared though. I mean, none of us have no church going clothes or nothing."

"Oh, don't worry about that," assured Annalisa with a smile. "Most churches these days are very casual. Some have a more traditional service where folks get dressed up, but at some point during the day there is also a contemporary service where folks just wear everyday clothes."

"I appreciate that Miss Annalisa," remarked Bertha.

"Well, yeah, I appreciate that too," agreed Willy. "But I guess what I'm trying to say is we don't really know no church folk . . . except you two."

Glancing at Annalisa, Alan gave her a look that revealed he knew precisely what Willy was going to ask next. But before either one could acknowledge the other Willy posed the question.

"So if it be alright with you folks, we'd all like to go to church with y'all this Sunday. Is that okay with you, Alan?"

-eight-

Standing behind the pulpit Sunday morning giving the announcements, Alan was surprised to see Willy, Bertha, and more than twenty others with them shuffling around the back of the sanctuary. They were causing quite a stir among the congregation, so when Alan caught Willy's eye, he waved them in. As is the case in many churches, all the seating in the back half of the sanctuary had been occupied first. Therefore, one by one, or sometimes two by two, Willy's entire group began filing up the aisle to the front rows and took their seats.

Teddy, standing next to Alan on the platform, leaned over and whispered, "Okay, Alan, what's going on here?"

"Nothing. These are some of our brothers and sisters in Christ I met at the coffee shop. They wanted to come to our church, and I assured them they would be welcome."

"When did this happen?" whispered Teddy, smiling at the congregation.

"We can talk about it later, Teddy." Then, turning toward the group, he exclaimed "Y'all come on in now. Willy, Bertha, welcome, we're so glad y'all are here."

The singing that morning was more vibrant than either Alan or Annalisa had experienced before. Willy, his family, and his friends were singing with all of their hearts and after each and every song several called out "Praise the Lord!" or "Thank you, Jesus!" So much so that Teddy got caught up in the enthusiasm and shouted, "Praise God!" a few times too. The whole atmosphere was a bit overwhelming to the song leader, a young man, who sold life insurance during the week. At one point, with an expression of semi-panic he gazed over at Alan looking for his help. Nodding his assurance, Alan mouthed, "It's okay," and then continued singing. When the worship leader finished his list of songs, he turned to Alan and shrugged his shoulders. Alan stepped to the pulpit, exchanged glances with Mrs. Utterback, the pianist, and picked up singing another three songs, ending with one he knew was Willy and Bertha's favorite, "Amazing Grace." Hearing this, Teddy lifted his hands toward Heaven and sang at the top of his lungs, while tears streamed down his cheeks. More than half the congregation followed suit. Alan, with eyes closed and hands in the air, sang his heart out. It was an exhilarating breath of fresh air, the wind of the Holy Spirit. It was as if Heaven itself were singing with them. However, not everyone shared the same opinion. More than a few walked out of the worship service that morning.

As the last stanza of the hymn was winding down, Alan started to quietly worship, "Praise you, Lord," and, "We worship You, Lord," as well as a few other phrases in Scripture, which came to his mind. Teddy, standing next to Alan on the platform, joined right in. Willy, most of his family, his friends, and a few in the congregation participated too. When the sound of their praising drew to a close, Teddy stepped up to the pulpit and prayed a prayer with such gusto that Alan was sure it must have shook the heavens. Peeking at the older, godly saint, Alan was certain his voice had boomed out many a time before around various parts of the country. That tone, that inflection must have been a godsend to countless souls in his day. And here he was, eighty years old, infused with new life that obviously awoke the heart of the evangelist within him. Teddy, standing behind the wooden podium with two hands holding on to the edges, one on each side, prayed for many minutes. Different ones shouting their "Amen," "Thank you, Jesus," or, "Praise the Lord," several times during his discourse with God. It was absolutely precious and filled Alan's heart with both joy and awe.

When Teddy had finished praying, he had the people sit down. Then he turned to Alan, put both hands on his shoulders, and declared, "The petals of the flowers are open. Preach it from your heart, brother, and let the showers of Heaven fall."

While Teddy gingerly stepped down the three stairs to take his seat with Margaret in the front row, Alan moved to the pulpit and pulled his folded sermon notes from the back of his Bible. Sensing a check in his spirit, he unfolded them placing them flat on the pulpit next to his open Bible. The caution wasn't going away. Glancing down at Annalisa, who was seated in the third row next to Bertha, he smiled when their eyes met. Her beaming face assured him that what he was sensing was the right thing to do. Catching a glimpse of Teddy's nod just before he began his sermon, Alan folded his notes and slid them back into his Bible.

"My brothers and sisters, I need you to pray for utterance, for the Spirit's anointing, or this is going to be a very short message." Alan paused for a few moments to allow each one time to pray silently. Then he spoke up again.

"You know, I must confess something to you. God uses the most unlikely vessels to accomplish His purposes.[1] We look on the outside. Isn't that right? Well, God looks on the inside. He sees the heart.[2] He uses what we think is weak to proclaim His strength. He uses what we would pass by as useless to declare His glory. In our weakness, He is strong. But what's the opposite of that? In our strength, is God ever weak? Never! But where I think I'm strong, I don't leave room for Him to work those things that only He can do. He calls into being those things which do not exist.[3] He softens even the hardest hearts. He turns the course of the mightiest rivers. Can He not change us? I believe we have more than enough evidence here today. Can you hear me this morning, my brethren? We're all in this thing together. None of us is better than the other. We just have differing gifts.[4] If our Lord Jesus were to enter through that door and walk down this aisle, would there be a single person still standing? Or would we all be face down, flat on the floor in worship and reverence?"

Continuing on for nearly an hour, Alan was surprised and delighted with the freedom he felt as he spoke. Not once did he look at his notes. The sermon moved smoothly from one point to the next, to the next, right up to the conclusion. He never raised his voice. He didn't have to. The depth of what the Holy Spirit was communicating convicted him as well as the congregation.

"Finally, my beloved brethren," he concluded. "If we can let go of thinking our natural attributes are somehow an asset to God, then I believe we can begin a whole new adventure with Him. It's an adventure of discovery for each one of us as we take a useful place in His Body, the church. He's given you, each one of you, a special gift. It's not a natural gift. It's a spiritual gift. Let's individually employ our gifts to build each other up in love. So what do you say? Are you up for a new adventure? A lifelong spiritual adventure with God?"

After closing with prayer, Alan stepped down off the platform and was immediately approached by Teddy and Margaret. Teddy shook his hand and advised, "We've got a lot of work to do, my brother. We need to get planning on how this is going to work out. Can you get together tomorrow morning here at eight o'clock?"

"Sounds good. I'll see you then."

Next, Alan made a beeline toward Willy and Bertha, who were talking with Annalisa. After telling Willy he wouldn't be at the Bible study, Alan encouraged Willy to teach the study himself. Willy was reluctant but with a few optimistic words from his wife, he agreed to take the responsibility for the morning once Alan assured him he would be back to lead the group on Tuesday.

Alan and Annalisa were engaged in several conversations as they made their way to the door. It seemed like no one wanted to leave the church. It was nearly two o'clock that afternoon when they arrived home. After changing their clothes and having a bite to eat, Alan went straight to the study and pulled out many of the notes he had accumulated over the last few years. He was feeling the need to get things somewhat organized before his meeting with Teddy. An hour or so later, Annalisa popped her head in with some iced tea.

"What are you doing, honey?" she asked softly.

"Well, I started reviewing and putting in order all my notes from the last few years. But before I got too far into it, I noticed something interesting."

"What's that?"

"Look here . . . at this twelfth chapter in the Book of First Corinthians. See how there are what I would call categories here? There are three of them. I checked the words in the original Greek language and they are, in fact, different words with very distinct meanings."

"Where are the words, Alan?"

"In, uh, verses four, five, and six. The first one is Gifts, the second one is Ministries, and the last one is Effects. Now, for something to be an effect there has to be a cause, right?"

"Yeah, I guess so."

"Well, what is the cause?" he asked her although asking himself as well.

"I don't know. Maybe there's a need, so the Holy Spirit gives something to help meet the need. You know, like someone has a difficult decision to make, and the Spirit gives a word of wisdom through another person that would help them make the decision."

"Wow, honey, I think you may have something there. Some of the other Effects in that list are healings, miracles, faith, word of knowledge, and a few more. I can see all of these would be in response to meeting a need of one kind or another. That's excellent."

"How about the other two lists then?"

"Well, the Ministries list is right there at the end of the chapter in verse twenty-eight: apostles, prophets, teachers and several more. I believe these are positions God has people fill as needed for the strengthening of His Body. And like Teddy, you move in and out of them as the Lord directs."

"Then where is the list of Gifts?"

"There's only one other list in the Bible and it's in Romans, chapter twelve." Alan quickly turned several pages in his Bible. "See, it's right here in verses six, seven, and eight."

"Yes, I can see that too, Alan. So I think you may be absolutely correct about that last list, the uh, Gifts list."

"Hmmm, I'm not quite sure. I mean, I think so when you look down the list. These are action words not effects or positions. Therefore, it's part of you. It's what propels or motivates you to do what you do. Really, I think it determines how you look at life. In our western culture we tend to think of ourselves as a title or a position, not as an action. You know, most folks don't say, 'I work on cars.' No, they declare, 'I'm an auto mechanic.' Or have you ever heard anyone say, 'I take out gall bladders?' Of course not, they proclaim themselves to be a doctor or surgeon. Now listen, here's what I think the Lord may be saying to us in these days."

"Yeah? I'm all ears," she encouraged.

"In the Old Testament, His Spirit spoke to His people through prophets, kings, and men and women of God, like

Deborah, Nehemiah, Gideon, and others. In the New Testament, He gave all believers His Spirit and through Him, spiritual gifts. Now in these three categories are His provisions to us, but they're not inclusive. There are many other blessings He has given us like love, grace, hope, mercy, and especially His Son, Jesus. Now, right here," Alan pointed at the page in his Bible, "He broke them down into three groupings or what I have called categories. They are Gifts, Ministries, and Effects.[5] It dawned on me that the only category we are using at church is Ministries, and we are only partially employing that category. Why? It doesn't make any sense to use only a fraction of the spiritual provision God gave us to walk this life. What if we could discover how to use all He provides for the building up of the Body, His church? What might happen then?"

"Wow, that would be amazing," she professed with her expressive eyes opened wide. "I would want to be a part of that wherever it was, our church here, or another church, or in a house, a barn, or wherever they met together. To be a part of a body of believers like that would be incredible."

"Well, that's exactly what I intend to propose to Brother Teddy tomorrow morning. I think after experiencing what happened today at church he will be open and receptive to giving it a try."

"Giving what a try?" she shrugged.

"This new approach to ministry, to being a church. Well, maybe it's a really old approach that has been lying dormant for centuries. I think it may be a more Biblical way of serving and growing His church though. I mean, instead of using only one person, or like in our case two people, there could be many different ones serving, based on their gifting from the Holy Spirit. And talk about a more well-rounded perspective of what the Lord may be saying to us. Just think of it. As each one is sensing how God may be leading them, they could express it through their unique gift. I'm not just referring to speaking, but communicating through demonstrating their spiritual gift. These aren't some sort of amenities that we can choose to employ if we want to. They are, for every Christian, absolutely essential to discovering the kingdom within you and walking together with our God and His people. Be it prophecy, serving, teaching, exhorting, giving, leading, or mercy, these gifts determine how we look at life, life's situations, and each other. Therefore, through your spiritual gift, you see everything and everyone from a unique point of view. But when all is done, we, His church, would have a more well-rounded perspective of the truth and what God is saying to us about it."

"I'm not sure I'm following you, Alan."

"Okay, let's say there is a car accident at an intersection with a traffic light," he proposed gently.

"Yeah?"

"And there are people who have witnessed the accident standing on each of the four corners of this intersection. They all saw from their limited perspective what happened, correct?"

"Yeah, I guess . . ."

"They couldn't see all sides of it at once, right? Only the part of the accident they could view from their corner."

"Yeah, I get it now."

"Well, one witness would declare one thing, and another would testify something a bit different. Perhaps one was looking at the traffic signal, but the other was watching the cars. Each would have something to report, and all four would be absolutely accurate according to their particular perspective. But what actually happened is the absolute truth. It's important that each witness testify as to what they experienced, but the truth of the matter is what actually occurred."

"So let me see if I'm hearing you right. In your story, uh, your example, each spiritual gift is like a person standing on the corner at the intersection. They have a certain perspective based on what they've experienced. The more witness statements the police officer obtained from each of the four corners, the more confidence he would have in determining what actually happened."

"Yes."

"Okay," she nodded. "Not to mess with your metaphor, but there's only four corners and there are seven spiritual gifts."

"Honey, whether it's four or seven isn't the issue. The point of the parable is with the testimony of many witnesses we can have a more defined perspective of the truth."

"And why is that so important?"

"Because our God is invisible. He has given us His Word, the Bible. A solitary person reads it from his or her own perspective. But if you had seven individuals, each with a different spiritual gift, all reading the same passage of Scripture, then the combined commentaries would offer a well-rounded perspective that would give better understanding of what God is communicating. At least I think it would anyway. That's what I'm hoping to propose to Teddy tomorrow morning in our meeting."

"I'll be praying, Alan. I hope he's open to hearing what you have to say."

"Me too."

Early the next morning, Alan spent time in prayer then gathered his Bible and headed off to church. Once he got settled in the meeting room, he put his notes and thoughts in order so he could be prepared for any distractions or issues which might arise and throw them off the topic he was hoping to discuss. Teddy arrived at precisely eight o'clock. After prayer, they started right in with their meeting.

"Alan, yesterday was a blessing I've been praying for decades would happen right here in our little church. But it has presented us with a problem or shall we say a challenge."

"I was working on that last night, Teddy. I have some notes and ideas here I would like us to go over together, if that's okay? First . . ."

"Hold on a second, Alan," he admonished in a sober tone. "That's not the challenge I'm referring to."

"No? What do you mean?"

"I received a phone call from one of the elders last night. He was unmistakably upset with the service yesterday. He wanted to call an emergency elder meeting right away. It took a while, but I finally got him calmed down. However, just as I hung up Maggie told me there was someone at the front door. Two more elders wanted to talk. They were fairly agitated too and demanded we have an elder meeting tonight to figure out what we're going to do."

"With what?" inquired Alan.

"With you," declared Teddy, gazing over the top of his glasses directly at Alan.

"With me? What did I do?"

"Well, they're bent out of shape because you invited those folks to the church."

"Number one, I didn't invite them. Two, 'those folks' are Christians just like you and me. They are our brothers and sisters. Willy and Bertha love the Lord. In addition to that I would dare say they have more love for His people than most of the folks that have been attending here for years."

"Easy, Alan. You're starting to judge, brother. You don't want to be on the wrong end of this thing. Remember who we're fighting. You can bet our devious enemy is at the bottom of this whole situation."

"Yes, you're right. Sorry about that. It just makes me so angry. They're really good people. Ask Annalisa. She'll vouch for them. I mean, we love Willy, Bertha, and their entire family."

"Well, brace yourself, my brother. There's more that may make you angry."

"What else didn't they like?"

"The service."

"What didn't they like about that? I thought it was awesome."

"Everything. Start to finish. They thought it was too emotional, unscriptural, and an improper way to worship

God. They are convinced God would never be a part of any such thing."

"Based on what?" Alan was trying to withhold his judgmental opinions by asking questions.

"Frankly? Their narrow perspectives, Alan."

"What do you think, Teddy?"

"I think the Holy Spirit came down and met with us in a way that I haven't seen in twenty-five years. I loved it and want more of it. But it's not up to me. This is an elder run church. I only have one vote, the same as you and the other seven elders. Three of them want you thrown out. They think you're trying to change this church into something they don't want. And the difficult part is, they believe God wouldn't want it to change either. So here's what I want you to do. Go home and you and that sweet Annalisa pray. Be back here at seven o'clock. I've been through these things before . . . I would encourage you to be early and to just sit quietly. It's what our Lord did. Follow His example. If they ask you questions, give them answers but watch your emotions. Those will get you in more trouble than you can handle. Remember, it's that wretched enemy of ours in the middle of this thing wreaking havoc. The believers who can recognize his schemes will be the ones to come out victorious."

"Okay, I'll try to be calm and quiet."

"Look, Alan, this is probably going to get nasty before it gets peaceful again. You'll need a thick skin, you and Annalisa both. Don't let them get to you. It's a spiritual battle we fight. It's not against flesh and blood. These folks aren't our enemies. They just don't understand yet what God may be trying to do here in our little body of believers. So fight with your faith. Resist the enemy when you need to, and he will flee from you.[6] Employ all your spiritual armor. Put it on and keep it on.[7] You're going to need it."

"Thanks, Teddy."

"Now go on home and love on that dear wife of yours. I'll see you back here tonight."

The entire day Alan struggled with thoughts of insecurity as well as emotions of anger and fear. He and Annalisa prayed together off and on throughout the day. Hardly eating any dinner, he left the house at six-thirty. He was surprised to find everyone was already there with the exception of Teddy, who arrived right on time. After praying for peace and unity, Teddy opened the meeting.

It was civil enough at first. But after several comments were made by some, and opposing remarks were volleyed back in return by others, the tempers started to flare. Teddy sat at the far end of the table, opposite Alan, as quiet as an ice hockey referee waiting for the fight to stop, so he can break in and bring order again. Several times an accusation was made in Alan's direction. He answered as calmly and accurately as he knew how. This had the adverse effect of stoking the fire in some of the furnaces, which got others fired up in their reactions as well. At one point, even Teddy got a bit riled up with those who were hurling accusations.

Lasting until almost midnight, the whole thing ended with two of the elders resigning, two others angrily marching out, and the rest, including Teddy and Alan, relieved that at least some agreement had been reached. In fact, it wasn't much of an accord at all, but it was some common ground as well as a commitment from the remaining elders to stay open to what God may be doing in their church body.

Teddy, who was visibly exhausted from the battle, closed the meeting with prayer. Then he quickly chased down two of the older gentlemen before they left. It was well after midnight when Alan pulled out of the church parking lot. He could see Teddy still standing on the front steps talking with the two elders.

Knowing Annalisa would be asleep, Alan was quiet as a mouse as he entered their home, got dressed for bed, and slipped under the covers. Frankly, he was entirely fatigued too. This type of meeting takes its toll on all involved. No wonder the enemy enjoys wreaking havoc among believers.

From his morning meeting with Teddy until the elder's meeting ended, it had been a completely draining day. While thinking their bed felt even more comfortable than he had remembered, Alan quickly drifted off to sleep. However, he was startled awake by Annalisa shaking him. "Alan, it's your phone. It might be one of the kids."

Staggering over to the dresser, he pulled it off of the charger.

"Hello?"

"Alan, so sorry to bother you," replied the stressed feminine voice on the other end.

"Oh, its okay, Maggie. Is everything alright?"

"It's Teddy, Alan. I think he's had a heart attack."

-nine-

Parking at the curb in front of Teddy and Maggie's home, Alan and Annalisa quickly hopped out, jogged to the front door, and lightly knocked. To their surprise, one of the church elders, Jake Beauregard, opened the door. Annalisa immediately sat down next to Teddy's wife on the living room sofa. Maggie then explained the situation to the two of them. After arriving home at one a.m., Teddy had articulated to Maggie that he had some pretty bad heartburn. She had suggested that he prepare for bed while she went to the kitchen to retrieve some chewable antacid. When she had returned to the bedroom, he was laying across the bed holding his chest.

"After I asked him if he was okay," Maggie expressed quietly, "he told me he had just sensed the Lord was speaking to him. I replied that I thought he may have had a heart attack as he was quite pale and clammy. He would hear none of it and asked me to quickly call you, Alan, along with three of the elders. Doc Watkins arrived first. He and Mary just live next door. He immediately went to the bedroom where he has been taking care of Teddy ever since. Jake showed up shortly after Doc. And with you two arriving, all we're waiting on is for Zachary Baylor to get here."

"Then what?" asked Alan.

"I don't know. I think Teddy will tell us what he's sensing," Maggie replied.

"He needs to be in the hospital," urged Jake.

"Oh, Doc and I both emphatically expressed that very thought to him several times, Jake. But he kept insisting that he needed to tell all of you what he had heard from the Lord."

"Did he tell you anything about it?" inquired Jake who was sitting across the room from the three on the sofa.

"No, only that he thought it lasted for several minutes," she replied with much anxiety on her face and concern in her eyes.

"Wow, that long?" expressed Alan in a near whisper.

"But it couldn't have, Alan, because I was in the kitchen for less than a minute. He hadn't even gotten undressed yet. How could it have been that long?"

"I don't know. Maybe it's something supernatural," replied Alan as he shook his head slowly. "I've had a couple of things happen to me over the years, but I can't explain how. And our clocks here on earth seem to be irrelevant when it comes to things of a spiritual nature."

Just then, there was a rap on the front door. Jake jumped up and let Zachary in. Alan caught Zachary up to speed while Maggie went in to check on Teddy. Doc Watkins, who was himself an elder, walked into the living room.

"How's he doing, Doc?" asked Alan for the group.

"Unexplainably, he's doing very well. He's perfectly calm and sitting up in bed. He hasn't slept a wink in over twenty two hours. You'd think an eighty year old man would be exhausted. However, he's wide awake and talking."

"Did he have a heart attack?" inquired Annalisa.

"Yes, I think so, honey," nodded Doc. "Perhaps a mild one, but it's difficult to be certain without running a couple of tests."

"Oh, Alan?" called Maggie from down the hallway. "Could you please come here for a moment?"

Glancing around, first at Annalisa then the others, Alan jumped to his feet when Doc flicked his chin as if to say "Get moving."

About to enter the bedroom slowly and not sure of what he would see, Alan's mind flashed back to first Stanley and then Betsy Taft. It all felt surreal, like he was reliving the same scenes again. It was scary to think of losing Teddy, especially at this point in the church's history. So much was stirring among the people now. How could they ever work through it all without a strong father figure, a pastor, a leader, a Moses, who could lead them through their own Red Sea? As he slowly pushed the door open, the whole room came into view. Teddy was sitting up in bed with pillows behind him and a huge smile on his face. He motioned Alan to come near.

"Alan, welcome, my dear brother."

"Hi, Teddy, how are you feeling?"

"I'm fine. Listen, I really feel the Lord has spoken something to me. Look, there are a couple of things we need to take care of right now."

"Okay, Teddy. How can I help? What do you think He's telling you to do?" asked Alan gently as he sat down in the chair next to the bed.

"I believe He told me to . . ." Teddy stopped abruptly and looking past Alan, he waved his hand. "Come on in here, gentlemen. We have some important business to take care of real quick."

The three elders shuffled their way into the bedroom with Annalisa peeking in from the door.

"You too, Annalisa, come on in here, sweetie, and stand next to your husband," urged Teddy. "Now where are the other two elders?"

"I called Seb but no answer. I left him a message though," replied Jake. "Then I dropped by his house on the way here, but there wasn't a car in the driveway. Maybe they're out of town or something?"

"Okay, well you tried. How about Joshua?" inquired Teddy with a concerned look on his face.

"I called him too," confessed Jake. "He wasn't cotton to any of it. I think he's still pretty angry. He asked me to call him in the morning and let him know what happened. Teddy, I think he and Jessica may be leaving too."

"Lord, bless them," breathed Teddy. Then he prayed quite the lengthy prayer, calling out to God for help in their time of need. When all had joined in with the final "Amen," Teddy started right in with what he believed the Lord was saying to him.

"Gentlemen, uh . . . pardon me, and ladies, I believe our Lord has given us some very distinct direction in His Word. He doesn't look on the exterior, on the outside. No, He sees the heart. He looks on the inside. We tend to look on the outside. I have something I need to confess to you all; I am guilty of this very thing myself. I have lived way too long judging what I see and not trying to perceive people and situations as God views them. He looks at what is invisible, way down inside of a person." Teddy paused to let this truth sink in before he continued while tapping on his chest.

"The greatest obstacles a person will ever have to overcome reside in here—the desires of his heart, the thoughts of his mind, the intentions of his will, and the fears of his emotions."

The only sound in the room was Jake's whispered, "Wow." Everyone stood spellbound, gazing at the sage, old saint, lying near death on his bed. It was a moment that none of them would ever forget.

"And how is it that we overcome them?" Teddy inquired as he glanced around at the silent faces transfixed on his every word.

"By faith," ventured Alan.

"Yes," agreed Teddy with a smile. "But how?"

The room was silent as Teddy paused again to allow this final question to sink in deeper.

"Where is the kingdom of God?" asked Teddy, trying to coax an answer from the group. His eyes darted around at each one in the dimly lit bedroom until he finally came to Alan.

"The kingdom is within you,"[1] Alan stated confidently.

"That's precisely right," Teddy nodded. "Therein lies the most simplistic of differences, and yet the impact on our lives is much greater than we comprehend. The battle is in here," he tapped again on his chest several times for emphasis. "It's not outside. It's not other people. It's not what they do that is our fight. It's how I respond that is the real battle. The kingdom of God is not meat and drink. It's not eating and drinking, but righteousness, peace, and joy in the Holy Ghost.[2] It's not external things. It's internal."

At this point, Doc spoke up. "What do you mean, internal?"

"Doc," continued Teddy, "Where does the Holy Spirit reside now? Where is His temple?"

"In every Christian."

"That's precisely right. We are His temple,[3] His house where He lives," affirmed Teddy.

"I agree," nodded Doc with a serious look that bordered on perplexity.

"Well, if that be true," posed Teddy, "and we know it is, and further we know His kingdom is within us, then that kingdom must be a spiritual kingdom, correct?"

All in the room were nodding their heads in agreement although none uttered a single word as they sensed Teddy was communicating something on a deeper level than what they were used to hearing.

"Great! We're all in agreement. This is wonderful. Okay, since we're all unified that this is a spiritual kingdom, and it's God's kingdom, and it is within each one of us, then will somebody please define the kingdom for me?"

Glancing around the room at the blank faces, Teddy's eyes stopped again at Alan. However, just as Alan began to speak Teddy placed his hand on Alan's shoulder motioning for him to be quiet. Raising his eyebrows and looking intently at the three elders standing at the foot of his bed, Teddy queried, "Gentlemen?"

The three men stared back at their older, bedridden pastor with a mix of wonder and a hint of shame in their eyes. Sometimes it's not easy for a saint to admit he doesn't know something. However, the second he lays aside his pride and confesses his lack of knowledge, he has just learned something new.

"I don't know," shrugged Jake with Zachary quickly following suit. It took several more seconds, but Doc also acknowledged he wasn't sure.

"Well, men, I'm in good company because I didn't know either until that night several months back when we invited Alan and Annalisa to come help with our church. They shared a few things with Maggie and me that were both intriguing and startling. I wasn't at all sure what to do with this new revelation, so I did nothing . . . until tonight."

"Tonight?" asked Doc.

"Yes, as you know, we had quite the heated meeting. Sadly, we lost two elders, and I think, maybe, one or two more may resign before it is all said and done. But why? As I sat there listening to the arguments from both sides, it dawned on me. It was like the time I walked to my shed late one night. I never would have seen the copperhead by the door if I hadn't brought my flashlight."

"I'm not sure I follow your meaning," Doc confessed with a wry grin.

"Alan and Annalisa brought us some light," declared Teddy. "We may have avoided being bit last night in our meeting if we had already begun implementing it."

"I don't understand," voiced Zachary in a quiet tone. "What light?"

"Spiritual light, spiritual kingdom, everything we're talking about tonight is of a spiritual nature. So when I refer to spiritual light, I don't mean an actual flashlight but an illumination of something hidden. Something spiritually discerned that to me has been unknown up to this point. Look, there are those that believe many things in Scripture are literally referring to actual things here on earth. You know, like some folks taking the verse that says the Apostle Peter was a rock that Jesus was going to build His church upon. Then, centuries later, they decided to build a church building on Peter's grave. When in fact, Jesus was making a declaration about Peter's faith, not where Christians should erect a future sanctuary. Do you understand, Zack?"

Zachary smiled, nodding his head.

"My beloved brethren, and I'm including you too, ladies, the kingdom of God is within you.[4] It is inside each and every one of us. His Holy Spirit, the same Spirit that was in Jesus, is in us. His Spirit lives in us today. His kingdom is within us, but it's a spiritual kingdom, not a physical kingdom. Remember when our Master stood before Pontius Pilate, he proclaimed that if His kingdom were of this world, His disciples would be fighting for Him. But as it is, His kingdom is not of this realm.[5] Yet that same kingdom lives inside each one of us. So I ask you again, what is the kingdom of God?"

Again the room was silent.

"Okay, then, here's the direction I think the Lord would have us go," proceeded Teddy with a smile. "We need to work on discovering what His kingdom is, and how we are to live because of it. What do you think?"

Maggie, who had been seated on the bed opposite Teddy, asked a question. "Is this what you sensed from the Lord, honey?"

"Yes, well partly anyway."

"How do you plan on teaching this, Teddy?" asked Doc with a hint of skepticism.

"I don't plan on teaching it. Alan will teach us."

"What?" I don't know . . ."

"Now, Alan," interrupted Teddy. "You have already learned more about this than the rest of us combined. And you've tried it to be sure it works. I mean, you have proof, not just theory."

"But, Teddy . . ."

"Alan, all you lack is the confidence. God will surely give you this as you need it. Share with the gentlemen what you shared with Maggie and me that night. You know, about the Gifts of the Holy Spirit, His Ministries, and His Effects, and all. Tell them how they should be used for the building up of His body, the church. And teach them about the Fruit of the same Spirit, as well as His weapons, and His spiritual armor."

Then turning to the elders, Teddy continued, "All of these, and more my brothers, make up the kingdom of God which is even now lying dormant inside each one of us. On this earth, the kingdom of God is not a place. It is the living relationship with our Father in Heaven as well as His abiding Spirit within us. The very same Spirit that was in Jesus. It is a myriad of elements and amenities, of character and wonders, of mysteries and assurances. No, the kingdom is not a place, my beloved. The kingdom of God is an intimacy. The more intimate you are with Him, the greater His kingdom expands in your life."

Alan, sensing courage welling up within him offered, "Well, I guess, I could . . ."

"Come on, Alan," coaxed Teddy, "maybe not tonight, but real soon. In our next elders meeting you could start laying out a plan for us. You have most of this memorized anyway. What do you say, my brother, are you willing to share what God has shown you over the years with your brothers and sisters in Christ?"

"Well. Of course, I am, Teddy. But . . ."

"Okay, then, we are now officially having an elders meeting. There are five of us in attendance, so we have a quorum. Now, for the first order of business: I move that Alan Michael Browne be ordained as the associate pastor of our church."

"Wait a second, Teddy," interjected Alan.

"Do I have a second?" urged Teddy gazing across his bed at the three elders.

"Second," called out Jake.

"All in favor signify by saying, 'Aye.'"

Everyone, including Maggie and Annalisa answered with a hearty "Aye" except Alan. He felt uneasy about the vote. As soon as things settled down somewhat he voiced his concern.

"Look, Teddy, shouldn't we set this decision before the people?"

"We will this Sunday. Leave that to me, okay? Meanwhile, let's all keep this quiet, okay?"

"Look," asserted Alan, "I will agree to this call to be the associate pastor with two conditions. First, that the people overwhelmingly agree to it. And second, Annalisa and I can leave when we feel the Lord indicating we're done with what He sent us here to do."

"Fair enough, gents?" asked Teddy nodding toward the three elders.

All three assented their agreement. But before he accepted their consent, Alan wanted to assure that they knew exactly what Teddy meant by making him a pastor.

"Gentlemen," propounded Alan. "I feel it's only fair to warn you of what you're getting yourselves into. This new way that Teddy has mentioned is not new at all. In fact, it's as old as the New Testament, although, it is new to our way of thinking about church. Plus, it will take some time to implement. However, it will no longer be the group dependent upon only one person. Rather, it will be each and every member doing their part to build up the whole. Our roles within the Body, the church, will no longer be based on positions, but on actions, on needs, on motivations, and the like. I know it may seem a bit peculiar now, yet it's Biblical and much needed within the entire church. There is only one Head of the church, and it's not Teddy, or myself, or anyone else. It is the Lord Jesus Christ, Him and only Him. It's up to us to understand how we function together under His kind and sovereign leadership. I'm looking forward to learning these things together."

"On a practical level, gents," expressed Teddy, addressing the curious looks upon the faces of the elders. "What Alan is indicating here is a different approach to ministry and how we function as a body of believers. The leadership will be based upon each one's spiritual gifting, not his role or position in society, or even in the church. Take you for example, Zack. You're an electrician down at the mill. That's not a leadership role, but you have a heart to serve others. Your spiritual gift is certainly Serving. Well, there are many in our church who need to hear what motivates a servant, what determines his actions, and how he sees needs before others recognize them. Now, Jake, you have a heart full of mercy, of empathy toward others. I believe your spiritual gift of Mercy is what determines how you perceive others, what they say, how they say it, and what they do. You, my dear brother, have one of the most valuable, yet unrecognized gifts of all. I want you, one Sunday soon, to share how you perceive situations and how you can befriend others without the slightest hint of judgement. Same with you, Doc. You are incredibly organized. Most folks are not. Just think how you could help others in our church with your spiritual gift of Organization."

"Well, what about you and Alan?" inquired Doc with a slightly critical tone.

"Alan has the gift of Prophecy," affirmed Teddy. "He has a unique ability not only to declare truth but to explain it in ways that others can understand. I think that's what really determines what he does and how he looks at life. And me, you can ask Maggie for verification, but I believe I have the gift of Exhortation. I continually want to help others stay encouraged and to remain hopeful."

"Well, how's this going to work, Teddy?" asked Doc, this time with more sincerity. "I mean, how are we going to plan and schedule this thing so the church can start learning about it."

Teddy laughed. "See you do have the spiritual gift of Organization." As everyone laughed, Teddy concluded, "I'm leaving that up to our new associate pastor. I'm sure he will be in touch with you soon. Right, Alan?"

The following Sunday they experienced a wonderful time of worship. As Alan was finishing up his message, Teddy, still feeling weak, rose from the second pew and walked up onto the platform. When Alan had asked God's blessing upon the people, concluding his benediction, Teddy waved the elders to join them on the platform too.

"Everyone, please have a seat," Teddy gently instructed, motioning his hand toward the congregation. "We're going to have a short meeting to inform you of several things that have happened this week. Some, to be sure, you have heard about, others we will share with you now. So please listen closely. Regarding last week's service, it is the general consensus of the elders that the Lord was moving in our midst, and we need to be open to His gracious leading. Subsequently, an emergency meeting of the elders was called to discuss what happened during the service. I will tell you quite frankly, the meeting was, at times, a very heated gathering. I'm sad to report, two of our elders have officially resigned and left the church. We wish them Godspeed and hold no hard feelings toward them whatsoever. It was simply a matter of the direction of our church. They thought we should head a certain way, and those of us who stand before you here believe God is leading along a different path. To be truthful, two of the five remaining elders feel a wait-and-see posture is prudent, so they have agreed to neither discourage nor promote this new direction."

At this point an elderly lady in the third pew raised her hand. Teddy acknowledged her, "Yes, Mrs. Whitworth."

"Who are the two elders still sitting on the fence?"

"Sebastian Haygood and Joshua Jernigan. Why do you ask?"

"Should they be elders if they're not in agreement?"

"Great question, Mrs. Whitworth. The answer is a definite yes. They are not antagonistic toward what God may be doing among us. They just aren't sure yet if it is truly His leading. Seb or Josh, would you like to add anything here?"

Joshua Jernigan moved to the microphone. "Mrs. Whitworth, and all y'all for that matter, Seb and I, well, we ain't against whatever this new thing is. We just don't know what it is. That's all. So we ain't against it, but I can't say that we are for it neither. I will say this though, just like I told Pastor Teddy, if I find out one way or the other, I'll tell y'all. Me and Jessica, well, we won't be shy about putting our shoulder to the wheel."

Teddy smiled and turning to the congregation asked, "Does that answer your question, Mrs. Whitworth?"

"For now it do!" she barked good naturedly. The entire assembly erupted in laughter. Once it quieted down, Teddy continued.

"Now, my beloved, there is one other piece of business we need to take care of. I'm sure everyone has been told of my little episode with my ticker the other night. Well, I'm doing fine. Doc Watkins thinks I should take it easy for a while and consider backing out of a few of my responsibilities around here. To which I replied, 'Why, Doc? I'm only eighty years old?!'"

The entire congregation broke into laughter once again. As silence fell upon the room once more, Teddy confessed, "In all seriousness, my friends, I do, with your permission, need to take it a bit easier."

Teddy paused as many were spontaneously voicing their love and admiration for their pastor. Before things got out of hand, Teddy called them all to order.

"Thank you for the kind words, folks. I really do appreciate, you all, and your prayers. Now in light of me working a little less, the elders and I have put forth, for your consideration, Alan Michael Browne as a candidate to be our associate pastor. He's been preaching here for several months, and we all have recognized he is gifted by our Father in Heaven to preach and teach His Word. Would you agree?"

Most of the assembly acknowledged their agreement. However, it was not near the response that either Alan or Teddy had hoped for. Teddy decided the decision to install Alan needed a vote of the membership. Therefore, he called for all members in favor of Alan becoming their associate pastor to signify by raising their hand and saying "Aye". Teddy asked Doc to count the votes and Zack to verify his numbers.

Although Alan tried not to look like he was counting too, he was most definitely taking his own detailed survey. Just before Teddy asked everyone to put their hands down, Alan finished his own calculations. He tallied eighty-seven votes in favor. As the hands went up for those who were opposed, his eyes darted around the congregation. This time there were a total of thirty-four casting their votes. He had been approved to be their associate pastor. But it wasn't the unanimous landslide he had hoped for.

Calling for the anointing oil and inviting all to circle around the front of the sanctuary, Teddy moved toward the steps with his arm around Alan's shoulder. It gave the appearance that he needed someone to help him down the stairs, but Teddy had another purpose in mind.

"We've got some serious work to do," he solemnly whispered to Alan.

Standing in the center of over one hundred people, with Annalisa by his side, Alan was anointed with oil by Teddy in the name of the Father, the Son, and the Holy Spirit. He prayed a most eloquent, heart-felt, and gracious prayer that deeply touched both Alan and Annalisa. In actuality, it was more than just Teddy's prayer; it was the fulfillment of what Alan had recognized as God calling upon his life many decades ago but had never felt he was competent enough to undertake. Yet today, Sunday, February 19, 2006, he was officially installed as a pastor. He felt as though at last he had arrived. He was overjoyed with the fulfillment of his lifelong dream.

But little did Alan actually know of all that would follow this momentous occasion.

-ten-

Without the daily Bible study at Willy and Bertha's coffee shop, Alan knew he would eventually lose touch with his new friends. He loved the closeness of the fellowship and the deep conversation, which revolved around the Scriptures. He certainly didn't want to stop attending the gathering. But unfortunately, it was precisely what he felt he needed to do. Monday, sitting at home having lunch with Annalisa, he confided in her.

"I absolutely love our times at the coffee shop," he admitted between bites of his tuna salad sandwich. "I thought what Willy shared this morning was such a blessing."

"Me too, Alan. I love how genuine everyone is around that circle especially Willy and Bertha though."

"Why do you think that, my love?"

"I'm not quite sure. It's like they are the father and mother figures for the rest of the group. It seems the others, particularly when you're not there, go to them for counsel and guidance."

"Well, that's good," breathed Alan.

"Why do you say that?"

"Because I think with all my new responsibilities at church, I need to back out of the Bible study."

"Really, Alan? Are you sure?"

"Yes, I believe it's the only way. I need to sit down with Willy and discuss this with him. I hope he doesn't perceive it as any kind of reflection on our relationship. I mean, I really care for him, Bertha, and the entire group. But I especially appreciate Willy."

"Honey?" she quietly urged.

"Yes?"

"If you're open, I think I'm sensing something from our Lord regarding all of this. I mean, I'm not a hundred percent sure it's Him, but I'm pretty sure it is."

"What is it, my love?"

"Well, if you're open?"

"Honey." Alan's tone gave evidence that his patience was beginning to fray. "You know I always want you to share your heart or what you think God may be saying."

"Okay, uh . . . I believe you might be falling into the same old pattern that you've seen before and have expressed to me many times, shouldn't be done, uh . . . at least in a church, I mean."

"What are you talking about, Annalisa?" His impatience was giving way to annoyance.

"It appears to me that you're laying aside something of much greater importance for something that you yourself have professed is of lesser significance."

"Honey, I'm not following you. Please just say it plainly, okay?" Alan managed a slight grin in an effort to show her he wasn't irritated, he just didn't understand her point.

After a deep breath, she again voiced her opinion, "I believe you are allowing your position as pastor, to get in the way of doing the work of a pastor. There, I said it. I hope it doesn't make you mad. But I really feel it is from the Lord, and you told me you were open to what I thought I was hearing, so . . ."

"It's okay, my love," he sighed. "In my heart of hearts I knew you were going to tell me almost precisely that. I thought maybe it would come across with a little more compassion. Regardless, I think it is what the Lord is saying. I don't know what to do about it though."

"Well, I'm not so sure either. However, I know that the goal of everything He is trying to teach us is love. Love must have objects for its actions, and those objects should be God and others. I don't think He would want you to turn away from those folks in the Bible study, so you can have more time for the administration of the church."

"Now, honey . . ."

"Wait a second, Alan. Let me finish, okay?"

Alan nodded his head although he wasn't quite sure he wanted to hear everything she planned to say to him. Sometimes, even though her spiritual gift was Mercy, he felt she could be rather brutal when it came to voicing her thoughts about something he wanted to do. However, he had learned two very key lessons over the years. First, to let her completely vent her heart on a matter. And second, that he should always wait before making a major decision, if she had a caution about it. He may be the head of their marriage, but she was the heart of it, and he loved her for it. Besides, each has its role and both are equally essential. Nobody ever lived without a head and a heart—it is precisely the same for a successful marriage. He smiled lovingly as he continued to nod his head, remembering that the heart has four chambers, so he might as well get comfortable because sometimes it took a significant amount of time to empty all of them. Early in their marriage he had noticed during a heated discussion they were having that she continually used the phrases: I think; I feel; I believe; and I will, to describe her opinions. Later, he determined these were four perspectives by which she needed to express herself. Once he had recognized this key revelation, that he needed to allow her time to work through her four chambers, there had been a higher level of harmony in their relationship.

"Anyway," she continued, "what if you were to find someone else to take care of the administration, so you could carry on with what the Lord has gifted you with, the proclamation of His Word. Alan, let's face it. You have the spiritual gift of Prophecy not the spiritual gift of Organization. You certainly learned that when you owned those bicycle shops, right?"

"Ouch, honey. Really?"

"Look, what did you explain to Teddy and Maggie the night he offered us the opportunity to come here to help?"

"You mean the way I was discovering how a church could be run according to the New Testament?"

"Yes. Remember how you told them God had worked in our church in Beulah right after Pastor Harrison left for the church in Savannah? You explained that the church was never designed to be run by a single person other than the Lord Jesus Christ. He alone is the Head of the church.[1] He gave each and every member of His church at least one spiritual gift to be used in the building up of His church in love. You even told me later, as we were driving home, you thought it was the goal of a pastor to work himself out of a job, remember?" She looked at him with eyes filled with love as she reached across softly grasping his hand in hers.

"Yes, my love, I remember," he smiled back assuring her they were on the same page in terms of what she was expressing.

"Well, I think you should continue to focus on proclaiming truth. You know, using your Prophecy gift. Let someone else, who is gifted in Organization, handle the administration. Someone like Doc. He could take care of those things . . . and probably much more efficiently than you could. Didn't Teddy tell you two to work together?"

"Yeah, he did."

"Then do it. You stay focused on keeping this ship headed in a spiritual direction. That's a big enough job in itself."

"It's not too big. I rather enjoy it. In fact, I much prefer it," he smiled with a shrug.

"That's because it's your gift, Alan. To another person, with a different gift, it would be a daunting task they would find completely overwhelming. But to you, it's a joy. It's like you get energy from it—it's food for you."

"Hmmm . . . I do sense the Lord is in what you're conveying. But what about the other things that need to be done?"

"Like what?"

"You know, the weekly upkeep of the building and grounds. There are several little repairs that I planned on doing, like tightening the loose door knobs, touching up the chipped and faded paint spots, and fixing the cracked window in the fellowship room. It's been broken since before we moved here."

"Don't Willy and some of the other folks need jobs?"

The room fell silent as Alan pondered all that Annalisa had communicated to him. His mind, in deference to his impatience, had adjusted slowly to her suggestions. But now, galloping along at a full trot, it was working through many of the obstacles he thought he might possibly encounter. After more than a minute, he finally responded.

"I think you may have allowed the Lord to work something much deeper than I had ever expected, my sweet Mercy gift girl."

"What do you mean?"

"I mean, remember our conversation with Teddy and Maggie when she answered that they were verbs and not nouns?"

"What were verbs and not nouns?"

"The spiritual gifts. You know, the list of them in Romans chapter twelve. They are actions, not positions. They are functions, not offices. There's the difference. I believe our incredibly kind Lord is providing us a way we can present this whole new approach to ministry, and it's not by explaining it, but by actually doing it. You see, my precious love, in God's kingdom, it's the doing, the action, that counts, not just the knowing.[2] I believe what He is telling us is this—if we are willing to do what He says, He will bring the words, the explanation, and the understanding."[3]

Jumping to his feet, Alan turned as if he was about to walk away. Then suddenly, he swung around and sat back down. Shaking his head, he reached across and held Annalisa's hand.

"What's wrong, honey?" she whispered.

"Nothing, except I completely forgot to talk this over with our Lord and ask Him for His wisdom."

Praying until he felt he was prayed out, he then urged Annalisa with a light squeeze of her hand. She continued where Alan left off asking God to show Himself strong and to make the way clear before them. As she was winding down, Alan began praying again. This leapfrog praying went on for the better part of thirty minutes. Then the two agreed with an "Amen".

"Honey, you are the most magnificent woman our Lord has ever created. It is both an honor and a privilege to be married to you. I mean it. Not only are you gorgeous, but you are wise beyond your years . . . which are quite substantial, by the way," he teased.

"Oh, Alan, you stinker. You always know just how to treat a gal," she laughed, throwing a dishtowel at him. "That was almost a Kiss-Slap-Kiss, but without the second kiss."

"Well, far be it from me to forget the second kiss," he laughed as he scooped her up in his arms and planted a long deep kiss upon her lips. As he lowered her back down, he whispered in her ear, "I love you with all my heart . . . I always have, and I always will."

She kissed him again. Then responded, "Me too, sweetheart. I love you with all my heart. And, Alan, thank you for loving me."

"What? Of course! There could be no other way."

That afternoon Alan worked on making a list of several members in the church who could and should take up at least one responsibility. He realized that by not presenting opportunities to these folks he was robbing them of blessings. The blessing of using their gifts or perhaps, for some, discovering their gifts, as well as the blessing of serving God's people, caring for His concerns, and giving to God and others of their time, efforts, and resources. When he had completed his list, Alan headed over to Teddy's house. He found him sitting on the front porch swing reading the Scriptures.

Pulling up in front, Alan hopped out of his car and called across the front lawn, "Hey, Teddy! How are you feeling today, my brother?"

"With my fingers," replied Teddy with a chuckle.

Alan laughed as he opened the screened door on the porch and stepped inside. Before sitting down in the chair next to the swing, he stretched out his hand to shake Teddy's.

"No, really. How you feeling?"

"Oh, pretty good for an eighty year old I guess. I'm looking forward to going home. This old body with its aches and pains, not to mention my other, uh, cardiac problem, is pretty limiting. If it wasn't for sweet Maggie, I would have already asked the Lord to take me on home. But as it is, I need to care for her. However, my house is in order, so when He calls, I'm ready."

"Hmmm . . ." Alan smiled as he nodded in agreement. "I remember a dear friend of mine, a few years back, expressing something similar. She was a godly woman," he breathed as he reflected on how much he missed her, her friendship, and her confident assurance when he was wrestling with a problem. As well as her amazing kindness . . . she was so incredibly kind. He sure did miss sweet Betsy Taft.

"Well, what have you got on your mind, Alan?"

"Uh, what? Oh, yeah . . . other than just visiting with you? Uh, I just thought to run a few things by you before proceeding any further. You got a few minutes?"

"Always, my brother."

"Teddy, several months ago you asked me about the situation with our pastor in California. I avoided giving you an answer because I didn't want to say anything derogatory regarding him. However, I do think there was something wrong. Something very wrong was going on there. I still don't think it was entirely his fault, but he had some responsibility in the matter as did the others who attended there. Here's what I believe God is teaching me through our days here in Wiggins as I remember what happened in California some twenty years ago—God has a model of how He has designed His church to function, thrive, and grow. The way we did it in California definitely wasn't it."

"What do you mean, Alan?" asked Teddy with a curious look on his face as he slowed the swaying of the porch swing to a stop.

"I think if there had been several members using their spiritual gifts instead of just one person, the pastor, the whole situation may have been avoided altogether. Now this will take a few minutes, but bear with me, okay?"

Teddy nodded but said nothing.

"Alright, let's set that aside as example number one," expressed Alan using his hands like he was gripping an imaginary box and moving it to one side of the porch. "Now, example number two: Do you remember what I explained had happened at our church in Beulah, there in Pensacola? How the pastor had left for a different church, and we couldn't find another pastor, so we divided up the responsibilities among several of the folks. Later, we discovered that some of the people were gifted to serve in particular areas. When each person stepped up to help, their gift effervesced and became more evident as it was employed to serve His Body. As long as the person wasn't serving in any capacity, their individual gift tended to lay dormant. So it was kind of by accident that we discovered each other's spiritual gifting and how very practical the gifts actually function. Before we knew what was happening, we believe God had us working somewhat within His framework, His design for a church. We found it wasn't a man's solution that was working. It was God's idea and His plan all along for how His church should operate."

"That's interesting, Alan. So this is part and parcel of this new way of ministry that you've been telling me about?"

"Well, sort of, but if we look at these two examples, I think we can deduce certain things about what God might be saying to His church these days. Number one, like in the first example from our church in California, when one person controls everything, there is ample room for something to go wrong. Only God is perfect. People aren't, and certainly not just one individual working alone. In a multitude of counsel is success.[4] And, I might include, less peripheral damage. We weren't the only ones who got hurt there. No one person can bear the load of the body of believers, nor is that God's design. Therefore, presuming it is not His design, there will be numerous problems that arise because the assumptions themselves are flawed."

"I agree with that, Alan. The burn out rate for pastors is significantly higher than any other profession. In fact, there are over a thousand of them leaving the ministry every month in the United States alone."

"They were never supposed to bear the entire responsibility, Teddy. That isn't how God designed it in His Word. Now look at example number two, our church in Pensacola. We were left without a person to pastor the church, so we had to come up with a plan or close the doors. We determined to have each one, who was willing to help, share the load. As we continued for several months, we discovered that this was something that lay hidden in the New Testament. More than that, it actually worked. More folks felt needed and as a result were very attentive to the overall well-being of the church. It was amazing to see how it operated without anyone planning anything other than Sunday services. And even that, we were starting to recognize, may not be exactly what our Lord wanted for His church. I mean, just read the Book of Acts. We're not to *do* church, or *attend* church, *we are* the church. Sunday services were not intended to be a show with performers singing and preaching while the rest of the folks sit and watch, like they were attending a Broadway show in a theater. I don't believe that was God's original design."

"This is quite amazing, Alan. I was just reading in the Book of Acts when you pulled up today. I think the Lord may be directing us into something new."

"Actually, Teddy, with all due respect to you, I think it is something as old as the New Testament itself. I really think this is the way His church is supposed to function. Now, I believe we have a great opportunity that has been presented to us—the opportunity to be the third example. To see if this really works."

"What do you mean?" replied Teddy.

"Out of the mouth of two or three witnesses a thing is established."[5]

"I agree."

"Well, the first example I shared was one man using his persuasion or coercion with very little input and participation from others. The second example was one done out of the need for survival with a moderate amount of participation. We now have the opportunity to be an example of what a group of believers can do if they each have the heart of a volunteer. What might the level of participation be if folks are given an opportunity without any influence pressing upon them other than the Holy Spirit's gentle promptings?"

"That is a fascinating proposition, Alan. But as a pastor you may work yourself out of a job," confided Teddy with a hint of skepticism.

"Actually, Teddy, I'm not sure you can make a case for a pastor directed church using the New Testament as the basis for your argument. Did you know that the word 'pastor' is only used one time in the entire Bible?[6] The same Greek word is sometimes translated as the word 'shepherd' but it's only used as a noun when referring to Jesus. He's our Great Shepherd. Every other usage of the word is as a verb, like when our resurrected Lord told Peter on the beach to shepherd His flock. It's an action word, not a position. I don't think the Lord wanted His church to function that way. I mean, with one person in charge and the rest in more of a passive posture rather than in an active role. That certainly is not the way His Body, the church, is supposed to function. In fact, I have read in several places in Scripture where God used the meek or the least seemly to reveal what He wanted to say. Can you imagine, God speaking through an average brother or sister in Christ?"

"Sure. He does all the time. I agree with what you are explaining here, Alan. But how will it work out practically. I mean, what are you going to do when folks show up for church service this coming Sunday?"

"Well, I'm not one hundred percent sure about that. However, I know we'll sing, worship, read His Word, and I'll give some thoughts for everyone to consider. I don't know if a sermon is appropriate though. I'm sensing maybe more of a 'Come let us reason together'[7] kind of discussion around a passage or maybe a chapter. What do you think?"

"That's an interesting concept," replied Teddy, with less skepticism in his voice now. "How did you come up with that idea?"

"Several times in the New Testament, we see the apostles and disciples working through an issue together. Sometimes an argument or disagreement ensued. Other times they arrived at a conclusion where all concurred with what God was indicating for them to do. Regardless, it was never just one person who decided, not even Peter, Paul, James, or John. The group prayed, discussed, and prayed again, asking for the Holy Spirit to make the answer clear. The whole concept of one person speaking on behalf of God is completely under the Old Covenant. It was a priest or prophet the Holy Spirit came upon who spoke or carried out His plans. Under the New Covenant, however, the Holy Spirit dwells within every believer. He can and will speak through each and every member of His Body as He deems necessary for the moment. In fact, that's what the whole group of 'Effects Gifts' listed there in First Corinthians chapter twelve is all about—the need of the moment. You know, Teddy, by definition, for there to be an effect there must be something that caused it. It's something to think about perhaps."

"Alan, I hear what you're saying," responded Teddy with a grin, "but I've been in ministry for many decades, and I know that most folks want a pastor to look up to, someone to follow."

"I understand, Teddy. I have needed one many times myself. Please don't misunderstand me, I'm not saying to eliminate all pastors. At least I don't mean to imply that. What I'm trying to communicate is this—there appears to be no Biblical basis for those type of positions within the Body of Christ. Jesus is the Pastor, the Shepherd, the Lord, and King. The rest of us, all of us, are His ministers, His ambassadors, His priests.[8] There's no hierarchy of clergy and laity mentioned. We are to be a kingdom of priests,[9] each and every one of us, from the most unlikely, to the most prominent of believers. Every one—no one is excluded. No one is less than another in the Body of Christ. It's His church. He bought and paid for it with His own life. Therefore, it should function as He intended. If every Christian was aware of this truth and encouraged to live by it, what might the church look like today?"

"I can appreciate that, Alan. But how would it ever work?"

"Well, I'm not absolutely sure. But the spiritual gifts play a key role—when they are functioning within the Body according to how the Lord designed, folks will feel their worth. You know, like they are valuable to the Body and an integral part for it to operate properly. Therein, they will find their purpose; they will also find their identity in the Body of Christ, His church. Granted, it was a different format under the old covenant. However, in the New Testament, there is no distinction. All are ministers, ambassadors, and priests according to their spiritual gift."

"How will you explain it in such a way that will motivate the people? How will you get them to be willing to participate, Alan?"

"I'm not quite sure, but I think the Lord is indicating that we shouldn't explain it. Rather, we should offer opportunities. You know, kind of like Gideon," chuckled Alan, unsure himself exactly how it was all going to work. "I really believe God loves the heart of one who willingly volunteers to fill a need. You know, He loves a cheerful giver."

"What?"

"Yes, sir. I believe we should express when there's a need, an opportunity, to help in a particular area and see who comes to the surface. People will volunteer for those areas, those tasks or assignments they feel the Lord has enabled them to do. As you know, He is the great Tugger of hearts. Then, I'm sure that after a few months we'll be able to recognize the various spiritual gifts when we see them in use."

"Alan," advised Teddy, "I think what you're proposing to do is Biblical. I certainly can see it in the New Testament. There's more than enough evidence for giving this a try. In fact, I do believe this may very well be the way our Lord designed for His church, His people, to function. But, my brother, you are going up against several centuries of church tradition, and you're going to upset a huge apple cart. I'm not saying it's been done correctly through the years, but it's several centuries of cemented mindset nonetheless. However, if you can do . . ."

"We, Teddy. If we can do," interrupted Alan.

"Yes, you're right. If we can, as His Body, make this transition, then, you . . . uh, we may have helped bring back a vital piece of how the Body of Christ was meant to function," nodded Teddy as he patted Alan on the knee.

"Yes, sir, I agree," assured Alan with a sober look on his face. "But what if we cannot make the transition? Then what happens?"

-eleven-

Just like a historian piecing together events of the past, or a police investigator at the scene of a crime, the key to a verdict is evidence. Alan knew he needed evidence to convince his congregational jury. This is what excited him more than anything else, the searching, discovering, and implementing, all for the sake of a deeper relationship with God. It was what first drew him to The **rojocci** Fellowship as well. To him, there was nothing more thrilling than opening up a whole new level of relationship with his Father in Heaven. It was like the first time he had realized he had offended Annalisa. He sought her out, confessed he was wrong, apologized, and asked for her forgiveness. The process had opened up an entirely new realm in their relationship. Besides, he discovered a clear conscience is a great asset.

Simply stated, to gain a verdict in a court of law, there must be evidence. This is presented to the trier of the case, so a determination can be reached as to its relevance. If it is found to be admissible, it will be used. If not, it is deemed inadmissible. Essentially, a verdict is reached regarding each piece of evidence.

In a science laboratory, a similar process can be observed. The scientist must first formulate a hypothesis.

Then, come the experiments, many experiments, to be conducted with each one either proving or disproving the validity of the hypothesis. For Thomas Edison, it had taken over four thousand experiments before he determined the specific elements needed for an electric light bulb. The result of all those experiments was what we refer to as proof. Our faith is much the same way.

The process goes something like this: First, we read something in the Bible, and we form an opinion, a hypothesis. This is similar to evidence. Second, by faith, we try it out in our own life situations. This, the scientist would call the experimental phase. In our courtroom of life, we are determining if this piece of evidence is relevant to our living case. Third, if we find that it works, helping to convince our internal judge and jury of its validity, we've proven it to be true. We believe it, implement it, and live our lives accordingly. Frankly, we all go through the same process several times every day with things like recipes, financial matters, health issues, or even deciding what to do this weekend. Perhaps the first time it took a bit of thought or planning. However, over the years, it has become second nature. It works the same way in the spiritual realm of life.

So to summarize: some new piece of evidence is presented to us in His Word. We run through a number of determinations or experiments to test its validity and reach a verdict, a conclusion of our own. What we had been unsure of before, having only read about it, we now are convinced of, having our own personal proof. Now we know and believe that it is true. This priceless pearl of truth, now, and only now, becomes a part of our permanent belief structure and decision making process. Up to the point of proving and reaching our own internal verdict, we remain uncertain, perhaps even doubtful at times. These are gaps in our spiritual armor. Chinks the enemy gleefully takes full advantage of.

Alan hated those chinks. He had dealt with them all his life. To him, they were reason enough to continue exploring, to continue seeking, to continue discovering all that the Lord had hidden in His Word. Much of his character had been developed during these diligent efforts of searching for the **rojocci** clues. Some were successful, others were less profitable. The first Sunday in August, another opportunity for growth walked through his door.

After finishing up his message to the church, Alan headed to the pastor's study to tidy up a few loose ends before leaving for home where he planned to have a restful afternoon. Leaving the door open, as was his habit, he had his head down and was writing a few notes when he heard a knock. Looking up, he eyed an unfamiliar man dressed in a navy blue pinstripe suit with a red and navy coordinating tie, neatly knotted under the collar of his white shirt.

"Reverend Browne?" The voice was polished with a hint of a gracious Southern drawl.

"Uh . . . "I'm Alan Browne. I'm not a reverend though."

"Well, are you the **rojoccian** pastor?"

"What? Uh, I'm not sure what you mean by that. I have been a part of the **rojocci** fellowship, but I wouldn't consider myself its pastor or anything."

"Okay, I guess what I'm trying to say, Mr. Browne . . ."

"Just call me Alan."

"Well, Alan, my name is Hugh Roseboughson. Would you be interested in some information regarding someone named P. D. who lived in Bend, Oregon, back in the 1800s?"

"What kind of information?"

"You see, Alan, last year I traveled out to Oregon in search of evidence regarding a peculiar document I had heard about while on a business trip in Seattle. Now, I want you to know, Alan, I was born and bred a Texan, what you might call a Southerner from the Deep South, if you get my drift. However, I now reside in a suburb of Denver, Colorado, and travel extensively with my business. Have you ever visited Denver, Alan?"

"No, sir."

"Well, it's magnificent, Alan, simply mag . . ."

"What do you do, Mr. Roseboughson?" interrupted Alan, who was giving indication that his patience was beginning to wear thin.

"Please, just call me, Hugh."

"Okay, what do you do, uh . . . Hugh?"

"My background is in engineering, avionics to be more precise. My partners and I started our company some fifteen years ago. I travel around to manufacturers, airports, and investors presenting our latest innovations as well as trouble shooting existing systems. My partners call me the rain dancer."

"Sounds very interesting," conceded Alan. "How can I help you, Hugh?"

"Yes, well, the travel gets quite tiresome, but occasionally I come across something I think may be of use to others. That's why I'm here, Alan, to help you. Now, I heard you have a chronic interest in antiquities concerning a little known group called The **rojocci** Fellowship. Is that correct?"

"Where did you hear that?"

"Oh, I think I was in an airport out west somewhere."

"Really?" replied an increasingly skeptical Alan.

"I can see you're a very busy man, Alan. So let me get right to my point. I have a copy of a relic that was discovered back in the 1930s in Bend, Oregon. It was written by someone only identified by their initials P. D. It's entitled 'The **rojoccian** Covenant.' Would you be interested in something like this, Alan?"

"Absolutely. May I see it please?"

"Oh, no. It's not for viewing, at least not without a price," explained Mr. Hugh Roseboughson through an annoyingly conniving grin.

"What?"

"I have it for sale, Alan."

"For sale?"

"Yes, I can let you have this copy by you simply making out a check, payable to me. Or, if you prefer a more discreet method, you can make a small donation to my children's college fund. How does five thousand sound to you, Alan?"

"Dollars?" barked Alan, his voice hitting a pitch several octaves higher.

"Yes. We can work out a payment plan for you, if that would be more convenient. Say one thousand a month. Or would five hundred work better? I'm very flexible. Which would work better for you, Alan?"

Jumping to his feet with an angry scowl on his face, Alan pointed to the door and answered in a stern tone. "It is time for you to leave, Mr. Hugh Roseboughson."

"If five thousand is too much, I could let it go for maybe half that. Now, if you will sign right here, I will send you a copy within ten business . . ."

"Out!" shouted Alan with controlled yet rapidly rising anger in his voice. "Get out now! Here, allow me to help you find your way."

With a strong grip on the man's jacket, Alan firmly escorted Mr. Hugh Roseboughson out the side door of the church building, sarcastically thanking him for visiting before he shut the door.

Once he was back in the study, Alan took a few minutes to calm down before returning to the items needing his attention. As the pile of papers on one side of the desk became smaller, the pile on the other side grew taller. Nearly finished, he rested back in his chair remembering what both Teddy and Annalisa had advised him to do. He had never considered administration one of his strengths. Actually, he was well aware it was one of his weaknesses. However, he had decided it was much easier to do what needed to be done, than to bother someone else with the chore. It was the same with all of these minor repairs around the building too. He figured he could just as readily take care of them as to go to the trouble of soliciting another's help. It was precisely at this moment in his thinking, when Willy stepped through the open door to the study.

"Alan, how you doing today?"

"Real good, Willy. And you?"

"Fine, we're all doing just fine."

"How can I help you, my brother?"

"Oh, nothing. I just heard you ushering that fellow out of here, and I thought to check in on you."

"Man, I appreciate that. I'm just trying to get ahead on this paperwork. Then, maybe sometime tomorrow I'll fix that . . ."

Alan stopped himself in mid-sentence. The topic he had discussed with Teddy on his porch not a week ago replayed in his mind like a television rerun. He knew the conclusion as well as all of the punch lines. Evidently, Alan pondered the mental scene a bit too long for Willy's comfort level because he interrupted Alan's daydream with a gentle nudge.

"You alright, brother Alan?"

"Huh? Oh yeah, I was just thinking. Hey Willy, what are you doing tomorrow afternoon? You got a couple of hours to help me out with a few repairs around the church building?"

"Sure enough," agreed Willy. "What time you want me here?"

"How's one o'clock sound?"

"I'll be here. You want me to bring any tools or anything?"

"You have some tools?"

"Oh yeah, I was in charge of repairs and the like when I worked at the mill. I can fix just about anything, and I love to do it too. In fact, Alan, I was noticing that door hardware on one of them front doors needs adjusting."

"You know how to fix panic hardware?"

"Oh yeah, I can take care of that for you. No problem at all."

"Willy, you are a Godsend."

"What you mean by that?"

"I mean, how would you feel about being the Lord's guinea pig?"

"I'll be whatever the Lord needs me to be. And if that be a pig, then so be it."

"Willy," laughed Alan. "I love you, man."

"I love you too, brother Alan," chuckled Willy. "You alright now?"

"Oh, yeah, much better."

That afternoon, when Alan arrived home, he shared with Annalisa first the story regarding Mr. Hugh Roseboughson and then, more importantly, the mysterious document the errant slickster was selling—a copy of something he called The **rojoccian** Covenant. This was the second time Alan had heard of the artifact, and frankly the news had piqued his interest.

"Did you get a look at it, Alan?" asked Annalisa from her spot where she sat crossed legged on the sofa.

"No, when he tried to sell me a copy of it, I somewhat forcefully invited him to leave."

"What do you mean?"

"I showed him the door in such a way that he couldn't get lost finding his way out," he smiled with a feigned look of regret upon his face.

"Oh, Alan . . ."

"He deserved it, honey. I know it probably wasn't appropriate, but he deserved it nonetheless. You can't charge others for that kind of thing. It's like back in the days of pew rents; it's not right."

"Well, it's over now. So I guess . . ."

"Now wait a second, honey. Let's not get sidetracked here, okay? I think what he was offering is invaluable, and it has a spiritual significance that may benefit thousands, if not millions. If the only way to obtain a copy is to buy it from that slick Hughie, then I say we need to set up a trip for the West Coast, and specifically Bend, Oregon, and find our own copy of The **rojoccian** Covenant."

"Could we see my family too?" questioned Annalisa with bubbling enthusiasm. "Maybe we could fly into San Francisco and visit for a few days, then drive north into Oregon. How's that sound to you, Alan? I mean, it's been three or four years since we've been back."

"That sounds like a wonderful idea to me, my love. Let me get things situated at church these next few weeks. Then, let's set something up. Maybe we could go for two weeks. How's that sound to you?"

"Oh, Alan, that is so exciting! I'm going to call my sister this weekend and let her know."

"I think that's a good idea, honey. See if she has some dates available when we could come. Just you, and me, and a trip out West, I can't wait."

The next morning at Bible study Alan confirmed with Willy the time they would meet at the church. Willy asked if he could bring John Abercrombie along. Alan welcomed the extra help. Later that afternoon, as they were finishing up the final items on the list, Alan marveled at how quickly everything had come together.

"My brothers, I cannot express to you how much I appreciate your help. I really thought it would take a couple of days to complete this list, but we finished it in less than three hours. Thank you both from the depths of my heart," smiled Alan with a healthy dose of sincerity laced within his words.

"Our pleasure, Alan," confirmed Willy as he and John began placing the tools in John's rust eaten Ford pickup. "In fact, me and John were noticing that grass need to be mowed. Them bushes looking a bit shaggy too. I thought if you need him, maybe John could come up here once or twice a week to kind of tidy things up. What you say to that, Alan?"

"John?" whispered Alan as he pulled Willy aside. "Why not you, Willy?"

"Oh, John don't have no money, and he needs to be having something that would make him proud, you understand. Besides, me and Bertha, we got a little coming in from the coffee shop and all. Truth be told, since we started the Bible study we be doing alright. The Lord truly blessing us that's for sure."

Alan and Willy walked over to the back of the truck where John was putting away the last few tools. Alan handed each man fifty dollars as he thanked them for their help. Then he turned toward John.

"John, would you be interested in taking care of the grounds around the church here? It would mean mowing the grass, keeping everything neat and trim, maybe even making a few repairs now and then. You know, keeping everything tidied up and all."

"I sure enough would, brother Alan," replied John with a huge smile beaming across his entire face.

"Well, it wouldn't pay much, but it would be something. Maybe it would work into a little business for you. You never know what God will do, if you're open to His leading. In fact, I would say that may be one of our biggest spiritual battles while we're here on this earth."

"What's that?" asked Willy leaning forward.

"The battle between doing what I want to do versus doing what God wants me to do. But I'll tell you a secret." Alan motioned for the two men to step a bit closer as he lowered his voice. "It's in the small steps. Many folks think they will submit to the Lord when it comes to something big, something major. But then, when something actually happens they are unable to yield to His will, and they wonder why. It's because we learn by taking small steps, little by little, just like a child learns the tiniest of lessons from infancy on through adolescence. We learn to trust Him as we are open to trying what He says to do, even when it doesn't make sense to us at the time. It's because when we step out in faith and see His hand working in our situation, we are assured of His faithfulness. Therefore, we're much more willing to trust Him the next time. It's baby steps really, one after another."

Although they were nodding their agreement, both Willy and John had perplexed looks on their faces.

Alan smiled and then continued, "Look, my brothers, Jesus taught His disciples a very straightforward principle that applies to us too—if you want to know the Father's will, you have to be willing to do it.[1] Next, you need to abide in it. You know, think about it all the time. Then, you will know the Truth and the Truth will make you free.[2] So you fellas willing?"

"Yes, sir," they responded in unison.

The following week Alan decided that Willy most definitely evidenced the spiritual gift of Giving. He noticed how Willy almost always looked for ways to give of himself to others. Even with the meager income he and Bertha scratched out at the coffee shop, he was usually quick to help someone who had a need as well. Alan was also aware that this particular spiritual gift was the only gift none of the elders possessed. This fact gave Alan an idea that he realized would shake the elders a bit, not to mention the church as a whole. He decided it was prudent to tread lightly. The following Thursday evening, the elders met for the regular monthly meeting. On his way to the church, Alan picked up Teddy.

During the short drive there, the two discussed several items they felt were important to bring to everyone's attention. When they walked into the building early, they were surprised to find the five remaining elders had already arrived. After a brief time of fellowship, Teddy prayed and then opened the meeting.

"Gentlemen, we as a church body find ourselves in a most interesting time of transition. Now, I'm not only talking about my cardiac issue. As you know, if anything happens to me or, should I say, when something happens to me, Alan will step right in to take over the pastoral duties. In fact, he has already done so to a great degree." Teddy nodded toward Alan, acknowledging his recent efforts.

"Setting that aside for the present, I want us to prayerfully consider the opportunity that I believe the Lord has set before us. I'm referring to this season of transition." Teddy, the consummate father figure, was smiling as he glanced around the room, his tone gentle, yet firm.

"What season are you talking about, Teddy?" inquired Doc with a hint of skepticism.

"What I'm referencing here, Doc, is returning to a more Biblical model of the church, the expression of His people. We, meaning Christians, have for way too many centuries, processed ministry like a business or a corporate structure. But that's not the way God intended when He designed the church."

"I'm not sure I'm following you," confessed Jake wearing an inquisitive look upon his face.

"Well, let me see if I can . . . yes! You, Jake Beauregard, you're a perfect example of what I'm trying to explain," pronounced Teddy with a wave of his hand in Jake's direction. "You have been an elder for what, about two years now?"

"Yes, sir."

"Well, you truly are a blessing to all of us. You have a compassionate and gentle way about you. Plus, you always seem to remember those folks the rest of us have overlooked. You, my brother, have the spiritual gift of Mercy. Now, why aren't we using this to its fullest potential?" posed Teddy, his eyes darting from one face to another.

"Uh, I don't know," replied Jake with a sheepish grin.

"Because we aren't giving you the opportunity to use it, that's why. Counseling and visiting folks have usually been left to the pastor. I'm not sure how you fellas feel, but I never thought I was very good at it. But that's precisely the point. Jake is. It's because of his gift. Therefore, he should be the one ministering to others in this capacity."

"What are you getting at, Teddy?" questioned Zack.

"Let me ask y'all a question. How many times is the word 'pastor' used in the Bible? I'm interested, my brothers. What's your guess?"

Zack guessed it was used about ten times while Jake suggested at least twenty. Two of the other three thought more than twenty times. Doc guessed twelve. Then, Teddy turned to Alan, who was seated across from him. "What say you, Alan?"

"Once. The word is only used once. It is translated as the word shepherd another fourteen times I think, but those times it is always used as a verb, not as a noun except when referring to our Shepherd, Jesus."

"Alan, what do you mean it's always used as a verb?" frowned Zack.

"I mean, let's see . . . remember in the last chapter of John's Gospel when Jesus asked Peter three times if he loved Him? When Peter answered yes, Jesus told him to shepherd His sheep. That's how the word is used, as an action, not as a position. That place, that position of shepherd, according to the Bible, is reserved for only One—the Lord Jesus Himself."

"Now wait a minute here, you two," barked Doc. "Are you proposing we do away with the position of pastor? I mean, I don't think that's right."

"Whoa, hold on just a minute," haggled Seb, his voice raised in protest. "We can't just go kicking out a pastor without a vote on this . . . and my vote is, no way. We need a pastor to preach every Sunday, and to visit us when we're sick and infirmed. What if someone ain't got no money for food or something, who they going to talk to?"

"Now easy gents," cautioned Teddy, holding up both hands in front of him with palms facing out. "No one is saying we're getting rid of a pastor. This is a transition from the old way of doing things, back to an even older way, which is found in the New Testament. Now, Alan has some information I want y'all to read before you pass any judgement on this. Listen to me as your older brother in the Lord. This is where the spiritual warfare begins—am I open to what the Lord may be saying, or am I closed and uninterested. Watch your hearts closely, my beloved. Sense what is rising within. Is it faith and love or is it fear and anger? It's not so much what is being presented that is the issue, but whether I'm open to what is being presented? This transition we are passing through is more about His kingdom within us, than it is about external things like how we do church."

The group sat stone still for several seconds pondering their sage, older brother's warning. The room was completely silent.

Then, quietly passing out several sheets of paper to each elder, Alan gave a brief explanation of the individual topics. The first page indicated the use of the words pastor and shepherd. Next, were the three lists of spiritual gifts starting with the Determination Gifts, found in Romans, chapter twelve. Alan and Teddy had named them so because these tend to determine how a person perceives life. The Effects

Gifts, designated in the twelfth chapter of First Corinthians followed. This list contained the effects of the Holy Spirit to causes we find in everyday life. Also, in the same chapter, Alan indicated the Ministerial Gifts, which are a number of the temporary roles needed within the church as a whole. Finally, Alan handed out a sheet showing the process of transitioning from a church which is led by, or administered by, one person to a church body which functions by using their spiritual gifts under the Headship of the Lord Jesus Christ. When he had finished explaining the information, the room once again fell silent. After a few seconds, Alan glanced over at Teddy, who gave a nod back, encouraging Alan to remain quiet and to continue to wait for this new revelation to sink into the hearts and minds of the elders. Within a couple of minutes, Jake was the first to speak up.

"I think this has some potential."

"Maybe," chided Doc. "But how are you going to force this down the congregation's throat? The same congregation, I might add, that has had the pleasure and blessing of a pastor for several decades."

"That's just it, brother Doc," contended Alan. "We don't force anything. We allow opportunities. Everything remains as is, except when a need arises we ask the body of believers if anyone senses an urging from the Holy Spirit to help. If no one responds, we'll do as we always have done; the pastor will handle it or call one of you gentlemen to help out."

The meeting continued on for another two hours with many questions, yet not enough answers. However, by the time they adjourned, all agreed to give this new, old way a try for a year.

Alan drove Teddy home and helped him into the house. They were greeted at the front door by Maggie, who assisted Teddy to the bedroom. After a few minutes she emerged telling Alan that Teddy wanted to talk with him.

Stepping into the dimly lit room, Alan stepped over and stood next to the bed where Teddy was lying. Maggie walked to the other side and held her husband's hand.

"Alan, my dear brother, we have known one another a long time. I remember when we first met out there in California. I sat in on a Sunday school class you were teaching. I thought it then and know it now; you have an anointing on your life. The Lord wants to bring about change in His church, and I believe you are one of many He will use to do just that. He wants to bring a freedom to His people that they have longed for, a new strength, a new power of the kingdom which lives within them. But sadly, they don't recognize that the very things they cling to, keep them from this new, more intimate relationship with the One who loves them more than they can imagine. It's really not their fault. They just lack knowledge. That's all. They don't understand."

Teddy paused to look lovingly at Maggie for a moment and then continued in a sober tone. "The time of my departure has come. I haven't always done what I should have, but I have loved the Lord and His people. Alan, now it's your turn upon the stage. You are mantled with the care of His sheep. I see where you are going, and I pray you get there. For if you do, you will have done the Lord and His people a great service. Now, bow down here, Alan."

Alan knelt beside the bed. Teddy, the great old saint, placed his right hand upon Alan's head and his left hand held Maggie's hand. "Alan Michael Browne, preach the Word and pay close attention to your gift. Use it for our Lord and the building up of His Body in love. Be strong, be a man, be courageous, be faithful, and above all else, be loving, kind, tender hearted, and forgiving of others. May the grace of our Lord Jesus, and the love of the Father, and the fellowship of the Holy Spirit be with you always."[4]

Turning to his loving wife, Teddy kissed her hand, blessed her in the name of the Lord, and thanked her for her love and all she had done for him through their years together. Then, he closed his eyes, rested back upon his pillow, and the man of God breathed his last.

Through tears, Alan whispered, "Precious in the sight of the Lord is the death of His Godly ones."[5] Then bowing their heads, he and Maggie wept quietly.

-twelve-

With Teddy's passing came a whole new set of sticky issues for Alan, the elders, and the church. The months rolled on but several nagging concerns continued to linger with no resolution in sight. Late one night, after Alan and Annalisa had long gone to bed, he got up and walked down the hall to their living room. Kneeling at the sofa, he humbly asked his Father in Heaven for some answers. The house was silent. The only noise was the refrigerator's motor occasionally clicking on and then, after a few minutes, shutting off.

"Here's the rub, Father. How do we get a group of your people to do for themselves what they have become accustomed to having someone else do for them?"

An inaudible thought drifted across his mind, "How did you accomplish that at the church in Pensacola?"

"That was different, Lord. We had to do it out of necessity because our pastor had left for another church."

After several seconds he sensed the Lord saying, "Well?"

"What do you mean, 'Well?' I don't understand, Lord."

"Didn't you promise Annalisa several months ago that you would take her to see her family in California?"

"Father, I can't leave on a trip now. The church would be in a mess by the time I got back."

181

The house was peacefully tranquil as Alan sat perfectly still listening to his heart for an answer. After several minutes, a still small voice drifted across his thoughts.

"You take care of your bride; I can take care of Mine."

A smile slowly began to break across Alan's face as it dawned upon his mind what the Lord was trying to convey to him. He leapt to his feet and started to softly praise the Lord for His answer. The praising evolved into singing. Alan's joy overflowed from their living room and wafted down the hall and into their bedroom. Soon, Annalisa appeared groggily shuffling across the living room toward Alan.

"Alan, what's going on? Do you realize it's after two . . . in the morning?"

"Honey, once again our gracious Lord has met us. He loves us more than we can imagine and has the answer to whatever problems may come our way. I used to struggle with thoughts of insecurities and fears. Then, it was our many money problems. After that, it was our situation with Julie and Roger. And recently, it's been a group of people called the church. Well, He's fixed it, honey. Just like He has taken care of everything else, He's given us an answer for this too."

"What do you mean, Alan?" yawned a barely awake Annalisa, rubbing her eyes.

"Honey, turn on your computer. I'll make us up some coffee. Let's see if we can get some airline tickets to San Francisco."

"What?! Really, Alan? Are you sure?" Now her eyes were fully alert and her countenance bright and hopeful.

"Yes, my love, and I'm so very sorry it took me so long to agree to this trip. Will you please forgive me, honey?"

"Yes, of course I will. But what brought this sudden change of heart in the middle of the night?"

"Jesus. It was obviously Him, loud and clear. Now, do you want a cup of coffee or hot chocolate?"

"Better make it coffee. I have a feeling we're going to be up for a while."

The following day Alan asked Willy if he and some of the Bible study group would help rearrange a few of the pews in the sanctuary. He was anxious to set in motion the agenda he and Teddy had discussed. However, once he arrived at the church and was on his knees unloosening the first bolt, which attaches the pew to the floor, Alan had a thought.

"Allow Me to shepherd My people."

Alan stopped what he was doing and looked up at Willy, who was standing at the ready waiting to move the pew. John and Jimmy stood at the far end preparing to carry this first one, among many, Alan had thought to relocate.

"Hold on a second, my brothers," hedged Alan with a bit of a sheepish grin. "I may have gotten ahead of myself here. Well, I mean, ahead of the Lord. Let's hold off on doing this until another time, okay?"

Once he tightened the nut back down on the bolt, Alan stood up and patted his dear friend on the shoulder. "I find it is so easy to get ahead of the Lord on some things. You know what I mean, Willy?"

"Oh yeah, I know exactly what you mean. It's much harder to sit and wait, than to just take care of it yourself," chuckled Willy.

"Very true, my brother . . . very true."

After the morning service on Sunday, Alan sat down with the elders for a brief meeting. He wanted to let them know he needed to head to the West Coast for a couple of weeks. The group quickly worked out a plan for the time he would be gone. They also encouraged Alan that if he needed any more time they could handle everything at the church. It was agreed that he would be back in three weeks to resume his responsibilities. Three days later, he and Annalisa were on a plane bound for the San Francisco International Airport and the beautiful Bay Area.

The air was cool and crisp when they stepped off the plane that sunny July afternoon. Only in a place like San Francisco could they find a chill in the air on a midsummer day. They both loved the west, but no place more than California. It wasn't just the climate, although it was especially pleasant. But more than that, it was the whole atmosphere of the outdoor lifestyle they appreciated.

Deciding to take some of the back roads to Annalisa's sister's home in Alamo, they headed across the Hayward/San Mateo Bridge in their rental car toward the East Bay hills. Exiting the freeway on Redwood Road in Montclair, Alan drove up the hill to Skyline Boulevard. The drive across this road offered views of the entire Bay Area including the city of San Francisco. They could even see the Golden Gate Bridge and the massive fog bank hovering over the Pacific Ocean. It was absolutely gorgeous.

After a quick stop at the huge boulder where Alan had proposed to Annalisa so many years ago, they were back on the road. Taking the left turn onto Pinehurst Road, they wound downward into the steep sided, heavily-forested, narrow canyon. The single lane road led through a stand of giant redwoods and into the tiny village of Canyon. Both Alan and Annalisa had always loved this little known burg nestled in the hills just east of the massive metropolis of the Bay Area. They stopped to take in the sights, scents, and sounds.

"The sun never shines down here," reminisced Alan as he looked straight up into the branches of a huge redwood tree.

"I know. I'm getting my jacket. You want yours?"

"Yeah, it's quite chilly. Listen to the creek. Can you hear it?"

"Oh, yes, it sounds beautiful. It's so quiet and peaceful down here, Alan. I love the smells too. It's so different from Wiggins. Don't you think?"

"Look over there," whispered Alan as he slid on his jacket. "If I'm not mistaken, I think that's a golden eagle."

"Where? I don't see it."

"Well, it kind of blends into the leaves, but look just above that gnarly notch in the tree. See the branch directly above . . ."

"I see it!" exclaimed Annalisa with a half-yelp. Evidently, she was loud enough to scare off the majestic bird. "Oh, no, I frightened the eagle away."

"Uh, no you didn't. That's a red tailed hawk, not a golden eagle," he chuckled. "My mistake," he acknowledged with a grin.

"Well, that's a relief," she smiled.

"What?"

"What?"

"Oh, nothing," he chuckled as he wrapped his arms around her. "I love being here with you. It's kind of like coming back home. Isn't it, my sweet wife?"

"Yes. Yes it is. In fact, remember that awful day we did that death march bike ride? That was brutal."

"It wasn't a death march. I mean, it was probably too long considering how little you had been riding, but we stopped plenty of times and had lots to eat and drink along the way."

"Alan, might I remind you, we left our apartment in Moraga at seven-thirty that morning. We rode through this very town and up that mountain to Skyline Boulevard. Then, we rode up to the top of Grizzly Peak before plummeting down the other side into Tilden Park. If that wasn't bad enough, we rode the entire length, up and down, Wildcat Canyon Road until we descended into Orinda. The only reason we stopped there was because my legs had seized up with cramps, and I couldn't spin the pedals any longer. However, you assured me, after nearly a two hour rest, that I would be able to make it back to Moraga."

"And you did. I was so proud of you. That was an awesome ride."

"It was an awful ride. It took us an hour and fifteen minutes to go the last four and a half miles. It was absolutely brutal."

"Well, maybe it was a bit long for your level of fitness at the time," he acquiesced with a smile.

"Have I ever wanted to ride with you again? I mean, on a training ride like that," she frowned to let him know she still remembered the agony.

"Uh, no, not that I can think of," acknowledged Alan with a guilty grimace on his face.

"Then, that should tell you something right there. Shouldn't it?"

"Yeah, sorry about that."

"Oh, I guess it wasn't all that bad." After a reflective pause of a few seconds she proclaimed, "Oh, yes, it was! It was an incredibly difficult sufferfest. But, I'm kind of glad I did it," she declared with a grin.

Drawing her close, he affectionately hugged her. She snuggled into him as they stood swaying back and forth, gazing up into the tree tops. It was one of those special moments they both would remember for the rest of their lives. However, it was starting to get dark in the canyon. Glancing at his watch, Alan suggested that they needed to leave soon if they were to arrive at her sister's home by six o'clock. They walked arm in arm back to their car and just before getting in, took one last deep breath.

As she exhaled, Annalisa pronounced, "I do so love it here, honey."

"Me too, my love, me too."

Fifteen minutes later they pulled into the driveway just behind Annalisa's sister Abigail, who had just arrived home in her mint blue Toyota Prius. Alan had hardly brought their car to a stop before the two women jumped out of their cars and ran for one another locking themselves in a hug that only sisters can replicate. Soon they invited Alan to join them, and the three had a joyous reunion.

"I'm so sorry I'm late," confessed Abigail as she unlocked the door to her contemporary styled home.

"Oh, that's okay," replied Annalisa. "We spent an hour down in Canyon on our way here."

"Canyon? What did you do that for?" remarked Abigail with an edge to her voice.

"We love it in there. It's so beautiful and really peaceful."

"Well, our firm represented a client in there who had a boundary dispute with a neighbor. It was a rather nasty battle. I don't care for the place myself."

Annalisa glanced at Alan who shrugged his shoulders. He then asked where he could put their luggage. Abigail directed him to the last door down the hallway on the left, and warned him not to open the other door.

"Oh?" questioned Annalisa.

"My roommate Grenoble's room."

"What? You have a roommate?" inquired Annalisa with a higher pitch to her voice.

"Yeah, we've been together for about three years. We met sometime after Dad died. Her help was invaluable in transitioning the law firm from Dad to me."

"She's an attorney too?" asked Alan with a chuckle.

"Yeah, she is, and a good one," defended Abigail. "What's so funny about that?"

"Nothing. I just got a picture in my mind of the two of you arguing," mumbled Alan, trying to curtail his level of amusement at the imagined scenario. "You know, two lawyers under the same roof . . . I would guess it makes for some animated conversation. That's all."

"Yeah, we do have some knock-down-drag-out, shouting matches. But it's okay. We get over it and continue on."

"Where does, uh . . . what is her name again?" asked Annalisa.

"Grenoble."

"Yeah, where does Grenoble work?"

"In Berkeley. She's an attorney for a nonprofit firm that helps people who can't afford to hire an attorney, accountant, or other professional. They mainly fight against the government bureaucracy and big money corporations."

"Wow, really?" inquired Annalisa in somewhat of a state of disbelief that her sister had a roommate like Grenoble.

"Fascinating," nodded Alan.

"What's that supposed to mean, Alan?" snapped Abigail.

"Nothing, other than I think what she does for a living is fascinating, Abigail. Why are you being defensive? Have I offended you or something?"

"No, no, I'm sorry. It's just I was afraid . . . oh, never mind. It's really nothing at all."

"No, what is it? Your sister and I have come to visit, you, and Mom. If I have done something wrong, I am sincerely sorry," assured Alan.

"No, it's nothing. Really, I couldn't ask for a better brother-in-law. It's just . . ."

"Yes, Abby," urged Annalisa.

"Well, I thought you guys would, you know, uh . . . judge me or something."

"Why would we do that?" questioned Annalisa softly. "We both love you with all of our hearts. Just because we haven't seen one another for a few years doesn't change that."

"I know, I know. But I'm in my fifties, not married, living with a roommate. You know, I thought you guys , well, you know . . . I mean, for crying out loud, Alan, you're a pastor of a church for Pete's sake."

"Yeah, but that doesn't mean I go around judging folks. My calling is to love others, not judge them."[1]

Just then, the three of them heard the front door open. A second later it slammed shut. Immediately, a boisterous female voice barked from the entry.

"Who parked their gasoline guzzling machine in my parking spot in the driveway? Don't they know I hate to park my Smart car on the street?!"

"That's Grenoble," confessed Abigail with an apologetic grin.

"She sounds, uh . . . assertive," Annalisa admitted softly.

Abigail shrugged and nodded her head. "We're in the kitchen, Grenoble. My sister and brother-in-law are here from Mississippi. Remember, I told you they were coming today?"

"She sounds French," whispered Alan with a smile.

"Kind of," Abigail clarified. "She's originally from Guadeloupe."

Just then, a tall, slender woman in her forties with a closely cropped blonde haircut and bright blue eyes walked into the kitchen. She headed straight for Abigail, greeting her with a kiss on each cheek. She turned to Annalisa and went through the same protocol. However, when she moved toward Alan she stretched out her hand and introduced herself as Grenoble Lefevre. Somewhat taken aback, Alan responded with a nod and a chuckle.

"I'm Alan Browne. Very nice to meet you, Grenoble Lefevre."

"What's so funny?"

"Nothing's funny. I just thought it was amusing how you kissed my wife and her sister but shook my hand."

"Do you have a problem with that?"

"No," retorted Alan. "Like I said, I thought it was amusing. Do you have a problem with that?"

"Alan?" pleaded Annalisa.

"No, I do not have a problem with you laughing at me," countered Grenoble with an exaggerated frown.

"Good, so where are we taking you two to dinner?" appeased Alan.

"Mom isn't here yet," intervened Abigail. "I told her seven o'clock, so she has another twenty minutes. Glass of wine anyone?"

"Absolutely," grumbled Grenoble, who still seemed upset.

"What do you have?" inquired Annalisa.

"A white zin and a merlot."

"Merlot for me," asserted Grenoble.

"I'd like a small glass of the white zinfandel," replied Annalisa with a nod.

"I'll just have a sip or two of Annalisa's if that okay, Abby?" offered Alan.

"Sure, no problem."

"Don't you drink wine?" asked Grenoble with an accusatory tone. "Or is alcohol a sin?"

"Well, that's a very interesting question, counselor. Annalisa and I have an occasional glass with dinner. However, it's not an issue for us whether we drink or not."

"What's that supposed to mean? Do you think I'm an alcoholic because I have a glass of wine each day when I get home from work?"

"No, I don't know you well enough, Grenoble, to determine whether you are an alcoholic or not. But I'm aware that alcohol, like many other substances, some illegal, others legal, has some addictive properties. I, for one, don't want to be addicted to anything. So it's not really an issue for me. Is it for you?" bantered Alan.

"No. I can drink whenever I want," Grenoble volleyed back.

"Good one!" laughed Alan along with the others. "But seriously, can you stop whenever you want? You know, it's like coffee . . . uh, I enjoy my hot cup of java each morning. However, if something happens where I can't have some for a couple of days, I'm not going to be bent out of shape over it."

"Oh, really?" smirked Grenoble. "Well we don't drink coffee in this house, Mr. Alan Browne. So you'll just have to drive down to the Starbucks."

"That's fine, Grenoble. Although, that's not really the issue."

"Oh yeah, then what's the issue, preacher man?" mocked Grenoble.

"The issue, the question I need to ask myself is: Is it serving me or am I serving it?"

The kitchen fell silent. After pouring the glasses of wine, Abigail sat down at the kitchen table. Annalisa, who hadn't uttered a word throughout the entire exchange between Alan and Grenoble, took a sip, then walked across and took a seat next to her sister. The two combatants were on either side of the room. Grenoble stood in the entrance to the dining room and Alan remained by the island. He smiled at Annalisa then turned toward his would-be opponent.

"Look, Grenoble, we're just here for a couple of days before we have to leave for Oregon. I'm very sorry we parked in your parking spot. I will move our car as soon as you give me a hug."

"What?!"

"We can continue this discussion later if you like, but for now, I really need a hug." This time Alan, with a smile on his face, held out his arms.

"Is this cat serious?" scowled Grenoble glancing at Abigail.

"Yeah, believe it or not, he is," replied Abigail frankly. "Look, Grenoble, I've known Alan a long time. He's a really good guy. He isn't one of those religious freaks who preaches at you or condemns you or anything. He and Annalisa just love the Lord Jesus Christ and try to live by His teachings. That's all. So, come on, give him a hug. He won't bite. I mean, you won't bite her, right, Alan?"

"Nah, I never bite on the first hug," chuckled Alan with arms still extended. "Besides, it's only a hug. Those guys both got kisses," he complained with a fake whine.

Grenoble took a long swig of her merlot and, after putting down her glass, haltingly leaned forward into Alan's arms for a stiff hug. She hugged him back briefly, and as they were backing away, she even gave him a quick peck on the cheek.

"Whoa," laughed Alan. "I feel like I'm part of the family again."

They all laughed together. Then, Alan hugged Abigail and followed with a hug for his precious Annalisa.

"Now, let me go move our gas guzzler out of the driveway," declared Alan with a grin. "Grenoble, may I have your keys please?"

"Oh, you don't have to do that. I'll do it later."

"Keys?" Alan held out his hand with a determined look on his face.

"Better give him your keys," suggested Abigail. "He's a preacher man. He won't give up, you know," she laughed.

With the keys to both cars Alan headed to the front door. The three gals chuckled as they sat at the kitchen table.

"He seems okay, I guess," confessed Grenoble.

"Alan?" questioned Abigail. "He's a really great guy."

"Yeah, he's a keeper," added Annalisa. "Uh, that's a Southern term. Means, I think I'll keep him around."

"You ain't no Southern gal," chuckled Abigail, trying her best to sound like a Mississippi Belle. "You were born and raised just down the street in Walnut Creek."

The three shared another laugh together. Just then, they heard the front door open again. Alan called from the porch.

"Mom's here!"

-thirteen-

After a satisfying dinner at a Walnut Creek steak house, Abigail, Grenoble, Alan, Annalisa, and her mother went for a leisurely stroll in the cool evening air. The sun had just set over the hills, and the faint fog tails crept along the ridge before flowing down into the warm valley where they dissipated into a cool breeze. Abigail and Grenoble walked ahead of Alan, Annalisa, and her mother, who was now in her seventies and couldn't quite keep up with the younger ones. Alan put his arms around both of them, and the three walked along at a somewhat slower cadence.

"Mom, you must have been one great mother to have raised a daughter like Annalisa. She is such a wonderful mother too. You would be so proud of her."

"I am proud of her, Alan. And I'm proud of you too. I love the way you two communicate with one another. You say so much by the way you treat each other."

"I wish, Dad could be here," confided Annalisa softly. "I miss him, and it feels so strange coming back, yet he's not here. I know it's been a few years since he passed, but we haven't visited since then. So I keep expecting to see him. You know what I mean?"

"Yes, honey, I do," comforted her mother. "It took me a couple of years before I stopped looking for him around the house or at church. I was at the grocery store last year when I saw the back of a man I could have sworn was your father. But as I got closer, I sneaked another peek and realized it was someone who didn't look like him at all. Things like that used to happen quite a bit but not so much anymore."

"Mom?" asked Alan quietly, "Would you like to go with us to Bend, Oregon, for a few days, maybe a week? We're leaving the day after tomorrow."

"Oh, no, travel wears me out, dear. Besides, I have my volunteer work at the church. Plus, some of the other widows and myself get together for lunch every week. Mrs. Lowenfels just lost her husband three weeks ago, so I need to be there for her. You remember her don't you, Annalisa?"

"Yes, I think so. Didn't her husband own a jewelry shop?"

"Yes, that's right. Nice man. He dropped over from a heart attack as he was closing the vault at the store one evening. They didn't find him until the next morning. He was stiff as a board."

"Mom!" blurted Annalisa.

"Well, it's true."

"Well, it might very well be true, but you don't have to be so graphic about it," complained her daughter.

"Annalisa dear, when you get to be my age you just say 'em as you see 'em."

"Oh, Mom, honestly . . ."

"Now, uh . . . back to our original subject," interjected Alan with a chuckle. "We're leaving early in the morning day after tomorrow if you change your mind. We'd love to have you along."

"What are you two doing up in Bend, Oregon?" her mother inquired.

"We're looking for some information about a man who lived there back in the 1800s," answered Alan.

"Does this have something to do with that **rojocci** Fellowship you two are involved with?"

"Yes, Mom," replied Annalisa. "At least, we hope it does anyway."

"You two be careful up there. I won't be going though," her mother commented as she patted Alan's arm, which he draped over her shoulder as they continued their stroll.

Alan and Annalisa decided to stay through the weekend, so they could spend more time with her mother and sister. Saturday and Sunday were spent driving around scenic areas as well as stopping at little cafés and bistros. Late Sunday evening, they even traveled to the top of Mount Diablo to watch the sun set. It was a magnificent sight for the clear weather allowed them a panoramic view all the way to the Pacific Ocean.

When they returned to Abigail's home, Alan and Annalisa finished packing up their luggage then walked into the main great room where Abigail and Grenoble were sitting on the sofa watching a movie on the television.

"We're all packed up and ready to go now," announced Annalisa as she plopped down in the overstuffed chair perpendicular to the sofa.

"Yeah, we're trying to leave early in the morning, before rush hour," added Alan.

"Good luck with that," jeered Grenoble. "Traffic around here on a Monday morning gets pretty heavy by five-thirty."

"Wow, we better leave even earlier then," replied Alan, glancing at Annalisa with raised eyebrows.

"Yeah, you better," murmured Grenoble.

"Let's go on to bed, Alan. We'll have to get up at the crack of dawn to leave that early."

"No, no, you guys stay up and talk a bit," urged Abigail.

"But we're watching a movie," grumbled Grenoble with an annoyed look on her face.

"Grenoble, I don't get to see my sister and brother-in-law but once every few years. I would like to sit and talk with them. We can finish the movie later."

"It's not your fault they rarely come for a visit," sassed Grenoble.

"Door swings both ways," responded Alan with a smile.

"What's that supposed to mean, preacher man?" mocked Grenoble.

"It simply means that the airlines fly both directions. That's all," shrugged Alan.

"Oh, you're a smart mouth, aren't you, Mister Christian?"

"No, just stating a fact. And by the way, I'm not a preacher. But I am a Christian, who happens to be in a position of helping others."

"Now what's that supposed to mean?" questioned Grenoble with a smirk on her face.

"It means that the Lord is using the spiritual gift He gave me in a way that is useful in assisting others to grow, spiritually speaking."

"What do you mean 'spiritually speaking?'" inquired Grenoble with only a slight frown across her face this time.

"I mean, everyone one of us, we humans, have a body, a soul, and a spirit.[1] The body is the most obvious part and is easily recognized. The soul is a little more, shall we say, nebulous? But essentially, it can be described as our personality, you know, our mind and emotions along with our will."

"Okay, then what's the spiritual part?" interrupted Grenoble with a slight hint of sincerity in her voice.

"Our spirit is the part of us that communes with God. You see, it was created in the image of God. God is a Spirit.[2] So our spirit is, how do you say, compatible with Him. You know, they have a family resemblance, kind of like Abigail and Annalisa. It's also the part of us where our conscience and our intuition reside. To me, it is the most fascinating, yet least studied faculty of human beings," explained Alan as he squeezed into the big overstuffed chair with Annalisa.

"Well, I don't really believe that," remarked Grenoble.

"That's okay. We live in a free country, and thankfully, you can believe whatever you want. However, just because you don't personally believe something doesn't necessarily mean it isn't true. It's possible you just haven't come to recognize it yet."

"Yeah, well . . ." blurted Grenoble.

"Look, Grenoble, you look very fit. You had to exercise your body and eat right to maintain that level of fitness correct?"

"Absolutely."

"You and Abigail are both attorneys, right?"

"Yes."

"Well, you had to study long and hard to pass that BAR exam."

"Yeah, well, what's your point?" bickered Grenoble.

"My point is, for you to benefit from a fit body, you had to train it, correct? For you to enjoy the assets of an intelligent mind, you had to work hard at it, right? It's the same with your spirit. You won't even know it's there until it is awakened and exercised. You know, trained by the One who created it."

"I don't believe any of that stuff," disputed Grenoble.

"Hey, that's okay. But if you were a three cylinder engine, you would only be running on two of your three cylinders. In fact, even less than that because your spirit is the most powerful of the three. There is a whole universe that exists called the kingdom of God, and if you are a believer in the Lord Jesus Christ, that kingdom lives within you."[3]

"What? That's ridiculous."

"Not to one who has experienced it," asserted Alan. "God has given each Christian a portion, a pledge, an inheritance of His Spirit,[3] who lives within the spirit of the believer. That same Spirit who raised Jesus from the dead lives in folks who believe. He lives in Annalisa. He lives in me. And He gives gifts to each one of us. These gifts are really just a portion of His Spirit revealing Himself."

"Gifts? What do you mean gifts?" questioned Grenoble with a hint of skepticism still in her voice, although she had scooched forward on the sofa.

"Grenoble, it is all about our relationship with God our Father through Jesus His Son. He loves you every bit as much as He loves me. He wants to have a friendship with you. He doesn't judge you, and neither do we."

"Yeah, well . . ."

"All you have to do is ask Him, and He will come into your heart,"[4] appealed Alan with genuine sincerity.

"Have you done this, Abby?" asked Grenoble turning to Abigail sitting next to her on the sofa.

"Yes, it was a long time ago, and I have kind of fallen away from it. But, yes, I'm a Christian."

"Really? Why didn't you ever tell me?" accused Grenoble.

"I don't know. Maybe because I was afraid of what you might think of me. Besides, it wasn't that important, not like it used to be," countered Abigail. "But, yes, Annalisa and I have been Christians since way back in junior high school or something."

"Whaaat?!" yelped Grenoble.

"Alan," prompted Annalisa. "Why don't you pray for us? It's getting quite late."

Reaching across, Alan took Abigail's hand while Annalisa grasped Grenoble's so that they formed a circle. Then Alan prayed. It was a time he would always remember when he felt the unction of the Holy Spirit praying through him. After closing with the Amen, Alan made a final suggestion.

"Do you guys have a Bible?"

"Sure, it's right over there on the bookshelf. Why?" asked Abigail.

"Would you do me one tiny favor? If you are willing, would you read the first three chapters of the Gospel of John. It's in the New Testament, right up front after Matthew, Mark, and Luke."

"I know where it is, Alan," quipped Abigail sarcastically.

"Oops, sorry. I just think you both would get a lot out of those three chapters. They're not long. It would take you maybe ten minutes to read."

"I think I can do that," offered Grenoble.

"Thanks, Alan," whispered Abigail.

"Sure."

"It's late, honey," pleaded Annalisa.

Everyone stood up and hugs were given all around. This time Grenoble even kissed Alan on both cheeks. Alan quietly laughed giving her an extra hug, and then all were off to bed.

At precisely four-thirty the next morning, Alan's alarm startled him out of a heavy sleep. After gently nudging Annalisa awake, he rapidly packed everything up since they were hoping to be on the road for Bend, Oregon, by no later than five o'clock. The house was silent as they tiptoed down the hallway to the front door. Annalisa stepped into the kitchen to leave a thank you note on the table before heading out the front door. Tears rolled down her cheeks when they pulled away from Abigail's house. Because the visit, at times, had been so confrontational she was disappointed that she and Abby hadn't been able to share their hearts with one another. Alan reached over and softly took her hand in his as they turned onto the freeway on-ramp heading north.

"Alan, promise me we'll come back soon to see my Mom and sister."

"I was thinking the same thing, honey. Although, it is true what I said. The airlines do fly both directions."

"Yes, I know, but Abby has been so busy with the law firm since Dad died. I don't see her or Mom making a trip to Mississippi anytime soon."

"Yeah, California and Mississippi are like two different countries. I think your sister would kind of freak out or something," chuckled Alan.

"Well, the Bay Area hasn't been a picnic for me either," she giggled while wiping away her tears.

"Honey, do you wish we still lived here?"

"Alan, what on earth? No, I am glad for all that God has taken us through together. I like this area, but I wouldn't want to live here again. It's too busy, too crazy, or too something."

"How about if we lived in Canyon?"

"Alan, for crying out loud. That would never happen. Besides, I don't want to live in a place where we'd rarely see the sun. I like where we live and what we're doing."

"Okay, just checking."

"You're too funny, Alan."

"Look, honey, if you'd like, why not take a nap? We have an eight hour drive ahead of us. I thought we'd head down the road for a couple of hours before stopping in Redding to refuel and to get something to eat. Work for you?"

"Yep, just wake me up when we're getting close," she yawned as she reclined the seat back to a position more comfortable for sleeping.

Interstate Five northbound from just outside the San Francisco Bay Area is long, straight, and flat for miles and miles. There's a ridge of the Coastal Range to the west and the open flatness of the Sacramento Valley to the east. A driver can turn on the cruise control and, with very little steering, be alone with his thoughts. Alan soon became absorbed in his own reverie. Drifting back, his mind dredged up many scenes from their early years of marriage when they lived in San Ramon. They once had driven this very stretch of freeway on their way to a stay in the Trinity Alps region. Remembering how Annalisa had screamed when she had jumped into Lake Shasta, brought a smile to his face as he passed a slow moving vehicle in the left lane. The snowmelt had filled the lake with absolutely freezing water, and she had bolted out of it almost as quickly as she had plunged in.

Thoughts of their church in Wiggins drifted across his mind. Before long, his smile turned to a more sober expression. There was so much that could go wrong while he was away. He hardly wanted to ponder what could be happening there. The Bible study group and how they were getting along was his main concern. But thinking about the elders, his thoughts became somewhat anxious, so he began to pray for each one by name. Just as he finished praying, a thought darted across his agitated mind.

"Maybe you shouldn't have gone on this trip. Don't you know the place is falling apart without you there telling everyone what to do?"

"What? Lord, that's not you. And it's not me. So it can only be . . . the enemy." These last two words he barked aloud and continued, "No, get out of my thoughts, you foul spirit of deception. Get out of this car . . ."

"What, honey?" asked a groggy Annalisa as she lifted her head to determine if they were close to their rest stop yet.

"Nothing, sweetheart, just fighting our enemy," replied Alan while he patted her hand. "How does IHOP sound for a late breakfast, uh, kind of a brunch? We'll be there in about twenty minutes."

"Sounds good. I am getting hungry," she yawned as she squinted out the tinted window into the bright California sunshine. "Where are we anyway?"

"Just a few miles south of Redding."

After breakfast, Annalisa drove for a couple of hours, so Alan could get some rest. The scenery was beautiful with Mount Shasta getting ever larger in their windshield. They crossed over the massive lake, which dons the same name as the mountain that feeds it. The brilliant blue waters reflected the sky above. Soon, they crossed into Oregon, and within a couple of hours they saw the Bend city limits sign. They found their hotel, a Hampton Inn by the river, and parked near the main entrance. Checking his watch, Alan confirmed it had taken them just over eight hours to drive from the Bay Area. They registered, carried their luggage to the room, and took a short nap before making their way down to the library.

Sifting through all the book laden shelves that may have had anything to do with The **rojocci** Fellowship in general, and the initials P. D. specifically, they left empty handed, having uncovered no new leads. Next, they decided to check with the Police Department. However, with only the initials as a clue, they found nothing. Not yet discouraged, they tried an idea Annalisa thought of when leaving the library. Pulling up in front of the Bend Historical Society, they hopped out of their car and walked into the old building. They were greeted by a very welcoming lady, who appeared to be in her late sixties or perhaps early seventies. She introduced herself as Mrs. Mildred Buttermore, historical associate of the establishment.

"How are you folks, today?" she inquired with a smile.

"Just fine, ma'am. How are you?" replied Alan returning the smile.

"Oh my, you folks aren't from around here are you?"

"No ma'am, we're from back east, uh, well southeast really," answered Annalisa.

"I could tell. No one around here, calls anybody ma'am."

"Our apologies, ma'am," Alan replied with a nod.

"Oh, no, not at all. I rather enjoy it. I think it has a respectfully courteous resonance. Thank you. Now how may I help you two?"

"We're looking for a document," announced Alan. "A paper about one hundred and fifty years old. It has something to do with a Christian fellowship called **rojocci**. We aren't sure, but we think it may have been written by a person who went by the initials P. D. Does any of this sound familiar to you?"

"No, I can't say that it does. How do you spell the word?"

"It's spelled, **r-o-j-o-c-c-i**," explained Annalisa.

"Hmmm . . . let me see here."

Evidently, Mrs. Mildred Buttermore was not only cheerful but was also extremely thorough as she delved into several files, book shelves, and boxes, all the while with Alan and Annalisa in tow. However, after more than two hours of scouring, the search hadn't availed them a single clue. There was nothing she could find in the archives that gave any indication of a document with the word **rojocci** in its title or that an individual named P. D. had ever lived.

"I'm very sorry, folks. I just don't have anything that resembles what you're looking for."

"Would you happen to know anyone that might have a clue about any possible lead concerning The **rojocci** Fellowship?"

"I can't think of anyone. I'm very sorry."

"Well, if you do, here's my card with my cell number. It's really important to us. We sure would be appreciative of any further help. Thank you so much," smiled Alan as he reached out his hand to shake hers.

The two explorers left the Historical building somewhat disheartened. They were sure someone must know something about the document they were looking for or perhaps the mysteriously elusive P. D. However, to this point they had struck out. Not even a hint of evidence had been uncovered that what they were searching for actually existed. They started back to the hotel puzzled and wondering where to turn.

Stopping at a hamburger grill, they sat outside and discussed their predicament. They considered heading back to the Bay Area. But decided instead to stick around Bend in hopes of stumbling upon something that could possibly substantiate that what they were searching for had actually existed. As they were finishing up their meal, they both agreed to give it another day before departing for the Bay Area.

The following morning they combed through the files and microfilm at another library. Then, they inquired at seven churches of varying denominations. But they struck out completely. They found nothing; not the tiniest trace of anything with even the hint of a resemblance regarding whoever or whatever may be the identity of the phantom-like P. D. and the tantalizingly mysterious document entitled The **rojoccian** Covenant.

Planning to leave at dawn the very next day, the two had a delightful early dinner at a local restaurant famous for its gorgeous view of Mount Bachelor to the west. Annalisa had a delicious Rainbow Trout Almandine and Alan a sumptuous Pasta Salad with Grilled Chicken and Pepperoncini. Just as he finished his last bite of the creamy dish, Alan's phone rang. Glancing at Annalisa, his expression indicated the number wasn't one he recognized. Upon answering, his eyebrows lifted upward and a smile broke across his face. It was Mrs. Mildred Buttermore, and she had news.

-fourteen-

Rising early, Alan and Annalisa were both ready to leave by seven o'clock. The drive to the address Mrs. Mildred Buttermore had given them was about an hour away. The mood in the car was cheery and optimistic as they pulled into the Starbucks drive-through just down the street from their hotel. Within minutes, they were headed north to meet a man named Dale Longleaf, who worked in The Museum at Warm Springs. The establishment, they discovered, was a beautiful tribute to several Native Americans tribes living in the northwest. Alan and Annalisa had been told Dale was a local amateur historian. They soon found out, though he was a historian, Dale was anything but amateur.

Dale greeted the couple with a smile upon his deeply wrinkled face. He was a soft spoken, gentle man, who walked with the same slow, deliberate cadence with which he conversed. Alan enjoyed Dale, like a hot summer day enjoys a thunderstorm. He spoke with a low rumble that was quite soothing if not altogether refreshing.

Dressed in his Native American attire, Dale spent most of the morning giving the two **rojoccian** explorers a personalized tour of the museum. They were absolutely fascinated by all of the colorful displays of beautiful artwork, clothing, and artifacts. Afterward, Dale walked them across the highway to the Tule Grill. Once they finished their delicious lunch of club sandwiches and chips, Dale asked if there was any other way he could help them. Alan had been stealthfully awaiting this moment and pounced upon it with the assertive intent of a mountain lion attacking its prey.

"Yes, Dale, we have been searching for an individual who lived in the mid to late 1800s. He or she was known only by the initials P. D. Does that sound familiar to you?"

"We're actually not even sure it's a person," added Annalisa. "But we think it is . . . uh, kind of anyway."

"Also, we believe this P. D. may have something to do with a historical document," clarified Alan.

"What kind of a document?" asked Dale in his unhurried style, half the speed of Alan's excited tongue.

"It's entitled 'The **rojoccian** Covenant.' Ever heard of it?" asked Alan.

"I have never heard of this document," Dale soberly replied. "However, I have heard of a man who went by these initials P. D. He was known for his kind heart."

"Really? Where did you hear about him?" inquired an enthusiastic Alan.

"He lived here in Warm Springs. He was well known among our tribe. He's what you would call a missionary, a Christian missionary. Arriving here in the 1870s, he moved into an abandoned cabin just west of town. Legend says he was somewhat of an outcast from his people because he was a man devoted to his religion. Even the white man didn't accept him, though he held to the same beliefs. While he slept one cold night in 1889, a fire rapidly engulfed his cabin destroying the entire structure. Some say it was the result of the values he lived by. Some say it was because he had converted some of the tribe to his religion. Sadly, the gentle, old man died completely alone."

"Oh, that's awful," exclaimed Annalisa slowly shaking her head.

"Where did they bury him?" asked Alan.

"Other than a few bones, there was not much left to bury. Besides, there was no one brave enough to go near the charred remains of the cabin. Much later, sometime in the early 1960s, a great forest fire raged through the area and completely reduced to ashes what had not been destroyed by weather over the decades."

"What a sad story," whispered Annalisa.

"Do you know what his initials stand for?" inquired Alan further.

"My grandfather, Standing Longleaf, used to tell me the legend of P. D. He explained that he was a great-hearted man, who had come from a vast distance to tell his stories. As children, my grandfather and his friends used to sneak away and spend hours at the old man's cabin listening to these tales of the majestic God of the skies and His precious only Son. Grandfather Longleaf said the stories made his heart warm within him. He and his friends called P. D., Papa Daks. The adults called him Preacher Daks."

"Daks?" repeated Alan quietly.

"Yes, he was from a tribe in the Dakota Territory," explained Dale.

"He was a Native American?" asked Annalisa, whose pitch just rose several octaves.

"Yes, he was," continued Dale in his solemn style. "As the legend goes, a traveling man of religion, a Christian, from across the Great Plains, who also belonged to The **rojocci** Fellowship, of which you seek, visited his tribe for several months and told the stories. As a young brave, P. D. believed the stories and was converted to the man's religion. Later he asked if he could travel with this man. The man agreed and they journeyed together for many years. The man taught P. D. all he knew about the majestic God of the skies. He also helped him learn how to speak English as well as how to read and write the language. The two were inseparable throughout the Northern tribes until one day in 1849."

"What happened in 1849?" asked Annalisa.

"The white man's cancer," replied Dale frankly.

"Cancer?" inquired Annalisa with a frown.

"Gold in California," Dale smiled ruefully.

"What's that got to do with P. D. and this traveling evangelist?" blurted Alan.

"The white man evangelist, as you call him, left for California after realizing that many of the white men had left wife, family, and home in search of gold. He feared most had fallen away from their religion. So with P. D. along, he packed up his things and headed to the great California land. Once they had arrived in Sacramento, he decided it best to part ways with P. D., figuring they could reach more people if they went in opposite directions. The very next day P. D. stood alone on the shore of the American River as he watched his only friend cross over and turn south toward

Sutter's Mill. P. D. headed north through Yuba City to Oroville and eventually to a mining camp up in the foothills of the Sierra Nevada Mountains named Dogtown."

"Dogtown?" asked Alan. "Where's that?"

"It's near what is now called Paradise. P. D. continued telling the stories and trying to convert the white man, especially those who had come from the east. He later traveled further north, working in the Trinity Alps. He lived in a stall in an old barn outside the town of Weed, under the shadow of the great mountain called Shasta. A few years passed by, then he journeyed here to Warm Springs, living out the last years of his life in the cabin I told you about."

"Wow, what an amazing story, Dale," expressed Annalisa shaking her head.

"Yes, but that is only a small part of it. My grandfather told me that wherever P. D. traveled and shared the stories, he was robbed and beaten. Sometimes he had nothing to eat or drink for days. He was kicked out of his rented room, chased out of towns, threatened with execution twice, and was actually hung once."

"Hung once?" repeated Alan in disbelief.

"Yes, as the story goes, he was beaten by a band of prospectors, who slung a rope around his neck and hung him from a tree. As the men rode off, the rope snapped. When his body slammed into the ground, P. D. awoke from his death."

"Oh, that's awful, Dale."

"Awful but true. He almost froze to death many winters because he had nowhere to stay. He endured the hot summers and shivered through the cold winters. He slept in trees to avoid wild animals and the men who would try to harass P. D. at night. He climbed across many mountain passes, forged many rivers, and was even swept over a waterfall on the Feather River after slipping while trying to cross. Oh, the suffering he withstood to tell the stories to those men. It causes one to wonder."

"I would like to have known him," confessed Alan sincerely.

The threesome walked back across the highway and up to the museum. Alan and Annalisa each hugged the aged man with the gentle yet wizened face and thanked him again for his recollections. As they turned to leave, Alan asked one more time if he knew anything regarding The **rojoccian** Covenant. Dale shook his head but made the suggestion that perhaps someone in Weed or Dogtown might know something. Determined to discover if this was true, early the next morning Alan and Annalisa packed their things and started for the tiny town of Weed.

Arriving later that afternoon, they checked into a rather crusty motel and immediately began asking anyone and everyone they met about P. D. and The **rojoccian** Covenant document. However, not one person was even remotely familiar with either. They were becoming discouraged and were beginning to believe The **rojoccian** Covenant to be a myth, especially considering that even Dale Longleaf had never heard of it. At one point the following morning, Annalisa gave voice to her frustration.

"Alan, I know we really hoped we would find The **rojoccian** Covenant, but I am beginning to think that it may be just a myth or some kind of fabrication."

"I would believe that, too, honey, except that fellow in Thomasville, Georgia, had heard of it. Before that, back when we went to Pfeiffer Station, Ohio, for The **rojocci** Manifesto we read about P. D. in that letter. And don't forget ole slick Hugh Roseboughson, who claimed he actually had a copy in his possession he was willing to sell me for an exorbitant price."

"Yes, well, maybe P. D. was a real person. Maybe he was beloved by many folks, who made him into a legend. And maybe The **rojoccian** Covenant is just a part of that legend," she shrugged.

"You may have hit the nail on the head, honey. But I'm not convinced quite yet. I will admit, I'm closer to believing your theory than when we arrived in San Francisco last week. But let's see what we find in Dogtown, wherever that is, before we give up totally. So many times in life it's the last unturned stone that reveals the answer."

Driving through the Trinity Alps the following day, they were glad to have gotten an early start. Stopping at stores, post offices, and churches, they inquired about P. D. and The **rojoccian** Covenant, but nobody had ever heard of either. Shortly after one o'clock, they headed south toward Paradise hoping to find the mysterious Dogtown.

After getting situated in a hotel room, they found a wonderful restaurant named Peter Chu's and settled in for some delicious Asian cuisine. Paradise was a delightful town at an elevation that was above the valley fog but below the mountain snow with a nearly perfect climate. They found the people to be very friendly and most helpful in their search. Attending a church the next morning, Alan and

Annalisa met an usher who confided that he knew someone who might have information regarding P. D. Following the morning service, the usher introduced them to a kind gentleman.

His name was Georges Champion, a Belgian, whose family had immigrated to New Orleans in the early 1800s only to move further west when hearing of the Gold Rush of 1849. They had settled in a tiny miner's town just up the mountain from Paradise. He had lived there all his life in the same home that his great grandfather had built in 1867. Georges, a petite, fifty year old, nearly bald man with a sprinkling of grey in his neatly trimmed goatee was full of all sorts of local historical lore as well as a vast amount of useless trivia. He spoke with a twinkle in his eye and the slightest hint of a French accent on his tongue. Alan found him quite amusing and entertaining. Annalisa found him too talkative and a bit annoying.

Georges invited them to have lunch with him. They accepted, and sat outside at a little bistro along Skyway, the name of the only main road in Paradise. About halfway through the turkey and cheese sandwich he was sharing with Annalisa, Alan asked Georges if he had ever heard of a place called Dogtown.

"Why, yes, of course, I live there myself," replied Georges.

"You do?" quizzed Annalisa glancing at Alan.

"See that sign over there?"

"Uh, which sign?" asked Alan.

"The one that declares 'Magalia One Mile.'"

"Yes," acknowledged Alan.

"Magalia is Dogtown. That is where I live . . . Magalia, uh, Dogtown. Initially, back in the 1850s, it was called Dogtown because a man bred dogs there. Later, however, the town folks didn't like the name so they chose, Magalia, a Latin word which means cottages. That's why it is called Magalia today. Although, I think around 1859, a fifty-four pound gold nugget was discovered down the hill along the Feather River. It was the biggest piece of gold ever unearthed. They called it the Dogtown Nugget, and it made the little town very popular. So even though the name had been officially changed to Magalia, it was still known as Dogtown for many years."

"You sure know your local history, Georges," remarked Alan.

Georges shrugged. "But of course. I have lived here all of my life, and I am the third generation of Champions born here. Why do you want to know about Dogtown?"

"Well, we are looking for information about a Native American named P. D., who lived back in the mid to late 1800s. We believe he may have stayed around here for a time."

"Preacher Daks?" inquired Georges.

"Yes! So you've heard of him?" asked Alan leaning forward.

"But of course. If it were not for Preacher Daks I would not be in the church today."

"Dare I ask what P. D. has to do with you attending church this morning?" ventured Annalisa.

"It was the love of Preacher Daks that saved my great grandfather. My great grandfather told my grandfather, who shared the message with my father, who passed it along to me."

"What message?" asked Alan.

"The message of God's love in sending us His Son, Jesus Christ, who died for the sins of the world and especially the believers,[1] of which I am one. That's what Preacher Daks shared with everyone who would listen . . . but there weren't very many of those folks in those days."

"Have you ever heard of something P. D. wrote called The **rojoccian** Covenant?" questioned a most hopeful Alan.

"Why, yes, of course I have. I have seen it with my own eyes."

"What? You have? Where?" urged Alan.

"My cousin's house. He has one of the original papers that Preacher Daks hand wrote himself before he left Dogtown."

"How long was he here?" questioned an intrigued Annalisa, her curiosity piqued even more now.

"As it was told to me, he walked into Dogtown in the spring of 1850. He didn't own a horse. Therefore, he walked wherever he went. Shortly after arriving, some of the miners brutally beat him for trying to share with them the Good News of Jesus Christ. He was left for dead along a dirt road. He lay on the ground for two days. The third day he picked himself up and slowly made his way down the hill to the Feather River where he nursed his wounds for nearly a week. The icy cold waters of the river were like a healing balm to him. Soon he was back up the hill and was, once again, telling everyone who would listen, the story of Jesus."

"He must have been an amazing man to have endured so much," exclaimed Annalisa shaking her head in wonder.

"Yes, I believe he was," agreed Georges. "That wasn't the only time he was beaten. Those who opposed his message were unimaginably cruel to him, yet he never gave up. Many years had passed when he met a man who had just received a letter from his home in Missouri. It bore devastating news. His wife and four children had died of a fever the previous winter. The man was overwhelmed with grief and had convinced himself that life wasn't worth living. Preacher Daks consoled the man by telling him of the One who gave His only Child, a Son, so that he could live. Then, laying his hands upon the man's head, P. D. prayed for his conversion."

"Did he get saved?" whispered Annalisa leaning forward.

"Yes, and he was the first one that broke the dam, so to speak. In the following months, many more miners were saved as well. One of them was my great grandfather. Then, one day, while sitting by the river, beaten no more, Preacher Daks sensed the Spirit calling him further north to tell others about Jesus. However, he didn't want to leave his new brethren without giving them a gift. So he prayed and asked his Father in Heaven for something appropriate for the young Christians, something that would strengthen their faith and help them on their journey. As he sat there by the river, he wrote The **rojoccian** Covenant. With the help of his first convert, he made a copy for each of the twenty-seven new believers. He gave this gift to every one of them before he departed for the north."

"What does it say?" asked Alan urgently.

"Although it is simplistic, it's really quite beautiful. It's more of a declaration of his faith than an actual covenant, but profound nonetheless," assured Georges. "I think the reason it has been called a covenant is because when people read it, many are compelled to dedicate or recommit their lives to the Lord."

"Do you remember what is in it?" Alan asked again.

"Well, rather than destroying its message with a butchered rendition from my less-than-perfect memory, let's get you over to my cousin Ulysses' house. He has a copy hanging on his wall."

"Really?" pried Alan as he stood up from the table. "Where does he live?"

"He's on up the mountain pass where the pavement stops and the dirt road begins. Continue another mile or two, and there will be a dirt lane leading off to the south. This curvy drive leads down the hill nearly a mile to his log and stone cabin. I better go with you though. Sometimes Ulysses gets a bit testy when he sees a vehicle he does not recognize pulling up to his house, so I think it would be better if the two of you ride with me."

Because it was taking much longer than he had expected, Alan was getting concerned that Georges didn't actually know where he was going. The three of them bumped and banged along the rutted dirt road, which had begun at the end of the paved road, for nearly fifteen minutes before finally turning right onto a smaller and more deeply rutted dirt road that led its winding way down a steep, forested slope. Georges announced that this was Ulysses' drive. After another ten minutes, they descended the final curve and there, among a stand of tall evergreen trees and many granite boulders of varying dimensions, stood a rustic log cabin with a stone foundation and a huge stone chimney to one side. It was a rather small house, more of a cottage really, but the setting was absolutely gorgeous. Looking past the cabin, from where they were parked above it, Alan and Annalisa noticed the beautiful scenery across the Feather River canyon to the south. As they got out of Georges car, they could hear the wind whistling through the needles of the pine trees and the sounds of the river farther below as it splashed and crashed its way ever lower into Lake Oroville near the valley to the west. The air was quite chilly for summer, and the scents were so pleasing that Alan stopped, closed his eyes, and with his face toward the brilliant blue sky, breathed in deeply several times. He imagined it was like being in Heaven. In fact, the only evidence that it wasn't, came when a gruff male voice bellowed to them from the front porch. Upon seeing the man was holding a double barrel shotgun, Alan quickly snapped to attention.

"You folks must be lost. Now turn that car around and get on up the hill," the gruff voice commanded.

"Uly," shouted Georges. "It's Georges, your cousin."

"Who?"

"Georges Champion, your cousin from down the mountain in Magalia."

"Come here a little closer, and let me get a look at you," barked Ulysses.

Walking slowly toward the front porch, Georges seemed less confident than when they were driving here just a few minutes ago. Alan and Annalisa chose to remain close to the car, just in case. Georges took one step onto the porch, and Ulysses let out a shout.

"Yes, yes, Georges! How are you doing, my dear cousin?"

"I'm fine, Uly. You had me a bit worried there for a minute."

"Oh, I'm sorry about that. My eyes aren't what they used to be. Come on in here and visit for a spell. What brings you up here this late in the day?"

"Well, I have these friends with me that wanted to meet you," confessed Georges, waving Alan and Annalisa up onto the porch.

"Me? What they want to meet an old coot like me for?"

"They're looking for The **rojoccian** Covenant. I told them you have a copy hanging on your wall. Do you still have it, Uly?"

Ulysses' face turned to a pasty white. He slowly lowered himself down on the porch swing and reverently whispered. "Bless the Lord, O my soul, and all that is within me bless His holy name."[2]

"Are you okay, Mr. Ulysses?" inquired Annalisa as she approached the ill looking man.

Ulysses, who appeared to be in his late eighties, maybe nineties, set aside his shotgun. Shaking his head, he gazed up at Annalisa. He looked utterly shaken.

"I'm just fine there, honey. Just had a bit of a shock, that's all," he confirmed.

"What's wrong, Uly? Your ticker again?" asked Georges.

"Nope. At least it don't feel like it's my heart anyway. But when you mentioned the old **rojoccian** Covenant, I nearly collapsed."

"Why?" asked Georges. "Don't you have it any more?"

"Oh, no, it's still hanging in there on the wall. I read it every day. But let me tell you something I ain't never told no one. You see, shortly after my Mabel died I was up all night praying and crying out to the Lord. I was so lonely. I was hurting so bad. I was so lost. Sometime along about dawn, I got really concerned that I was going to be alone for the rest of my life. What was I going to do? Who would take care of me if I got injured or fell sick? How was I going to cope without my sweet Mabel? I didn't want to live another day. I walked over to The **rojoccian** Covenant hanging on the wall and held up the candle so I could read it. As I finished reading, a soft voice entered my thoughts. It reminded me that He was more than able to handle all that concerned me. He told me to carry on, to take one day at a time, and that He would give me a sign when my life's course was coming to an end."

"What would the sign be?" asked Georges leaning forward.

"He told me a couple, a husband and a wife, would come from a great distance to gaze upon the document."

Then, turning to Alan and Annalisa he asked, "Have you folks come from a great distance?"

"Yes, sir," nodded Alan. "We live in Wiggins, Mississippi."

"Are you folks married?"

"Yes, sir, for more than twenty five years," Alan replied.

"And you've traveled all this way just to see The **rojoccian** Covenant?"

"That's right, sir," replied Annalisa softly.

Ulysses peered up at Alan and Annalisa with a slight smile on his face. "Then you folks come on in, and let me show it to you."

-fifteen-

W alking through the door into Ulysses' cabin was like taking a step back into the late 1800s. Other than the few rays of sunshine, which filtered in through the two south facing windows, there was very little light in the main room of this four room house. On several walls, animal skins of various sorts were displayed. However, their purpose was not to reveal the skills of a successful hunter, but to provide insulation and retain the heat within the home during the long mountain winters. Although Ulysses had running water, there was no electricity or phone service. He couldn't even get propane for his stove and water heater because the company that supplied it refused to navigate his somewhat treacherous drive. Therefore, everything was heated by the fire in the fireplace, giving explanation for the enormous, neatly stacked pile of split firewood on the front porch. Admittedly, it was a primitive lifestyle, but one Ulysses had known and enjoyed for decades.

Once their eyes adjusted to the dim interior, Alan and Annalisa glanced around the tiny cabin. As Annalisa stepped forward, she tripped over what she thought was a fuzzy ball of some sort. Grabbing hold of Alan's arm, she recognized the ball to be the fur covered head of a giant black bear, whose massive skin covered a good portion of the floor in the main room.

"That's okay there, Miss Annalisa," pardoned Ulysses. "I kick old Bartholomew in the head every day."

"Who?" asked Annalisa.

"That big guy laying there on the floor, my Mabel named him Mr. Bartholomew Black. And that big old head of his seems to get right in my way no matter which way I'm heading."

Everyone in the room chuckled while Alan resumed his inconspicuous inspection of Ulysses' home. He turned to notice a makeshift kitchen next to a door that revealed a toilet and sink within. The last of the three doors in the home led to Ulysses' bedroom. On the wall next to his bedroom door, hung a wooden framed document covered with clear glass. Alan took Annalisa's hand, and they began moving slowly toward it. His eyes focused on the handwritten words, which almost appeared as scribbles upon the old faded and tarnished paper.

"That's it," pronounced Ulysses with a sense of accomplishment in his voice that revealed the pride he felt in having kept this meaningful keepsake intact since receiving it from his grandfather.

"Wow, that's amazing," whispered Annalisa.

"Yep, I can't vouch to whether it's an original, but I think it is. My grandfather gave it to me after my father died. When was that, Georges, some fifty years ago now, wasn't it? He claimed it was one of the ones that Preacher Daks' friend had copied and had handed out to his good friend . . . our great grandfather, right, Georges?"

"Yes, of course. That is my understanding anyway."

"Do you mind if we take a photo of it?" asked Alan gingerly.

"No. Do whatever you want. It's yours," declared Ulysses with a grin.

"What? Oh, no we couldn't. This belongs in your family," exclaimed Alan shaking his head.

"Mabel and me never had no children. So I don't have anyone to leave it to."

"Well, what about Georges?" asked Annalisa.

"No, no," exclaimed Georges. "I cannot give it a place of respect, a place of honor worthy of the meaning. Besides, I have no one to leave it to either."

"You never had children?" questioned Annalisa.

"Oh, but yes. I am so sad to confess to you I had a son, but he was killed in the war in the Middle East several years ago. If he were alive, he would have wanted it. But, alas . . ."

"I'm so sorry, Georges," breathed Annalisa, pausing briefly before posing her next inquiry. "So how about your wife?"

"Broken hearted, she left me shortly after the news of our son's death arrived. I don't even know if she is still alive or where she lives, if she is," shrugged Georges with his arms stretched out to each side with palms up.

"Look," asserted Ulysses as he sat down in one of only two chairs in the home, "The Lord told me I should give it to a particular couple at a specific point in time. Clearly, the couple is you two, and the time is now."

"I don't know what to say," expressed Alan softly. "This is a tremendous honor."

"Thank you, Mr. Ulysses," whispered Annalisa as she reached down to give the old man a hug.

"Now that right there, Georges," laughed Ulysses, "That was well worth giving away my beloved treasure. Do you have any idea how long it's been since I had me some feminine attention?"

"But of course," laughed Georges. "Too long. I know because sadly I am in the same way," he protested, glancing in Annalisa's direction.

"Thank you too, Georges," grinned Annalisa as she gave him a half hug, patting him several times on the back.

"You have made my day. No, ma cherie, you have made my year," chuckled Georges. "Alan, you are a most blessed and fortunate man to have such a lovely and beautiful woman to walk with through this life. Don't you think Uly?"

"Yes, I do," affirmed Ulysses. "But, Georges, I think you are embarrassing our charming guest."

"My apologies," offered Georges. "But, of course, Alan knows he is a blessed man."

Alan acknowledged Georges with a nod and a grunt but continued to gaze at the artifact hanging on the wall in front of him. Scanning the precious words, his eyes took in every detail like a seasoned investigator searching for the tiniest of clues. He quietly gasped when he caught the reflection of his face centered in the glass. Pausing for a moment, he then read the words softly and reverently for all in the room to hear. It was one of those poignant moments in life that Alan knew he would long remember. Annalisa walked over to him, looped her arm through his, and resting her head upon his shoulder she listened with rapt attention.

The rojoccian Covenant

I am nothing, one soul within myself
And have but one life to give, one strength
If He's chosen to set me upon life's shelf
Who am I to question how long the length.

Now hear the voice that cries too deep
With words only His Spirit understand
As alone, yet many invisible they keep
My soul, my body when trodden to sand.

There is One more close who knows my pain
Who I am not worthy to glance upon
It is He so sweetly, so surely I gain
Everything clear and pure when life is done.

So don't give credence to grumble nor complaint
Knowing your Father never sleeps nor rests
But soldier on, yet stronger on, never faint
Under sore affliction, trials, and tests.

Now one last word I boldly declare
The beauty of all His teachings be
This one thing most sublime if we will dare
His love for you long ago He decreed.

Lord, ne'er will I give up, nor will I flee
From the way for me You have chosen
Surely Your love, Your grace, Your sovereignty
Mingled midst bold faith my life Handwoven.

Preacher Daks
Dogtown, California 1857

Just as Alan had finished his respectful recitation, Ulysses shuffled across the room, reached up to the brown wooden frame, lifted it up off the nail, and kissed the glass.

"That's the first time in my recollection this has ever been moved from that wall." Then turning to Alan and Annalisa he proclaimed, "And now, my **rojoccian** friends, it is yours. I sense I will soon be released from my bondage to this earth. I give this to you both with my heartfelt blessing. It has been hidden away in this cabin for way too long, Now, take it and proclaim it to others, who will hear its timeless message."

Handing the framed document to Alan, Ulysses laid one hand on Alan's shoulder and his other on Annalisa's shoulder. Then he prayed pronouncing a blessing upon the two of them.

"May God bless you and keep you and make His glorious face to shine upon you and be gracious unto you. May He lift up His countenance upon you and give you His peace from this day forth and forever."[1]

When Alan and Annalisa looked up, the once dingy cabin seemed to be softly glowing with a radiant light. Everyone was completely silent. A hush had fallen upon them that even talkative Georges didn't want to disturb. It was obvious to all four of them, the Lord was there in the room with them. Within a few seconds, Ulysses, weakened from standing, shuffled back to his chair. Alan and Annalisa turned their attention once again to the spiritual antiquity Alan held in his hands.

"Mr. Ulysses," asserted Alan quietly, "I really don't know what to say other than thank you. Thank you so much for this. We will treasure it all the days of our lives and with your permission, we'll make copies so that others may be inspired and encouraged by it too."

"Absolutely," acceded Ulysses. "You make as many copies as you like. I pray it will inspire millions to come to the Lord and others to return back to Him."

"Thank you for that, Mr. Ulysses," replied Annalisa with a smile. "We receive it as from our Lord."

A reverent stillness once again fell over the room. However, after a couple of minutes it was interrupted by Georges, who urged them to leave soon as it was getting late. He warned them that the dirt roads were much worse to navigate in the dark than they were in the daylight. So they exchanged hugs, and Alan prayed a short prayer. Then, the three set off from Ulysses' cabin into the light of the early mountain evening.

"Alan?" asked Annalisa leaning forward from the backseat of Georges car.

"Yeah?"

"Did you notice the . . ."

"Yes, I did," he interrupted, knowing where her question was headed.

"Notice what?" inquired Georges.

"The spelling of **rojoccian** on the poem," answered Annalisa pointing at the document still in Alan's hand.

"Yeah," quipped Alan. "In 1857, when the poem was written, **rojocci** was spelled **r-o-j-o-c-k-i**. It wasn't until after World War II that it was changed to the current spelling used today. This makes me quite suspicious that this may be a copy and not an original."

"But, of course it is an original," protested Georges. "It was handed down to Ulysses by our ancestor. Besides, look there, I can see the faded line indicating the letter 'k'. Hold it at an angle, Alan, and you can see it too."

"I think I see it, Georges. Look, Annalisa, do you see that faint vertical line by the second 'c' right there?" Alan held the framed document up at an angle for her to view from the backseat.

"Yes, I see it," she exclaimed. "And that 'c' looks more like a 'v' turned on its side."

"But, of course you can see it," bellowed Georges. "Of a truth, it is an original."

"That's a relief," sighed Alan. "It must have been the lighting in Ulysses' cabin. It was so dim I couldn't view the details clearly. But now in this sunlight, I can see it perfectly. Not that it matters that much. I mean, Preacher Daks still authored the poem, but now I believe this one we have here to be one of the original copies."

Annalisa flopped back in her seat with a chuckle as Georges started the car up the rutted dirt road to the top of the ridge. Once back on the smooth surface of the asphalt roadway, Alan asked Georges for Ulysses' address explaining that he and Annalisa would like to send him a thank you card in a couple of weeks to let him know what they have done with The **rojocci** Covenant.

"But he does not have an address," replied Georges.

"How does he get mail?" asked Annalisa.

"Mail? What mail? He does not get mail."

"How does he receive letters or packages? How does he pay his bills?" she inquired.

"Bills? He does not have any bills. What bills would he have? He has lived that way for so long. Before his wife died, the two of them took some money and opened an account at the bank. It was the first time they had ever possessed a bank account. They did not know what to do with it. They could not even write a check. I had to help them."

"Then why did they open an account?" asked Alan.

"Because the government required them to do it so they could pay their yearly taxes."

"Ulysses pays income taxes? On what?" inquired Annalisa.

"No, no, not income tax, but the property tax," replied Georges cranking around to see Annalisa in the back seat. "The many acres his cabin sits upon has increased in value since he has lived there. It is worth a lot of money."

"Well, if we write a letter for him, will you see that he receives it?" questioned Alan.

"But of course, I will hand deliver it myself. You have my word on it. Let me give you my address when we get back to your car at church, okay?"

"Yes, thank you, Georges," Alan voiced his agreement.

After a late breakfast the following morning, Alan and Annalisa loaded their luggage into the car and drove down the hill into the Sacramento Valley. Choosing to travel a different route back to the Bay Area, they took a diagonal course across the plain and entered the coastal mountains on a curvy, two lane road. They loved driving the smaller, less traveled roads, particularly once they were in the mountains.

Dropping down into the Napa Valley, they stopped at a delightful restaurant named The Rutherford Grill for an early dinner. The weather was warm but arid and very pleasant, so they chose to sit on the patio. Alan ordered a delicious salad with grilled chicken. Annalisa selected her favorite, a filet mignon grilled to perfection. Their conversation had all but ceased when, after taking a bite of chicken and dandelion greens, Alan posed a question.

"What time are your sister and Grenoble expecting us tonight?"

"Not until later this evening. I told her we would arrive sometime after dinner."

"Well, I was thinking since we haven't done anything, you know, touristy on this trip, what if we checked out the Wine Train?"

"Oh, Alan, that would be such a blast. Let's do it! Do you know when it departs and how long it takes for the round trip?"

"I think it lasts for about two hours."

Just then, they heard a low rumbling noise. In less than two minutes, the Wine Train lumbered past on its way back to the station in Napa.

"There it is, Alan. Let's go!"

"Wait a second, honey. We have to pay our bill first. Now, where is that waiter of ours?"

Passing the train on their way to Napa, Annalisa finally settled down, somewhat. She was so thrilled they were planning to do something just for fun that she could barely contain her excitement. At the station, they stood in the short ticket line. After a few minutes, they were boarding the train's dining car. A pleasant man dressed in fine attire seated them at a table next to a window. Within seconds a waiter appeared, handed them menus, and poured two glasses of water. Having already eaten dinner, they ordered a rather expensive delicacy entitled The Dessert Sampler Tray. It contained an assortment of six delectable after-meal delights including Annalisa's favorite: cheesecake with strawberry topping and chocolate sauce. She was in heaven from the first bite until the last.

As Alan watched her delight, he realized one of the most important things he loved about her—the fact that she was so totally different from him. She was cute, pretty, and sweet all wrapped up in a beautiful petite package. Her heavenly moments were times with their children or alone with a good book, especially while relaxing in a hot bubble bath. Alan on the other hand, considered heaven no closer than when he stood upon a high mountain, breathing in the cool, crisp air and basking in the deep warmth of the sun's rays. He was certain the scents of the mountain air had to be similar to the fragrance of the air the angels breathe in Heaven. Plus, the views from high atop a lofty peak were so vast and expansive, that it reminded him of his proper place in God's great universe.

Turning from this pleasantly panoramic place in his mind, Alan again focused his attention on his precious wife. The thoughts of her almost always made him smile. And gazing at her temporarily slumped back in her chair, after consuming the last bite of her favorite dessert, absolutely fascinated and delighted him all at the same time. He marveled at how she could take such rapturous pleasure in a piece of cheesecake. Just then, she opened her deep brown eyes and sat up in her seat. She smiled across the table, confirming her love for him. He returned the smile as his mind drifted back to when they had first met. He remembered they were so opposite that the attraction was immediate and magnetic. And the closer they were drawn to one another, the more the attraction was irresistible. Although very different, they were, he decided, a match made in Heaven.

The two hour train ride passed all too quickly. Before leaving Napa, they stopped at a winery to purchase a bottle of Merlot for Abigail and Grenoble. Then they headed for her sister's home, arriving shortly after sunset. Laughing out loud, Alan pointed first to the empty parking spot in the driveway, and then to Grenoble's car out by the curb. With much good natured ribbing from Annalisa, Alan decided to pull into the driveway. Knocking on the front door, they were greeted by a cheerfully, boisterous Grenoble followed by a beaming Abigail. After too many joyous hugs to count, they were finally invited into the living room where the three gals plopped down on the sofa, with Alan taking a seat across from them in the comfortable, overstuffed chair.

"Well, did you find what you were looking for, you guys?" asked an enthusiastic Grenoble.

"Actually, we did," boasted an excited Annalisa, slapping her palms on her knees and pounding her feet on the floor.

"Where is it? Do you have it with you?" asked Abigail.

"It's in my suitcase," replied Alan. "I wrapped it in layers of my clothes so it wouldn't get damaged."

"Damaged?" questioned Abigail.

"Yeah," confirmed Alan. "There is glass covering the parchment."

"Can you get it? I would like to see it?" begged Grenoble anxiously.

"Sure," nodded Alan somewhat surprised at her change of attitude toward him.

Returning from the front hallway, where he had left the suitcases, Alan gently handed the wood framed antiquity over to Grenoble, who was sitting between Abigail and Annalisa. The two friends read it silently as Annalisa eyed Alan. He once again had taken a seat in the enormous chair. Her curious look was one of bewilderment mixed with an expectation of joy. She then leaned over Grenoble, so she too could view the poem again. About a minute later, Abigail, with tears in her eyes, glanced across at Alan and then back to her sister.

"This is so beautiful, you guys. It brings tears to my eyes."

"Yes, it touches my heart deeply too," confessed Grenoble as she wept softly.

"Grenoble, please don't take offense, but I just have to ask you, why the change in your disposition? Did something happen while we were gone? I mean, we noticed you even parked your car in the street, so there would be a space for us in the driveway. What's going on?"

"Oh, I don't know," Grenoble hesitatingly replied.

"We talked about this, Grenoble," urged Abigail. "You said you would tell him if he asked."

"Well, it's nothing. Abby and I . . . we had a talk."

"A very open and honest talk," confessed Abigail.

"Yes, it was," agreed Grenoble. "I will admit that . . . it was way out there."

She glanced at Alan and then at the two sisters sitting on either side of her.

"Uh, look . . . after you left," began Grenoble, "I felt awful about the way I had treated you. I had truly expected you to argue back. But when you treated me so nicely, it made me feel really bad. Anyway, the day you left, Abigail and I had a deep conversation about things I know very little about. I mean, when you talked about how the spirit part of us communes with the Spirit of God, it kind of freaked me out. You know, it kind of scared me. So that's what we talked about. As we were finishing up, she reminded me of the chapters you mentioned we should read in the Bible. So Abigail got the Bible off the shelf, turned to the first chapter you suggested, the Gospel of John chapter one, then handed it to me, and walked out of the room."

"I went in my room and started praying," added Abigail.

"Yeah, and the most amazing thing started to happen," proclaimed Grenoble with a smile spreading across her face.

"What's that?" questioned Annalisa leaning forward.

"My heart began to melt. I mean, honest to God, the liquefying of a solid was occurring right inside of me. It was a miracle, an absolute miracle."

"Really?" inquired Alan with an expression of amazement.

"Yeah, yeah, it all happened when I got to the third chapter and Jesus and that guy Nicodemus were talking. As I was reading, it was like Nicodemus had my voice and Jesus had Alan's. I could actually hear Alan speaking the words I was reading. It was so unnerving, so convicting I knelt down and tried to pray. But I was really struggling. So I told God, you know, uh . . . Jesus, that if He wanted me saved, He needed to bring Abby into this living room. I told him I wasn't going to go get her. No, if He really wanted me to believe in Him, He needed to perform this little miracle for me."

Both Alan and Annalisa were staring at Grenoble with mouths agape. Her eyes sparkled as she spoke, her face was as radiant as if a brilliant light were shining upon it. Abigail sat next to her smiling brightly with tears streaming down her cheeks.

"So just as I finished saying that to the Lord Jesus," continued Grenoble, "you know what happened?"

"What?" whispered Annalisa.

"I felt a hand on my shoulder. I started trembling. I knew who it was. It was Abby, and she didn't say a word. She just knelt down beside me and prayed for me. When she was done, she prayed with me to receive the Lord into my heart. It was the happiest and most precious moment of my life. I literally felt all the cares and hurts I have carried for so long melt away and disappear."

At this point, Alan sprang up and gave Grenoble a huge hug. Soon the two sisters joined in. There were smiles, tears, hugs, and kisses for everyone, including Alan. It was a memorable evening they would speak of for years to come. In fact, three days later on the flight home it was practically their only topic of conversation.

"Can you believe how good our God is, honey?" marveled Alan slowly shaking his head.

"Yes, He is so very gracious and incredibly kind to love a woman who was so clearly, at least initially, uninterested and even antagonistic toward Him. And look at her now, it's like she isn't even the same person. It's amazing, absolutely amazing."

"I agree and I'm trying to keep my mind on that joyous news instead of what may await us at home."

"What do you mean, Alan?"

"Well, I must admit, the closer we get to landing in Mississippi, the more I feel a heaviness creeping in. I wonder how the church is doing."

"Oh, I'm sure everything is fine. Doc or one of the elders would have called if anything major had happened. I wouldn't be concerned. Let's just rejoice in our wonderful news—Grenoble was lost and now she is found!"

"Thanks for that, honey. That's just what I needed to hear."

The weary travelers arrived home very late that evening. After unpacking, they fell straight into bed. Waking up late, they quickly had a bite to eat and then headed, jet lag and all, over to Willy and Bertha's coffee shop to join the Bible study. As soon as Bertha saw them enter, she jumped up and fixed their favorite morning beverages. There were hugs all around and stories to tell on both sides. As the Bible study adjourned, somewhat later than normal, Willy asked if he could have a private word with Alan.

"Sure my brother, what's up?" asked Alan.

"Well," replied Willy with a sheepish grin. "We had a little problem at church last Sunday."

-sixteen-

Whatever fond thoughts Alan had been entertaining about returning to his responsibilities at church flew right out the coffee shop door, and an extreme heaviness came rushing in to take its place. The burden got heavier and heavier as Willy began to explain what had happened in the morning service four days earlier. Willy described how Doc had visited the coffee shop one morning to ask him to bring a few men over to the church that Saturday afternoon. When Willy had arrived with two of his friends, he found Doc and Seb removing the pews from their rows and arranging them in a circle.

"Now, I know you didn't want them pews moved, Alan, so I tell Mr. Doc that he and that other elder shouldn't be doing that. He say that them elders had all agreed, and that you would be happy with it too. I wasn't too excited about helping them, but when Beldon and Jimmy jumped in I figured I better help with it too or they going to think I be trying to stir something up."

"That's okay, Willy. You did the right thing. I'll have a talk with Doc and see what's going on. Don't worry about it, okay?"

"Oh, I ain't too worried about it, Alan. But before you go sitting down with Mr. Doc, maybe you should hear what else happened."

"There's more?"

"Oh, yes, sir. And it ain't good neither."

Alan moved a bit closer and spoke in a softer tone. "What else happened, Willy?"

"Well, sir, come Sunday morning, everyone started filing into the service, and they see them pews moved around and all. Some of them folks don't like they pew moved, you know what I saying, Alan?"

"Oh yeah, I hear you, my brother."

"So before we even commenced to singing, a couple of them men, sorry I don't know they names we haven't been attending long enough for me and Bertha to get acquainted with everyone you understand? Well, anyway, they start complaining and then another joined in and then another. It got right nasty. And before you know it, about half the church done up and walked out."

"What?!"

"Yes, sir. Then Mr. Doc got up and say a little prayer and dismissed us all that was left there standing. Alan, we still going to hold services at that church or do me, Bertha, and our kin need to find us another church?"

"No, no, don't worry about that, Willy. Let me talk with Doc and Seb. I'll see what's going on. We'll work this out, okay?"

"Okay, if you say so."

Turning to head out the door, Alan motioned to Annalisa that he was ready to leave. Then, swinging back around, he patted Willy on the shoulder. "Thanks for telling me, Willy. I really appreciate it, my brother."

"Sure enough, Alan. Hope everything turn out alright."

"It will. Nothing surprises God. He already knows all about this."

As soon as they got in the car and well out of sight of the coffee shop, Alan told Annalisa all that Willy had reported to him. She was shocked with the response of the congregation and asked if he knew who among the church had actually left the service. Not knowing anything other than the few details Willy had presented, Alan confessed to her that he had sensed something might be wrong last Saturday when they drove up the hill into Paradise, California.

"What do you mean, honey?" she asked as he closed the front door to their cozy home.

"Well, I wasn't sure at the time, but I was feeling uneasy about something at the church. I just didn't know what. But according to Willy, that was the same day Doc had them move the pews around in the sanctuary."

"So what's the problem? You mentioned to me, more than once, you wanted to do something like that."

"Yeah, I know. We had even discussed it in a couple of our elders' meetings. We had been trying to discern if the various components of what we had been doing at church were in line with the Scriptures. We had come to the conclusion that many of the things we do were being done more out of tradition than from a New Testament church model. One of those things was sitting in a sanctuary in a configuration that was set up like the seats in a theater."

"I'm not sure I understand, Alan."

"I don't believe you can defend a posture of passivity for a congregation using the New Testament as your basis. It's just not in the Scriptures, honey."

"So that's why you wanted to move the pews into a circle?"

"Well, kind of . . . uh, yes, I guess so. You see, in the New Testament every member of the body has an active role. There isn't a place for a complacent believer. It was my hope that by moving the pews out of a non-active, entertain-me format and into a participatory focused arrangement, folks would be encouraged to take more initiative in their roles as members of the body of Christ and thereby foster an environment that is more conducive to an active and growing faith."

"Then why are you so concerned that they moved the pews?" probed Annalisa.

"Because I sense something is afoul."

"What are you talking about?"

"Remember the day I went over to the church to move the pews?

Annalisa nodded.

"Well, as you know, I didn't move them. Do you remember why?"

"Yes, you mentioned something to me about how you thought it wasn't God's timing."

"That's right, honey. And based on the evidence that half the church walked out of the service the Sunday after they had moved the pews into a circle, I think God was telling me to hold off on shifting things around for good reason."

"Why do you think He wanted you to wait?" she inquired.

"I'm not sure. Maybe so He would have a chance to prepare the hearts of the people for something He knew would upset many of them."

"Wow, really, Alan?"

"Yes. Just think of the time before we got engaged. Or the couple of years before Roger asked us for our blessing to marry Julie. Timing was and always is critical in God's economy. Sometimes He indicates moving forward in faith. But in other circumstances, waiting is what's needed. Often we've found He stretches us like the wine skins of old. That's why He says it is so important to be like a new wine skin,[1] to always be pliable, so we are able to be stretched without cracking. At times, He calls us forward, other times He says wait. Regardless, timing is most important to Him, and I'm fairly certain Doc didn't consider this when he decided to rearrange the sanctuary."

"You really don't think so?"

"No, I don't. But did he do it out of ignorance or out of malice? That's my biggest concern."

Alan and Annalisa spent some time in prayer together. Then he sat down with the Scriptures to listen for the Lord's counsel. Later that afternoon, he drove over to the church and walked into the sanctuary. He was quite pleased with what he found. For the most part, everything was arranged the same way he would have chosen to configure it himself. He tried several different locations around the circle and got comfortable with the whole shift in the seating. At one point, he was so delighted that he broke out in laughter.

Nearly thirty minutes had passed when he dropped down to his knees and asked the Lord for a supernatural ability to handle whatever was coming just around the next corner. As he was finishing up, his phone rang. It was Jake, one of the church elders. Once he welcomed Alan back home, he told him all that had happened Sunday, and how he hadn't known anything of it until he walked through the doors that particular morning. Jake further stated that he had been told by another elder that Doc had taken it solely upon himself to change the seating arrangement.

Back at home, while having dinner with Annalisa, the phone rang again. This call was from yet another elder. Essentially, his assessment of the situation lined up with Jake's. Now that Alan had three witnesses, he knew it was time to telephone Doc, who strangely enough had not contacted Alan. Before he picked up the phone, Annalisa confessed that she had fielded seven phone calls that afternoon from families in the church wanting to know what was going on. She had waited to tell him because she didn't want to burden him, at least not until he had finished dinner.

"What a mess!" he bellowed. "What a huge mess and all over a seating arrangement. Really?! I mean, can the enemy really destroy a church over how its pews are arranged? Is our level of love and commitment to one another based upon whether we stare at the back of someone's head or view him face to face?"

"I'm sure God's got it all in control, honey."

"Yes, I know He does. But I may be the one He uses to fix it. And that ain't going to be no fun walk in the woods," he complained in a loud voice using his best imitation of a Mississippi accent.

Waiting until after he had calmed down considerably, Alan picked up the phone at five minutes after eight o'clock and called Doc's number.

"Hey, Doc, how you doing this evening, my brother?"

"Oh, hey, Alan. Doing pretty good. How was your trip?"

"Amazing trip. Wait until you see what we brought back with us."

"Yeah?"

"Yeah, it's a beautiful piece of work."

"That's nice, Alan."

"Yeah, real nice. Hey, Doc, I heard it got a little exciting at church this past Sunday?"

"Uh, yeah, something was kind of happening there."

"Yeah, that's what I heard too. What say you and I get together tomorrow and talk about it for a few minutes, okay?"

"Uh, tomorrow? Uh . . . I don't really have any time tomorrow."

"Okay, how about tomorrow evening. You name the time and the place, and I'll be there."

"Uh . . . well, let me look at my schedule here . . ."

"Doc," Alan interrupted using a resolute tone. "We need to talk, and we need to talk now."

"Uh, okay . . . I guess I could meet you before my first appointment in the morning. Let's say about seven thirty."

"Okay, good. At the church work for you, Doc?"

"Yes, seven thirty at the church is fine."

"Great. See you then, my brother."

As he hung up the kitchen telephone, Alan looked down at the dull linoleum floor and shook his head once. Then he gazed out the window, deep in thought.

"Well," he whispered to himself. "This should be interesting."

Annalisa's mouth was hanging wide open when Alan entered the living room. He walked across the shiny hardwood floor and sat down next to her on the sofa. Her eyes had followed him all the way from the kitchen to the sofa. He glanced in her direction and noticed for the first time her gaping, silent orifice.

"What, honey?" he inquired with a scrunched up face.

"Uh . . . you were incredibly nice to him, dear."

"Why wouldn't I be?"

"Well, I thought you said he may have, you know, sabotaged the church."

"He may well have, my love. But I don't know that for a fact. So until I know, there's no need to be nasty. I mean, I was upset, but then I realized God is more than able to get to the bottom of this situation."

"Good for you, Alan."

"Thanks. I also learned from being an employer all those years, there's never a reason to be accusatory or abusive. The truth almost always comes out one way or another. Let's see what our meeting tomorrow morning brings."

Arriving at the church, Alan chose to wait for Doc in the sanctuary. It was a lesson he learned long ago—never be the last one to arrive at an important meeting. Entering several minutes late, Doc apologized as he sat down several feet away from Alan. They exchanged polite greetings and cordial questions about their families before the conversation got around to the arrangement of the room in which they were seated. Alan quizzed Doc thoroughly yet with courtesy. Once Alan had determined that Doc had indeed taken the initiative to move the pews into a circle, he then asked Doc why he had done it.

"Well, we had discussed it in the elders' meeting, so I didn't think it wouldn't be a problem."

"We had decided in the meeting to hold off on it, remember?" Alan firmly jogged Doc's selective memory.

"Yes, I do recall something like that. But I thought this was a good idea, and frankly so did Seb. So like it or not, we did it."

"Doc, what would make you think that it was a good idea, when the leadership, of which you are a part, agreed to wait?"

"Look, Alan, you may think you run this church, but you don't the elders do," snapped Doc, who was obviously indignant that Alan would question his authority. "And further, I have been an elder longer than anyone on the board. How long have you been here, a year? You shouldn't even be an elder, and if it weren't for old Teddy, God rest his soul, I dare say you wouldn't be one!"

"Doc, what does your decision to move these pews have to do with me?"

"You're the one who came in here with all your highfalutin ideas. How you thought the church wasn't run right and all. Yeah, you, Alan, telling old Teddy that your way is better than what we've been doing here for generations. It's your fault, Alan Browne. You're the reason these pews are moved around like this, and I wanted all the church to know exactly what you're planning to do around here!" accused Doc with anger and resentment oozing out of every word.

"Oh, that's not good, Doc," Alan replied softly. "You haven't hurt me, my brother. You've hurt the church. The church isn't mine. It's the Lord's, and He has some pretty strong feelings toward her."

"Yeah, what's that supposed to mean?" demanded Doc with a sneer.

"What I'm trying to say is this: that in an effort to cause difficulty for me, you have unknowingly created a situation that may very well cause the church you love some major problems."

"If you believe that kind of thing," smirked Doc.

"Listen to me, Doc. I'm trying to appeal to your conscience. I'm trying to reason with your sense of right and wrong. Do you really believe in your heart of hearts that what you did was right?"

"Sure, why not?"

"Do you think God would be pleased with your actions and, more importantly, your attitude? I mean, be honest here, Doc. If your son did something like this would you be proud of him?"

Sitting quietly, Doc stared across the sanctuary with a blank look on his face. Alan prayed silently while glancing at Doc every few seconds. Suddenly, Doc stood up and headed for the door. He placed one hand upon it, pushed it open, and abruptly stopped. He gazed down at the floor for several seconds. Then he allowed the door to gradually close. He stood there stone still. From his pew, Alan watched and prayed. Doc, with one palm still pressed against the door, began to slowly shake his head. Turning toward Alan, he sauntered back across the sanctuary floor.

"Alan, you're right," he sighed. "What I did was wrong, and I did it with malicious intent toward you. I'm very sorry. I don't have any good reason other than I was getting really frustrated with the way things were going around here. Frankly, you make me mad, Alan. You really do."

Alan nodded his head acknowledging what Doc was expressing.

"I mean, my family and me, we've been attending this church for decades. Back in the 1950s, my own father was one of the founding fathers who purchased this land and built this building. Now you come in here stirring things up. Why can't you just leave well enough alone?"

Tears were brimming in Doc's eyes. Alan shifted in his seat, ready to respond to Doc's question.

"Listen, Alan," Doc continued, fearful that Alan was going to say something to put him in his place. "I do apologize for what I did, but not for my feelings about what you're doing in this church. I'm sorry. I really am, but I think what you're doing is wrong."

"Okay, Doc, I can appreciate that."

"Well, okay then." Doc stood and thrust out his hand toward Alan, who was still seated. "You'll have my letter of resignation in the morning. I won't cause any further trouble. I hereby resign my eldership."

"Not accepted," replied Alan in a solemn tone.

"What?"

"I'm not accepting your resignation. Look, Doc, who can be more helpful fixing this than an elder who loves this body of believers as much as you do? You are the perfect person to begin putting this church back together. So, no, your resignation is not accepted."

"Uh, Alan, I don't know what to say," he replied with a sheepish grin.

"Well, the first thing we need to do is to call an elder meeting and get this train back on its tracks."

"What are you thinking to do?" inquired Doc with a tone that clearly indicated he wasn't open to any further change.

"I don't have any idea but God does, and He will make it clear if we allow Him to share His counsel with us. But nothing good is going to come out of quitting. We're great allies you and me. We just need to figure out how to work together."

Springing up, Alan gave Doc a hug. Then, the two men walked out, agreeing to set an elders' meeting as soon as possible. The very next evening, the six elders gathered at the church to discuss the crisis. To his credit, Doc spoke up on his own initiative and asked for the forgiveness of the other men. Shortly after, Seb confessed to his part in the incident. What followed was a sweet time of fellowship, prayer, and recommitment by each elder to do his utmost to heal the wounds in their church. Alan asked for ideas and was slightly disappointed to receive only suggestions for more social activities. One was for a pot luck picnic, another for a bowling league, and yet another was for something they called a weekly Bunko game.

Trying to promote an atmosphere of healing, Alan was concerned with events that were based on competition. "In every competition half the participants lose. And not everyone enjoys losing," he reminded them.

The elders decided on a pot luck picnic with a friendly softball game where no one would be allowed to keep score. Alan, however, contemplated how he could promote a more spiritual focus in his messages each Sunday. Adjourning the meeting earlier than normal, Alan headed home with a light and joyful heart. He sat down on the sofa next to Annalisa, who was quite curious as to how everyone had gotten along at the meeting.

"It was amazing, honey. I really think the Lord is helping us work through this. First Doc, then Seb, then just about everyone else confessed something to the group. It was a wonderful time of cleansing, healing, and fellowship."

"Oh, I'm so glad, Alan."

"Yeah, me too," he admitted with a nod. "This Sunday, we're going to announce a pot luck picnic. The guys think some social events would be a good idea to promote unity. I'm leaning toward going a little deeper spiritually in the sermons."

"What was decided about the pews?"

"That's an interesting topic. It was batted around the table like a ping pong ball in the World Table Tennis Championships."

"What?!" laughed Annalisa.

"Yeah, I just thought that one up," chuckled Alan. "Funny thing . . . it was just like that at the meeting. Ideas being slapped back and forth all evening."

"Well . . . what was decided about the seating arrangement?" she prompted with a smile.

"We're going to leave a smaller circle of pews up front. Then toward the back we'll have four rows on either side of the main aisle facing forward. I think it may solve the problem. At least it's a step in the right direction. Doc actually came up with the idea."

"Wow, really? Maybe it was a good idea to forgive and forget, honey."

"Yeah, I think that's always a good idea."

"Now, guess what I did to help?" she smiled sweetly at Alan.

"Uh . . . called all the ladies and asked them to pray?"

"Well, come to think of it, I actually did call several of the gals and suggested it would be good if we all prayed for God's love, peace, and wisdom to be evident during the meeting. I had an interesting talk with Bertha too. I dropped by the coffee shop this afternoon about an hour before she closed up."

"Yeah? Are they doing alright?"

"Oh yeah, they're doing great."

"Why do you say it like that, honey?"

"Because I showed her The **rojoccian** Covenant. I had a couple dozen copies printed along with a short biographical paragraph I wrote regarding Preacher Daks and how God led us to discover the document. When Bertha read it, her heart was deeply touched right then and there. She took her copy and hung it in the front window of the coffee shop for all to see."

"She did what?"

-seventeen-

While leading the Bible study at the coffee shop the next morning, Alan was surprised to see that most everyone who came through the front door stopped and took the time to read The **rojoccian** Covenant. Judging by their thoughtful expressions, it appeared to him that the insightful, old poem was causing quite a stir. It was gratifying to see how the Lord was using the simple words written by a humble man long ago, to affect so many lives today. One such person, a businessman known for his harsh dealings with others, broke down that morning while reading it. Unfortunately, he hurried off before Alan finished the lesson and had a chance to greet him. However, to everyone's delight, he and his entire family entered the sanctuary the following Sunday.

Two days later, as the Bible study was concluding, Bertha leaned over to Annalisa and asked if she had any more copies available. She went on to explain that yesterday afternoon the owner of the dry cleaners, several doors down, came in for a cup of coffee. Upon reading the poem, tears began flowing down her cheeks. After composing herself, she asked if Bertha had an extra copy, so she could display one in her establishment too. Annalisa provided Bertha with enough copies to hand out to anyone who might be interested. Before the week was out, there were more than a dozen businesses that had posted The **rojoccian** Covenant in a prominent location.

Over the next few months, something extraordinary began happening at the church. Little by little, families were coming back and, even more surprising, new families began attending as well. Doc informed Alan that this was highly unusual. Although he wasn't positive, Doc was fairly certain it had been over a year since a new family had visited their church. Challenging the congregation from week to week, Alan continued presenting messages with deep spiritual content. He wasn't sure why, but the town of Wiggins seemed to be buzzing; and it appeared the church had something to do with it.

One Saturday morning, as he was pondering all that was occurring in the town and in their church, Alan sat down at the kitchen table to write a letter to Ulysses Champion. He again thanked the kind old saint for his generous gift, the ancient copy of The **rojoccian** Covenant. Then he explained in detail all that was happening in their town in general, and in their church in particular. At one point, Alan walked across the living room, took the framed document off the wall, and carried it back to the kitchen table. He read it over and over, asking the Lord to reveal to him what it was that was so special about this little poem.

"Lord, why does it touch the hearts of so many people? What is it that connects with something deep within each person?"

Waiting expectantly, Alan reined in his racing thoughts, slowing them from a gallop to a trot and then to a walk.

Finally, a hushed calm rested upon his mind. Listening, as he had learned to do years ago when hunkering down in a coastal cottage during Hurricane Opal, Alan sensed the Lord's presence. After several minutes, a gentle thought came into his mind.

"It speaks of My kingdom—**The kingdom within you**."

Alan continued to listen but was having some difficulty keeping his thoughts at bay. Thoughts that were louder and more demanding than the soft voice of the Holy Spirit. After several minutes of settling down, he once again asked the Lord for clarification.

"Please, Lord, what do you mean?"

"It's a spiritual kingdom. It does not consist of material things but of righteousness, peace, joy,[1] and the fruit of the Holy Spirit in your life. Qualities like love, faith, goodness, gentleness, patience, and many others.[2]"

"Hmmm . . ." thought Alan aloud as he pondered the depth of what he was sensing in his spirit. Glancing down at the written words of the Native American Christian Missionary, who died some hundred and fifty years ago, he slowly read it through again.

"Oh, I think I see it now, Lord. Preacher Daks' writings reveal the work You are doing in each heart. The first stanza speaks of our surrender to You. The second, indicates trust. The third, shows the power of hope. The next stanza defines the need for patient endurance. Then the fifth, declares love, Your love for us. Finally, the last stanza is all about faith."

Alan sat at the kitchen table with tears in his eyes and a smile on his face as the tide of this revelation ebbed upon the shores of his mind.

"Yes, there's your kingdom within: Surrender, Trust, Hope, Patience, Love, and Faith. This explains why the words Preacher Daks penned touch folks in such a visceral way. Each quatrain speaks to a deep issue of the heart. They are heart issues and major themes in the Bible."

Holding the wood framed document in his hands, Alan gazed out the window. He was rather pleased with this new revelation. Just then, another thought dawned upon his mind.

"Who gave Preacher Daks the ideas to write upon the paper?"

"You did, of course, Lord," whispered Alan.

"I am Spirit, and those who worship Me, must worship Me in spirit and in truth."[3]

"Thank you, Lord. I appreciate what You are saying. I will endeavor to live my life by Your truth and by the leading of Your Spirit."

"My Spirit spoke to Preacher Daks' spirit, and he wrote down what he perceived. When another person reads those words, My Spirit can speak to their spirit."[4]

"Oh, I get it now, Lord. It touches deep down where few other things do. So it is a particularly sensitive place. Thank you for that insight, my dear Father."

It was just like Betsy Taft had told him long ago; the spiritual side of life controls all other aspects of our time here on earth. But it is invisible and, therefore, difficult to see how it functions, until you see the change in a person's heart, just like the tough businessman who was deeply moved while reading The **rojoccian** Covenant. Afterward, his relationships with his children were renewed and his marriage, which had been cold and distant because of years of neglect and bitterness, experienced a miraculous healing. All of this was outward physical evidence of a spiritual transformation that had taken place within him.

Alan also remembered old A-Dub's advice given decades ago before he and Annalisa were even thinking of marriage. The wise gentleman had expressed, in his direct manner, that it was not possible for Alan to compartmentalize his life. What he said and what he did, especially when no one was around, revealed who he really was. He also told him he couldn't act one way at church, another way at home, and a different way at work or he would just be deceiving himself. If Alan was going to behave like a Christian at church, then he should act like it at home too. And if he was spiritual in those two places, then he better be spiritual at work as well.

"The spiritual influences all others areas," A-Dub had declared.

Having become convinced of this very principle, Alan understood more clearly why Preacher Daks' words, inspired by the Holy Spirit, had the power to touch lives on a deeper level. It was as if Spirit was speaking with spirit.

Leaning back in his chair, with a contented expression on his face and an abundance of gratitude in his heart, Alan lifted his hands and began softly singing a hymn to God. Finishing the song, he silently basked in the presence of the Lord. Startled by a loud knock on the front door, Alan, who was balanced on the two rear legs of the chair, slipped backwards and crashed to the floor. With his head now pressed up against the wall behind him, he was temporarily trapped in a laid back position, similar to an astronaut in his capsule ready for lift-off. After wriggling from side to side, he was able to free himself and quickly made his way to the front door just as the person on the other side knocked for the third time. Reaching for the knob, he swung the door wide open.

"Surprise!" shouted the chorus from the front porch.

Pushing the wooden screened door out of the way, Alan bounded over the threshold and threw his arms around Julie and Roger. "You're right!" agreed Alan with a laugh. "This is a surprise, a wonderful surprise!"

Alan invited them in and poured the three of them some iced tea. He expressed with delight how thrilled their Mom was going to be to see them.

"Oh, we already saw her, Dad," professed Julie just before taking a swig of her chilled beverage.

"You did? Where?"

"We dropped by the church on the way in," explained Roger. "There were a couple dozen cars there. The doors were unlocked, so we walked on in. Man, were we surprised to see about thirty women in the sanctuary praying."

"Yeah," exclaimed Julie. "And who came up with that seating arrangement? That's genius, Dad, no kidding."

"A couple of the men at church did. Well, really it was the Lord. It was His idea."

"I would have thought that was you, Dad," Julie chuckled. "That has you written all over it. You're always coming up with creative alternatives like that."

"Nope, I can't take credit for anything good around here, only the boo-boos," he laughed. "I guess you guys shocked Mom."

"Oh, yeah, she gave out a little yelp, slapped her hand over her mouth, and then ran over toward us, almost knocking us down with her hug," voiced Julie, who, with a laugh, threw herself into her father's arms, mimicking her mother's hug.

"How long can you guys stay?"

"Well, if it's okay, about five days," replied Julie.

"Absolutely," urged Alan. "We'll get the spare room set up for you."

"Oh, no, we don't want to impose. We can stay out at the hotel on the highway."

"No, we won't hear of it. We have plenty of room."

"Uh, Dad?" asked Roger quietly. "I would really like to see The **rojoccian** Covenant. I've heard so much about it. Do you have the poem here?"

"Yeah, sure, hang on just a second, Roger."

Coming back into the living room from the kitchen, Alan handed the wood framed document to Roger, who was sitting next to Julie on the sofa. The two of them read it silently. Then Julie, with tears in her eyes, looked up at her father.

"This is so beautiful."

"Yes, I would have to agree. It is really special."

"It sure is," agreed Roger without looking up.

"Why do you think so?" asked Alan. "I'm really curious why it affects folks the way it does."

"I think for me," responded Julie, once again looking down at the framed paper, "it speaks of a journey. An adventure, not without its difficulties, that a lone person, yet invisibly supported by those who care for him, must travel.

As I read it, I felt the 'person' was actually me. These words encourage me to never give up, to never quit, no matter how hard the way seems. Finally, they speak of love, God's love for each and every one of us, but especially for me. They convey how much He cares for me and if I will only persevere to the end, I will see His tapestry woven within the very fabric of my life."

Both Alan and Roger stared at Julie with mouths agape. Alan was shocked that someone he had raised could be this perceptive and intuitive. Roger was also amazed his young bride was such a spiritually sensitive woman. Suddenly, he felt somewhat threatened by her insight.

"Wow, hon, where did you get that from?" inquired Roger with a sheepish grin on his face.

"Oh, I don't know. I just thought that was what it meant. That's all."

"Get used to it, Roger," chuckled Alan. "Her mother is precisely the same way. It used to astonish me when she would come up with some of the things she'd say. But I have come to realize it's all part and parcel of being married. I have come to really appreciate her insights. They are absolutely amazing and have sometimes warned me of hazards in the road ahead."

Roger let out a partial sigh and then went back to reading The **rojoccian** Covenant. Julie winked at her father, which made him smile even broader.

That afternoon when Annalisa arrived home, the four of them talked of things concerning Roger and Julie. In particular, Roger and Julie shared how they wanted to live their lives for the Lord. Roger explained that he believed he was called to the ministry. Along those lines, Alan asked him some very pointed questions. Alan also expressed that what they had been experimenting with here in Wiggins, was more of a Biblical model. He perceived that Roger's vision of ministry was askew and lacking understanding. His view of getting up in front of a group of people each week wasn't quite the entire ministry ball of wax. Although he recognized Roger's sincerity, he wasn't convinced his son-in-law was ready to handle such a demanding responsibility.

After dinner, the four settled down in the living room. Before picking up the conversation where they had left it, Julie handed her parents a small, gift wrapped box.

"What's this?" questioned her mother.

"Oh, just a little something we thought the two of you would enjoy," suggested Julie, struggling to hold back a smile.

Brimming with curiosity, Annalisa, with Alan by her side, unwrapped the little box. She lifted the lid and unfolded the tissue paper to find a peculiar looking black and white photo.

"What's that?" asked Alan, straining to view the photo.

"Not what, but who?" Julie emphasized, wearing a huge smile.

"Who? Are you serious?!" shrieked Annalisa. She jumped up from the sofa and began doing a high-stepping version of her happy dance. "Is it a boy or a girl?"

"Whoa!" blurted Alan. "You mean to tell me I'm going to be a grandpa?"

"Yes, Dad, that's what we're telling you, and we think it's a girl."

"Oh my living soul, I can't believe this," shouted Annalisa as she dashed across the room and threw her arms around Julie and Roger. Alan immediately followed suit.

"So, how far along are you? Have you selected any names yet? Are you having any morning sickness? How are . . ."

"Mom," interjected Julie. "Let me answer the first question before you go bonkers with fifty more, okay?"

Annalisa nodded her head with a radiant smile on her face. "Well?"

"I'm about thirteen weeks along. I had a couple of minor issues early on, but the doctor says everything is right on track. We wanted to tell you face to face, but I had some intense morning sickness which made it difficult to travel until now. I'm feeling much better this week though."

"So, you're okay?" breathed Annalisa.

"Yeah, Mom, everything is fine, and we're really excited. We've been thinking of naming her after Roger's mother."

"Gertrude?" asked Annalisa, desperately trying to conceal the somewhat critical thoughts flitting through her mind.

"No, Mom. We're considering his mother's middle name. It was Grace. And if it's okay with you, we want her middle name to be the same as your middle name."

"Grace Michele Ballinger," Annalisa proudly announced. "I just love that, you two. It's absolutely precious. Don't you agree, Alan?"

"I love it, and what a wonderful tribute to your mother, Roger."

"Yes, I was really touched when Julie suggested it. As you know, my mom meant the world to me, and now we'll have a little one to carry on her legacy."

Alan placed his hand on his daughter's head and began to pray a blessing upon her, Roger, and the little one in Julie's womb. Roger and Annalisa quickly laid their hands on Julie as well. When they had finished, Alan had a suggestion.

"We need to have a dinner out to celebrate. What say Mom and I take you two down to Gulfport tomorrow night for some seafood?"

"That sounds wonderful, Dad," exclaimed Roger, patting his father-in-law on the back.

"Sounds good to me, too," agreed Julie. "However, I need to be careful with what I eat. It appears that some foods were the source of my morning sickness."

"Don't worry, my little pregnant mama, we'll stay away from Cajun," smiled Annalisa who glanced at Alan for confirmation.

"Works for me," he quipped.

The very next morning Alan and Roger sat on the front porch sipping coffee while discussing all things concerning ministry. Roger had a lot of questions, and Alan felt it very important that Roger know the realities of living a life of ministry. Roger's first question was concerning spiritual warfare.

"It's a real fight, son," responded Alan with a sober tone. "But you're not using your fists, so to speak, you're using your words, your thoughts, and your spiritual weapons. It's a battle which employs every bit of your faith. Because it's a faith fight.[5] Our foe is not powerful, but he is very cunning. Although at times, it may seem like we're battling against stubborn, hard hearted people, we're not. They're just susceptible to the enemy's suggestions, ideas, and images. We don't wrestle against flesh and blood.[6] Oh no, it's not people. It's our relentless adversary. He's always pressing and needling everyone. And if we don't resist him, he'll push even harder. Furthermore, if someone is unable to see through the fog of war and recognize, in a very practical sense, who it is they are really fighting, then he's beat them already. The result is that they usually give up the faith fight feeling defeated and discouraged. Do you understand, son?"

"Ummm . . . I'm not quite sure," mumbled Roger with a shrug.

"That's okay. Let me see if I can explain it a bit clearer. Let's say you and a friend are having a disagreement about something. Perhaps he's causing you some discomfort or difficulty. Over time, you begin to perceive him as an enemy and several unfortunate circumstances between you only seem to confirm your warped opinion. Before long, there is a division with others taking sides as well. He's pulling on the horns, you're pulling on the tail, and all the while the wretched enemy is milking it for all it's worth by invisibly manipulating all. But if you don't have eyes to see, you are convinced it is the other person's fault, and the minor rift between brothers becomes a gaping chasm. In that case, the enemy won and you both were defeated. In fact, everyone involved lost as well."

"Wow, I never thought of it like that before."

"Look, son, leadership is not for the young believer. It's for those who are more mature; those who have the scars of battle and have lived to show others the way to victory; those who, because of practice, have their senses trained to discern good and evil.[7] Now that's only my opinion, but if you search the Scriptures, I think you'll find the overall principle to be evident."

"What do you mean, Dad?"

"I mean, that nasty, evil one, has no ethics, no morals, no sportsmanship. Plus, he lies, cheats, steals, and destroys. He looks for the chink in your armor, and that's where he'll strike. He is ruthless and doesn't have one minuscule amount of compassion. He couldn't care less if you think what he has done isn't fair because he's cheating anyway and refuses to play by any rules. All he wants to do is destroy you, and he'll laugh at you as your ship is going down, all the while piling more weighty burdens on you so you sink faster."

"What do you mean chinks in my armor?" inquired Roger leaning forward.

"He attacks you where you are most vulnerable. Let's say you struggle with being prideful or perhaps lust has been an issue for you. He'll see to it that you have plenty of opportunities to express both."

"But suppose I've worked through those issues, and they aren't really a problem for me. Couldn't I be in the ministry then?"

"Roger, the Scriptures say we all stumble in many ways.[8] I'm not telling you to avoid a life in the ministry. We are all ministers. I'm just letting you know what to expect. And in my opinion, a younger man is so much more vulnerable to the enemy's assault, than one who has a whole backpack full of experience. Don't get me wrong, you don't have to be in church leadership to be the recipient of his arrows of deception. Every believer is guaranteed in the Scriptures to be in the fight. But when you're in leadership, the whole process is on display for all to see, like a movie being shown on the big screen for everyone to watch and comment on."

"I think I'm getting a clearer picture here. But David was a young man when he defeated Goliath."[9]

"That's true. But what many Christians don't realize is that later David was almost killed by several of Goliath's relatives. David had to be rescued by his friends, who were themselves mighty warriors.[10] In fact, Roger, this brings up a very important point that I would like you to always remember—there are no lone rangers in the Body of Christ. Whether you are a pastor or not, we Christians are all in this together. You are not separate from your congregation. We are members one with another. Jesus Christ is the Head, and we are all equal members of His body. I have come to see, by personal experience, His wisdom in establishing the church with Him as the Head. He has also given us seven spiritual gifts which advise and implement His directives to His people. These make for a functioning expression of His will. However, those who are endowed with these gifts are not holding positions but are working as equal members within the whole group."

"You mean, like we did in our church in Pensacola?"

"Yes, that's exactly right. Except in Pensacola we adopted this out of need because we found ourselves without a pastor. Here in Wiggins we didn't have to do it out of necessity. So it's been more of a prolonged process. But yes, seven compared to one against our adversary gives us much better odds in this spiritual fight."

"Okay, I understand . . . I think," chuckled Roger.

"Look, son, I love you with my whole heart. You're not just a son-in-law to me. You're my son. You and Julie are precious as are our other children. So what I say to you, I say from a heart of love, not to discourage you but rather to make you aware of the severity of the battle. Not only are you young, with little experience in this fight, but you have a young wife, a young marriage, and a young child on the way. These are all vulnerabilities, which the wretched enemy will take full advantage of."

"Wow, Dad, I didn't even think about that."

"Sure, it's similar to when you go to purchase a home for your family. You don't buy it because it's pretty or because you like the colors . . . well, not entirely anyway. But as you are considering the new house, you think through as many scenarios as possible. Perhaps you notice there's a creek along the back fence that floods on occasion, or maybe there are several large trees that could fall on the home in a strong wind. Then, when you go inside you may discover the HVAC system is flawed, and the appliances are worn out. These are things you contemplate because you want to make a wise decision, not just for yourself, but for your wife and children too."

"Hmmm . . . that's a good point. I didn't look at it that way before."

"I understand. But remember this, okay? It's one thing to work through the labyrinth of issues with your wife and children in the privacy of your home. It's an entirely different matter when you're on display in front of your entire congregation. Although I believe Christians are the most loving people on earth, they are still people, and sometimes their opinions get in the way of their love."

"So if I have to fight this fight you're talking about, I agree, it would be better to do it in private. I wouldn't want my faults on display for the whole church to see."

"Just remember, Roger, it's not just you in the fight, but Julie, and any children you may have in the future. Their struggles will be on display for many to observe as well . . . and all in living color too."

"That's not good. Can you tell me more about this spiritual war?"

"Well, the first thing to recognize is that we don't know it all, not that we should approach this in a fearful way, but in a sober, humble way, realizing who it is we're fighting—a defeated foe. But he's an invisible defeated foe, so he's got the drop on you. Although, if you resist him, he has to flee.[11] He and his cohorts are powerless against you, if you don't allow them any sway, any ground. Now that's a big 'if' because he's so cunningly evasive and deceptive. I mean, let's face it, that despicable one has been messing with humans for centuries, no actually longer, for millennia. Oh, he's crafty. But not like they portray him in movies or those end time novels. The war is in your mind. It takes place in your thoughts. He'll run an image through there to promote a desire or a fear and, within seconds, if you give it any credence, he's got you off and running on some tangent. However, if you resist the enemy, using the Scriptures as your weapon, he will turn tail and flee. It's like my good friend Willy says, "I resist. He gone," Alan chuckled.

"So how do you actually resist him?"

"Remember, it's a faith fight. So by your faith you call out and forcefully inform him, 'No, I'm not going to think that. I'm not going to do that. I resist you in the name of Jesus, you foul spirit of . . .' whatever you're being tempted with. If it is pride, call it pride. If lust, call it lust. Or if it is worry, or gossip, or selfishness, whatever it is, call it by that name. Then, in a firm tone tell your adversary, 'No!' and command him to get out of your thoughts, your room, your house, or wherever you're experiencing the fight. And finally, when you have done all you can do, then stand firm.[12] Be steadfast, immovable, with your helmet of salvation protecting your head, your breastplate of righteousness guarding your heart, standing with your shield of faith raised up, which can extinguish every flaming arrow of the enemy, and take hold of the sword of the Spirit which is the Word of God, having it ever at the ready.[13] This is all part of His kingdom within you, Roger."

"That's powerful stuff, Dad."

"It's all in the Scriptures, my beloved brother. It just takes time to learn how to apply them. That's why I don't recommend younger believers to be in leadership. It's not that I don't love their enthusiasm. I do, but that exuberance isn't what can accurately divide the Word of Truth; its years of study and practice, trial and error, and a faith that has endured through many and varied struggles. Even so, I truly believe we always need one another. When the seven spiritual gifts listed in the Book of Romans are functioning as our Lord intended, we are much more effective as a church. No one man should be burdened with carrying the whole load himself. The Lord didn't design us for that. Each one has his part, not a responsibility to do it all."

"That's very interesting," admitted Roger, rubbing his hand on his chin. "You really think those gifts are for the modern church?"

"They're absolutely essential. Think of a major corporation. They have a board of directors, which would include several members with varying areas of expertise. One may be an attorney, another an accountant, others may have backgrounds in real estate, operations, sales, or marketing. A well rounded board makes for sound decisions and a strong company. I believe God had something like this in mind when He created the seven spiritual gifts. And I'll tell you a little secret I've been working on. In the Book of Revelation it speaks of the seven Spirits of God.[14] There are also seven indicated in the Book of Isaiah[15] too. I'm thinking somehow they both tie into the seven spiritual gifts."

"Really?"

"Yeah, it's pretty exciting to ponder the possibilities."

Just then, Annalisa poked her head out the front door. "Hey, honey, sorry to interrupt, but Doc is on the phone. He says it's real important. He's come up with a solution to our problem on Sunday mornings."

"See that, Roger, Doc is our elder who God has gifted with the gift of Organization. Evidently, he already has a problem solved that I wasn't even aware of yet," chuckled

Alan. "Although to be honest, for Doc to call, it must be something big."

-eighteen-

Hopping up from the front porch swing, Alan patted Roger on the shoulder, opened the door, and then headed inside. On his way across the living room to the kitchen, he took a detour to where Annalisa and Julie were sitting on the sofa scanning a baby catalog of some sort. He bent over and gave Julie a kiss on her cheek. She raised her eyes and cast a loving gaze his way. Annalisa, however, threw up her two hands in silent protest as if to ask, "Where's mine?" Chuckling, he gave her a quick peck before heading off to the kitchen.

"What was that for, Dad?" asked Julie.

"I love that husband of yours," called Alan as he entered the kitchen to answer the phone.

"Hey, Doc, how are you doing today?" asked a cheerful Alan.

"I'm well, Alan. Hey, I think I've got a solution for our problem on Sunday mornings."

"What problem is that, Doc?"

"We don't have enough seats for everyone in the sanctuary. Didn't you notice last Sunday? We were nearly maxed out."

"Well, sure. I was pleased there were so many people, but there's still room for a few more. Don't you think?"

"A little, but what about next week and the week after that? How about next month or even next year? We need to think about these things now before they get out of hand."

"Thanks, Doc, that's planning ahead alright."

"Just using my spiritual gift, Alan."

"Yes, you are. Hey, speaking of spiritual gifts, we're still missing one of the seven gifts on the elder board. I've been praying about it, and I have a great idea for who may fit in perfectly."

"Yeah? Who?"

"Well I'll leave that for the elders meeting this Saturday. For now, tell me what you've figured out for the influx of new people."

"The solution is the fellowship room."

"What?"

"Yeah, we can take out that wall between the sanctuary and the fellowship room. I know that's a load bearing wall, but I figured we could install a beam and put in one of those accordion-style, movable walls. We can close it for meetings like the ladies prayer group and our elders meetings. Then, it could be opened when we need extra seating space on Sunday mornings."

"That's a great idea, Doc. I wonder how much that would cost?"

"If we remove the wall and install the beam ourselves, we'd spend about about twenty-eight hundred. Those walls aren't cheap, you know."

"Hmmm . . . I'm curious, Doc. Where are most of these new folks coming from?"

"From what I can tell by the checks in the offerings, and asking around a bit, they're mostly from the Wiggins area. However, there are quite a few from down in the Gulfport area as well as a dozen or so from up in Hattiesburg."

"That's interesting. Both of those locations are forty-five minutes away . . . in exact opposite directions. Let's discuss this at the elders meeting, okay, Doc?"

"Works for me. See you Saturday morning."

"Hey, Doc? Thanks, I really appreciate you thinking ahead . . . and using that gift of yours."

"Thanks, Alan. Have a great day."

Walking back through the living room on his way to the front porch and to a patiently waiting Roger, Alan glanced over at Annalisa and Julie. They were still sitting on the sofa. However, now they were looking at baby furniture on Julie's laptop.

"You were right, honey," exclaimed Annalisa with a smile.

"What?" Alan stopped at the front door waiting for her reply.

"You were right about Doc. He really is a good guy, isn't he?"

"Yeah, he is. We all need a helping hand at some point in our lives. I'm really glad Doc decided not to leave."

Proceeding out to the front porch again, Alan and Roger continued their conversation for more than two hours. When they came in for lunch, Annalisa and Julie entered the discussion, which mainly focused on the topic of fighting the good fight of faith. At one point, a very perceptive Julie made a comment that had both Alan and Annalisa smiling from ear to ear.

"So that's why you guys have always enjoyed that whole **rojocci** thing. It's like practice exercises in schoolwork or training on the track—it develops in you a desire for more, a determination to never quit, and the perseverance to always keep fighting, no matter what comes your way."

"Other than the joy of discovering some of those wonderful historical documents, that's precisely it, Julie," responded Annalisa, a proud smile spreading across her face.

"Yeah, I want you guys to know I have a fire proof box," announced Alan. "It's where I've saved all our **rojocci** items. Inside are all of the old scraps of paper from when I discovered the meaning of each letter. There's also Stanley Taft's little draw-stringed, leather satchel with his original, rain-stained, scotch-taped paper. Plus, I stored the photographs of every page of that historical book we found at the general store in Pfeiffer Station, Ohio, as well as a copy of The **rojocci** Manifesto in the box. The original **rojoccian** Covenant that Ulysses Champion gave us is in there too. The one in the frame on the wall is a copy we had made in Montgomery, Alabama. They did a nice job. Don't you think?"

"Yeah, it fooled me," confessed Roger staring at the document from his seat in the recliner.

"But everything else is in the box, Dad?" inquired Julie.

"Yep. That's where I keep **The rojocci Papers**."

"Well, there are several copies of both the Covenant and the Manifesto posted around town," confessed Annalisa. "In fact, Bertha told me just last Sunday she heard there were copies in Hattiesburg, Jackson, Montgomery, and Birmingham. Then Willy mentioned that his cousin had seen The **rojoccian** Covenant in Atlanta posted in the front window of a restaurant in downtown."

"Oh, I don't know about that," interjected Alan with a bit of cynicism. "But I have heard it is spreading throughout the south. Doc told me last week he saw The **rojoccian** Covenant at a hardware store in Gulfport. It made me smile."

Saturday morning the elders gathered at seven o'clock for their meeting in the conference room at church. After a short time of fellowship, they prayed for several minutes. Alan opened the meeting with the observation Doc had related to him regarding the congregation outgrowing the sanctuary. With this brief introduction, Doc took the ball and ran with it proving, from his organized study of their situation, a change would be needed relatively soon. He then handed copies of the proposed changes to the room in which they sat. All seemed open to the proposal although Alan had some other ideas for the elders to consider.

"Gents, I think Doc's solution is appropriate for the problem at hand. The costs seem reasonable, and I think there would be minimal distraction to the people. The last thing we need at this point in the life of the church is for folks to get their minds off spiritual matters and on to building projects. So in the short term, I agree with everyone here, we should move forward with Doc's solution. However, in the long run, I'm talking years, I really don't see the Lord wanting us to build our own little empire here in Wiggins."

"What's that supposed to mean, Alan?" questioned Seb, with three of the elders looking on with guarded interest.

"Well, Doc tells me the majority of our new families are traveling from either down in the Gulfport area or out of Hattiesburg to our north. Regardless of their origin, both distances are about forty-five minutes away."

"Okay, so what's your point, Alan?" asked Seb.

"My point, brother Seb, is this, it would be better for those folks, and anyone they would be ministering to, if the church they attended was closer to their own homes. I think it's quite possible that sometime in the future we will be helping others to start a work in those locations. So we shouldn't go too far with any building projects here."

"I actually can see that, Alan," agreed Doc.

"Thanks, Doc. However, I think we may be getting the cart before the horse in our little experiment here in Wiggins," warned Alan with a smile.

"What do you mean?" asked Jake quietly.

"I mean, our leap of faith in trying to determine if the Lord actually wants His church led by a group of seven believers, each with one of the spiritual gifts, and these seven elders functioning within the Body, not separate from it. Or, is the Lord satisfied with one individual in a position of leadership who advises, delegates, and instructs the congregation in what he believes God is saying to them? In both scenarios Jesus is the Head, the Shepherd. But which case more resembles the New Testament model?"

"I think we've proved that, Alan," pronounced Seb. "We've been functioning this way for nearly two years now.

I think I can speak for all of us that the spiritual gifts work way better and more importantly, they actually work."

"With all due respect, Seb, we don't really know that yet."

"What?"

"Where's the seventh gift?" posed Alan frankly. "There are only six of us. We need one more, and that person has to have the one gift we are missing here at this table."

"What are we missing?" asked Josh, who had been silent up to this point in the conversation.

"I know what we're missing, gentlemen," ventured Jake. "We don't have the spiritual gift of Giving on this elder board. We're lacking the Giving gift, and that's not good."

"Really?" asked Seb scrunching up his face indicating he wasn't sure he understood.

"Yes," affirmed Doc. "Now, Alan, correct me if I'm wrong here. Seb, you have the spiritual gift of Exhortation. Josh, yours is Teaching, and Jake, well everyone knows your gift is Mercy," Doc pointed out as he continued around the table. "Alan has the Prophecy gift and, Zack, you are obviously the biggest Service gift I have ever known. So there, as you can see we're missing one spiritual gift, the gift of Giving."

"Yeah, guys," agreed Zack. "We need someone with the spiritual gift of Giving in here before this church gets much larger."

"Anybody have any ideas?" asked Doc.

The room fell silent. After about a minute, Jake spoke up.

"How about Willy Jarvis?"

"Yeah, he has the gift of Giving in him as thick as my wife's gumbo," proclaimed Seb.

That brought a chuckle from the group. Then everyone began to silently nod at the thought of Willy and Bertha. Alan asked the elders to privately discuss it with their wives and devote the decision to prayer overnight. If they were all still in agreement in the morning, he would ask Willy and Bertha if they had a few minutes right after the Sunday service for a brief meeting.

The next morning everything went off without a hitch and after a short ceremony in which the elders and their wives laid their hands upon Willy and Bertha, the elders now had a person with the gift of Giving on the board. It was surprising to some, though not to Alan, that Willy fit in perfectly with the group of elders. He and Bertha brought a breath of fresh air to the Board. In his very first meeting, Willy encouraged the elders to consider the idea of becoming a tithing church. The notion had never occurred to them. However, recognizing it was Biblical, they voted unanimously to have Willy present it to the congregation. Using the parable of the sower and his seed, he did a brilliant job. The entire congregation wholeheartedly supported the idea and cheerfully became a tithing church, giving at least ten percent of everything received in offerings to other ministries in their community and throughout the world. It was a Biblical principle they had not recognized until Willy presented the idea to them, and they all were blessed because of it.

Willy and Bertha along with the help of Jake and Doc also organized and opened a thrift store for the more needy folks throughout their county. They not only sold items at a deep discount, but gave away clothes and food. They even helped with utility bills and rent for those less fortunate. Again, the Lord blessed their efforts toward helping others.

Within a year or so they opened a church ministry in Hattiesburg and six months later another church in Gulfport. These began with seven individuals who were appointed to the leadership, each with one of the spiritual gifts. Both ministries were self-sustaining within a year of commencement. The two churches continued to grow and after a few years birthed other new churches as well. All were using the same model that Alan had discovered lying hidden within the Scriptures.

"Looks like your dream about that apple tree was prophetic, my love," acknowledged Alan one Saturday morning at breakfast.

"It wasn't me, Alan. It was the Lord. But I'm really glad he used me to express it to you. I'm glad I wrote it down because this has all been pretty amazing. Don't you think?"

"I sure do," he smiled. "In less than ten years, the Lord has used this little work here to grow six new congregations. It's very gratifying to be a small part of what He's doing in the world."

"I agree. For the most part it has been a delight."

As the years slowly rolled by, like the Mississippi River flows in winter, the church in Wiggins enjoyed relative peace and harmony. It continued to grow both spiritually and numerically. Little by little, Alan relinquished his role of giving the Sunday morning message so the other elders could begin taking turns at the pulpit. It was amazing to see how the Lord wove beautiful, harmonious messages using several messengers. Alan, now in his mid-sixties, traveled much less, only once every two or three months. When he did, he still told the **rojocci** stories. His timeless message of encouraging others to never quit believing, to never give up hoping in the Lord, and to continually keep growing in faith was almost always well received, even in the staunchest of congregations.

After finishing dinner one evening in early November, Alan and Annalisa stepped out onto their front porch just before sunset. He took his traditional spot on the swing; she sat cross legged on the rocking chair with her face lifted toward the warmth of the setting sun, willing the last rays of its heat to shine upon her face. The picture of her resting there, was one he had seen several times before. His mind drifted back over their precious history together. Tears welled up in his eyes as he thought of a much younger Annalisa, climbing up on the boulder on top of the mountain in Western Maryland the first time they had hiked together. She was as beautiful now as she was then. In fact, he determined, sitting there basking in the view, she would be the one person on earth he would miss the most when he left for Heaven. Sure, he would miss the kids too, but he knew they would have their spouses and their families to comfort and encourage them. Annalisa, he decided, would be the only reason he would ever have to gaze out of the windows of Heaven.

Closing his eyes, Alan pondered his life and how the Lord had led him all along the way. He thought of his wonderful parents. Then of Stanley Taft, who had first shared with him "The Quiet Road" and had hinted at something Alan had mistakenly called the "Road Jockey." Next, his mind brought up the image of Betsy's face as she explained the mysteries of The **rojocci** Fellowship to him. She was such a dear, saintly woman whom he had never forgotten. He would always remember old A-Dub too. He was a godly man, who had steered him in the right direction at a critical time in his life. Smiling, he thought of his Youth Pastor, Fred, and his crazy antics. "He really was a good guy, Lord," he acknowledged silently. But other than Annalisa, he realized Betsy had made the greatest impact for the Lord in his life. Her kind thoughts and gentle grandmotherly way of being sweet, yet firm, was just what he needed during a time when he was floundering with what to do with his life.

"Oh, thank you, Lord," he sighed.

Opening his eyes, Alan glanced over at Annalisa, who was still in her favorite position. He turned toward the sun, which was nearly touching the horizon and closed his eyes. Once again his mind began to slowly drift to days gone by. Floating upon his memories, he meandered back to when he had first met Joey Hinote. He had been a most cherished friend, who had helped Alan through many a discouraging and disappointing time. "I sure did love that guy, dear Lord," he softly whispered. "We were like David and Jonathan."

"What, honey?" asked a relaxed Annalisa.

"Oh, nothing, just thinking out loud."

"I love these evenings together. Don't you, Alan?"

"Yes, I do, sweetheart."

"When did it become so popular to be busy?" she asked with a tone that bordered on disappointment.

"What?"

"You know, why do folks think being busy is such a good thing?"

"I'm not sure what you're getting at, honey."

"Well, I was at the store," she continued with her eyes still closed, face toward the last bit of warmth from the setting sun. "And I saw a couple of the ladies from church. When I asked how they were doing, each one answered, 'Busy, I'm so busy.' But more than that, they proclaimed it as though being busy was a noble and desirable quality. It was like they were proud they were so busy."

"Yeah, unfortunately I've noticed that in the last few years too. I feel like I'm in a relative calm, as though in the eye of a tornado, while the rest of the world whirls chaotically around. Honey, I believe that's a perfect illustration for the kingdom of God within us too. All my thoughts, emotions, plans, fears, and desires are swirling around a perfectly quiet and still center. That center where I am in constant communion with Him. It's the anchor of my soul, a rock both sure and steadfast, never moving, always solid, and worthy of my complete trust.[1] But if you don't have that confidence in Him, you can get so caught up in the world's hapless hurricane. So, come to think of it, I guess, for many, the answer would be, 'Busy, I'm so busy.'"

"Good point," she interjected. "But I wonder what ever happened to answering, 'Fine,' or, 'Well, I am doing well.' Seems almost everyone answers, 'Busy.' Then rarely do they ask how the other person is doing."

"Hmmm . . ."

"It's almost like being busy is an excuse for being impolite. And frankly, I wouldn't say this to anyone else but you, Alan . . . it kind of hurt my feelings."

"I'm sorry, honey. I'm sure the ladies were just preoccupied with their errands or something. It's like Pastor Fred told us at the retreat way back when we first met, 'You are, of necessity, *in* the world, but don't be *of* the world.' Remember? You know, it's like you're in the tornado. Just don't get caught up in it. I think that would be a bit of a rough ride," he chuckled.

"I'm grateful we have time to think and ponder life together. I enjoy talking about the things of God. You know what I mean?"

"Yes, I agree. Although you still crack me up sometimes with the way you think, how you can jump from one topic to another, like a hummingbird from flower to flower."

Annalisa shrugged but said nothing; she only acknowledged his comment with a smile while still facing the sun, her eyes closed.

"Sometimes I miss old Teddy. You know, honey?" he asked softly.

"Yes, he really was a godly man who loved the Lord and the people too."

"Yeah, there were several times over these last few years when I wished I had him to talk to, you know, for counsel and advice."

"Hmmm . . ."

"What's that supposed to mean?" he asked opening his eyes to see her response.

"It means, I think our loving Lord took him at the precise moment when you needed to depend more on Him and less on another person."

"Really?"

"Yes. That's what I think anyway," she shrugged.

"Man that makes me wonder if I'm in anyone's way? I sure hope not. I mean, I've really tried to be a hands-off kind of guy. You know, to allow the Lord to lead His people. I know folks look to me for advice and all, but I really try to point them to God and His Word."

"I think you do an excellent job, Alan. You didn't used to be like that. But you've really improved in that area since we've moved here."

He sat silently gazing at the love of his life. To him she was absolutely perfect. He loved her with all of his heart. After the last few moments of sunlight passed, Annalisa opened her eyes and turned toward Alan with a smile on her face.

"I love you, Alan Michael Browne. I am so proud of the man you have become. You used to be so insecure and suspicious, and your quick wit and sarcasm could make things rather difficult at times. If you know what I mean? But you are a godly, loving man, who wants to help others and to do the right thing no matter the cost. I really am so very proud to be married to you."

"Thanks, my sweet Annalisa Michele Browne. You are a joy to be married to and the love of my life. Throughout our many decades together, I have seen how the Lord has used you, more than any other person in my life, to develop His character in me. I cannot express in words how extremely grateful I am to God for knitting our hearts together as one. I do recognize it is a precious gift from Him. And I want you to know something, if our Lord gave me a million lifetimes to live over and over again, I would want to live every single one of them with you."

"Me too, honey," she smiled. "Me too."

-epilogue-

Several months had passed since I had last seen Alan and Annalisa, so I was eagerly anticipating a visit with them. Since they had moved to Wiggins nearly a dozen years ago, our visits had become less frequent. This was due to the distance between our homes more than any other reason. Upon my arrival, they warmly welcomed me into their cozy home. Alan's eyes, although much older, still reflected the kindness of the heart within. Annalisa, ever the cheerful one, sat in their petite living room with a sincere smile upon her attractive countenance. I'm sure I could not enjoy two people more. They both literally exude graciousness and are truly delightful in every sense of the word.

Evidenced by the twinkle in his eyes as we chatted, Alan still enjoys sharing all things **rojocci** with anyone who will listen. However, the time he needed to recover after each speaking engagement had become disruptive to their ministry. So when they receive an invitation to speak at a church or retreat now, they apologetically decline and offer to send a little booklet they've created. These, he assured me, had been well received.

I was pleased to learn that moving back to Pensacola was on their horizon. Alan explained that they still owned the old house they had bought from Joey Hinote several years ago and were looking forward to living out their days there. Sadly, Alan informed me that Joey had passed away early one morning while praying at his kitchen table. The doctor said it was a heart attack. Joey's wife, Pam, was convinced that he had prayed himself through the gates of Heaven. Regardless, the notion of one moment praying in your kitchen and the next talking to God face to face clearly appealed to Alan. Even so, his eyes brimmed with tears as he recounted to me the news of his dear friend. He expressed that other than Annalisa, Joey had been his best and closest friend.

As the room fell silent, I reached into my bag and pulled out the final volume in The **rojocci** Papers Trilogy. This last book of their lifelong story I had entitled *The Kingdom Within You*. They were thrilled and asked me to autograph the copy for them. I implored that they return the favor on my personal copy, which they told me they would if I promised to stay for dinner. I agreed knowing full well they wouldn't let me leave on an empty stomach. They are not only gracious, but are stubbornly so.

Driving away later that evening, my heart was a bit heavy with the realization that I wouldn't be as close with this remarkable couple as I had been over the last several years. I have so enjoyed the opportunity to learn of their journey with the Lord and to share their story with you. They are just plain ordinary folks that took a chance on God and His Word, launching out in what they have many times called their "Adventures With God".

Several miles down the road, while merging onto Interstate 10 heading east toward Pensacola, my heaviness began to lift, giving way to a spirit of rejoicing. Something truly amazing suddenly dawned on me. With God's help and inspiration, I had done it—I had done something I never thought remotely possible. I had written their life's story and had done so in three volumes, no less. Me, a guy who would be the first to admit, English composition has never been my cup of tea.

With a grateful heart, I started singing a little chorus of praise to my Father in Heaven. Surprisingly, what I had dreaded would be a dismal drive home, became a joyous trip. A huge sense of accomplishment had washed over me like a swelling tsunami of satisfaction. For I had proved, by personal experience, like Alan would have definitely advised me to do, that the Scriptures are actually true and pertinent for today. Don't get me wrong, the entirety of His Word is true, whether I have proved it or not. But having experienced it for myself, I can assuredly and wholeheartedly proclaim, if for no one other than myself, that His Word is living and active. Not only has it proved true for others, but it really worked for me too. A step of faith is what is required to obtain a magnificently joyous revelation of His mysteries hidden within the Scriptures. And He chose to reveal this to insignificant, at times unbelieving, disobedient, ordinary me. You see, I discovered ...

"His strength is perfected in my weakness."[1]

Footnotes

Prologue:
1. Matthew 6:33

Chapter One:
1. Matthew 7:1
2. 1 Timothy 1:5
3. Galatians 5:6
4. 1 Timothy 1:5
5. 1 John 4:8
6. 1 Corinthians 13:13
7. Mark 12:29-31
8. Luke 17:20-21
9. Ephesians 4:26-27

Chapter Two:
1. 1 Timothy 6:12
2. Mark 12:29-31
3. Proverbs 6:23
4. 1 Thessalonians 5:23
5. John 4:24
6. 1 Timothy 1:5
7. Mark 12:29-31

Chapter Four:
1. Ephesians 4:11
2. Romans 12:6-8

Chapter Five:
1. Hebrews 11:8
2. 2 Corinthians 10:5
3. 2 Corinthians 10:7

Chapter Seven:
      1.   Hebrews 10:25

Chapter Eight:
1. 1 Corinthians 1:27-28
2. 1 Samuel 16:7
3. Romans 4:17
4. 1 Corinthians 12:11
5. 1 Corinthians 12;4-6
6. James 4:7
7. Ephesians 6:11

Chapter Nine:
1. Luke 17:21
2. Romans 14:17
3. 1 Corinthians 6:19
4. Luke 17:21
5. John 18:36

Chapter Ten:
1. Colossians 1:18
2. James 1:25
3. John 7:17
4. Proverbs 11:14
5. Matthew 18:16
6. Ephesians 4:11
7. Isaiah 1:18
8. 2 Corinthians 5:18-20
9. Revelation 1:6

Chapter Eleven:
1. John 7:17
2. John 8:31-32
3. Psalms 116:15

The Spiritual Benefits
of
the Kingdom Within You

Psalms 103:2

Luke 17:20-21

Determination Gifts: (Charisma) 1 Corinthians 12:4; Romans 12:6-8
Prophecy, Serving, Teaching, Exhortation, Giving, Leading (Organization), Mercy

Effects Gifts: (Energema) 1 Corinthians 12:6-12
Word of wisdom. Word of knowledge, Faith, Healing, Prophecy, Discerning of spirits,
Various tongues

Ministerial Gifts: (Diakonia) 1 Corinthians 12:5, 27-31; Ephesians 4:11-13
Apostle, Prophet, Evangelist, Teacher, Worker of miracles, Healer, Helper, Administrator, Various tongues

Fruit of the Holy Spirit: (Karpos) Galatians 5:18-25
Love, Joy, Peace, Patience, Kindness, Goodness, Faithfulness, Gentleness, Self-control

Weapons of our Warfare: (Hoplon) 2 Corinthians 10:3-5; Ephesians 6:10-19
Belt of Truth, Breastplate of Righteousness, Preparation of the Gospel, Helmet of Salvation, Sword of the Spirit (which is the Word of God), Prayer

The rojocci Papers

Acronym

i=insights

c=Christian

c=cherished

o=overlooked

j=Jesus

o=of

r=receiving

The Seven Tenets of

The rojocci Manifesto

1. **Love is the calling.** Matthew 22:35-40;
1 Corinthians 13:13; 1 John 3:24; Colossians 3:14; 1 Peter 4:8

2 **Pray first and unceasingly.** Luke 18:1-8;
Colossians 4:2; 1 Thessalonians 5:17; Ephesians 6:18

3. **Check first your heart when searching the Holy Scriptures.** Hebrews 4:12; Proverbs 4:23; 2 Thessalonians 2: 7-13

4. **Thankfulness is the evidence of trust.** Colossians 3:16-17; 1 Thessalonians 5:18; Hebrews 13:15

5. **Generosity toward others, frugality with self.** 2 Corinthians 9:6-7; 1 Thessalonians 4:9-12; Proverbs 19;17

6. **Judge yourself, allow God to judge others.** Matthew 7:1-5; Romans 14:4; I Corinthian4:5

7. **Freedom is an offspring of the truth.** John 8:31-32; Galatians 5: 1, 13-14; John 14:6

The rojoccian Covenant

I am nothing, one soul within myself
And have but one life to give, one strength
If He's chosen to set me upon life's shelf
Who am I to question how long the length.

Now hear the voice that cries too deep
With words only His Spirit understand
As alone, yet many invisible they keep
My soul, my body when trodden to sand.

There is One more close who knows my pain
Who I am not worthy to glance upon
It is He so sweetly, so surely I gain
Everything clear and pure when life is done.

So don't give credence to grumble nor complaint
Knowing your Father never sleeps nor rests
But soldier on, yet stronger on, never faint
Under sore affliction, trials, and tests.

Now one last word I boldly declare
The beauty of all His teachings be
This one thing most sublime if we will dare
His love for you long ago He decreed.

Lord, ne'er will I give up, nor will I flee
From the way for me You have chosen
Surely Your love, Your grace, Your sovereignty
Mingled midst bold faith my life Handwoven.

Preacher Daks
Dogtown, California 1857

about the author

R.J. Graves, Jr. and his wife, the lovely Mrs. Graves, met on the mission field in 1978, he a Virginian, and she from Northern California. They have been married thirty-seven years and have six wonderful children, three of whom are married and have blessed them, to date with three precious grandchildren.

Over the years, he has held many roles in church leadership, including teaching and preaching. However, he most enjoys leading interactive Bible studies. He believes, "Come, let us reason together," is every bit as pertinent today as it was centuries ago. He loves family gatherings and delights in walks with his wife Susie, and their dog Pumpkin. When he finds the time he likes to ride his bicycle and dabble in woodworking.

After college, R.J. began his career as a carpenter's apprentice. He quickly obtained journeyman status and also worked as a park ranger in California, being elected president of his police academy. He has held numerous management and executive positions throughout his more than forty year career mainly in construction. His gifts and calling are to exhort and encourage fellow believers to consider greater possibilities and the mysteries of a deeper life in our Lord Jesus Christ.

You can contact him on Facebook at www.facebook.com/rojocci or at: www.therojoccipapers.com if you have any questions or comments.